MIDLIFE WITCH HUNTER

THE FORTY PROOF SERIES, BOOK 6

SHANNON MAYER

HiJinks

FOREWORD

Author's Note:

Note: I'd call the first three chapters a prologue, but some of you readers don't like to read prologues (weird, I know), and if you don't read THIS prologue, you'll really be ducked for the rest of the book and series. I mean . . . do you want to miss out on things? Important things? I just don't understand why you'd skip a prologue. I mean, I can see skipping acknowledgments, author's notes, shit like that. Who cares, right? Let's be honest, if you're still with me now, at this point in a long-ass author's note, you are a step above. A real loyal reader who is just waiting for me to spill some unreal secret that you won't find anywhere else.

Like that I have TWO new series starting in 2022.

FOREWORD

One is paranormal women's fiction, and the other is urban fantasy. Just in case you were wondering. I might even have covers for them at the back of this book somewhere.

Anyhoo, on with the show, as the saying goes ;)

Midlife Witch Hunter, Forty Proof Series Book Six
All rights reserved
HiJinks Ink Publishing
www.shannonmayer.com

All rights reserved. Without limiting the rights under copyright reserved above, no part of this publication may be reproduced, stored in or introduced into a database and retrieval system or transmitted in any form or any means (electronic, mechanical, photocopying or otherwise) without the prior written permission of both the owner of the copyright and the above publishers.

Please do not participate in or encourage the piracy of copyrighted materials in violation of the author's rights. Purchase only authorized editions.

This is a work of fiction. Names, characters, places and incidents are either the product of the author's imagination or are used fictitiously, and any resemblance to actual persons living or dead, business establishments, events or locales is entirely coincidental.

Original illustrations by Momir
Mayer, Shannon

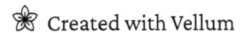

Created with Vellum

ACKNOWLEDGMENTS

I love this series. I love Bree, Feish (pronounced FISH), Crash, and Robert. I love all the characters and they have in some cases come straight out of my real life. So, thank you to the assholes in my life for helping me create realistic bad guys. As for the good people, the loyal and love-you-through-anything people, thank you for reminding me that there is always a light in the darkness.

Most especially, thank you to the love of my life. My little boy, who is my reason for working as much as I do. He is my biggest light, and I can't wait for him to be able to read my books.

When he's like ... thirty.

CHAPTER
ONE
CRASH

I left Bree there, at the fort. Gathered up my army and left her, because I could not bear to see the hurt in her beautiful eyes. Hurt that I'd caused. Because I was bound to the Dark Council. I didn't hold with what they were planning, but it didn't matter—I had no choice but to stand with them, which meant I could not stand by her side.

The goblin city inside of the realm of fae was as good a place as any for me to lick my wounds, yet it still wasn't where I wanted to be.

"Boss man, that was a frackus, wanninit? Demons! Damn, I'd have never thought your girl would bring demons to stop us!" Leland popped around a corner and strode into my room. Tall and slender for a goblin, he was not well liked, and the others often treated him as though he were a half-breed.

"Leland, not right now, and she's not my girl." I

uncorked a bottle of ogre beer with my teeth and spat the cork to one side. I downed three long pulls from the bottle, yet even that powerhouse booze didn't do more than make me wobble.

I wanted to sleep.

To put it all from my mind for a little while and pretend that I wasn't alone again.

"Yeah, but it was fun, boss! We all had a good time! I like her, you know. She's got some grit." Leland strode across the room and took the bottle from me, sniffed it and curled up his nose. His bright blond hair stood straight up all over, as if he'd been playing with electricity.

I closed my eyes and drew a deep breath. "Leland, get out."

"Nah, I thinkin' that is a bad idea." It sounded like he pushed the beer to the side, across the table in front of me. "You've got problems, and ogre beer won't really be helping to solve them."

I opened my eyes, and he was sitting on the table where the beer had been. It was not a welcome replacement. "I'm well aware of that."

"I think you should go down to the smithy and bash some steel. Make a new weapon." Leland grinned, flashing a mouthful of sharp teeth. "Maybe something for your girl? She seems to like sharp things."

"She's not my girl," I repeated, hearing the Irish in my voice deepen. Anger was not my friend lately. Another day, I would have put more effort into making him leave me alone or convincing him that Bree was not my girl. The problem was she had my heart in a way I'd never experienced before . . . and I had given my loyalty to those who would see her dead.

My jaw clamped shut, the urge to hit something nearly overwhelming. I turned away from Leland. "Maybe I *will* bash some steel." Pushing past him, I made my way through the goblin castle, down across the main street, and to the only smithy in the realm of fae. I'd built this smithy with my own two hands when I'd first realized that I was different from the other fae, different even than the goblins and darker fae. When I'd first realized that I didn't fit in anywhere. It had become my refuge, my place of solitude and my place of growth.

I'd brought men from the human world here—blacksmiths who taught me how to work metal. Farriers who taught me how to bend steel in the most efficient way possible. Metalsmiths who taught me how to work the finer metals into detailed art and dainty jewelry.

The large iron doors to my home, my sanctuary, were cracked open, when I knew I'd left them closed.

My hand slid down to the sword still attached to my hip. Sliding my fingers around the hilt, I pulled it free slowly, silently. In my mind, I could hear Bree muttering about all the 's' sounds and the thought made my lips tip upward.

Even now, I couldn't let her go.

Stepping sideways, I pressed my back to the door and held my breath. Someone was moving around inside, clinking the metal pieces together.

Touching my shit.

Jaw tight, I stepped through the door, opening it farther as I went and then quietly shutting it behind me. Whoever was in here wouldn't be leaving without going through me.

The forge was dark, lit by nothing more than the banked coals that remained wherever I set up shop. That light was not bright enough to illuminate the entire room, and I waited near the door.

"You'd best consider what your life is worth," I growled.

A low, masculine chuckle echoed through the space. "Ah, *mais oui*. So much *courageux* from you, Blacksmith."

"Louis?"

What in the name of all that was fae was the necromancer doing in my forge? I rolled my eyes and lowered my sword. I snapped my fingers, and the banked flames burst to life, roaring up and revealing the scrawny French necromancer standing directly next to the forge.

He didn't flinch, didn't step back.

I frowned. That did not fit with the Louis I knew. "What are you doing here?" I tossed my sword on the work bench. I would need to clean it. Vampire blood was almost as bad as a demon's blood. It could etch blades if given enough time to sit, and my blade had been coated in Joseph's gore. Thinking about him conjured an image of him in my mind—I could see him holding onto Bree, threatening her, and my breath and heart both hitched.

"I came to discuss your current situation with you." Louis flared his nostrils wide and smiled as he tucked his hands behind his back. "I believe you owe your allegiance to the Dark Council, yes?"

I fought off the flinch and gave a slow nod, even though I wondered why he was bringing this up. "I do."

"And they are controlled by . . . remind me again?" The way he was speaking told me he already knew. Louis was power tripping.

"Clovis," I said.

"Correct, and I work directly for Clovis, which means *you* work for *me*." Louis's smile widened, and he touched a hand to his chest. But his glee slid away when I didn't respond. "You. Work. For. Me." He snapped the words with each step that he took closer to me.

I raised an eyebrow and stared him in the face. "I don't. Get out of my forge."

The Louis I knew would have left in a huff, stomping his feet and cussing me out in French.

This new version of Louis got right in my face. "You will take this—" he shoved something heavy into my hand, "—and you will finally make the crucible. The

Dark Council will no longer remain in the shadows. You will do your part to make sure of it."

My hand closed around the object, feeling the stone, and knowing exactly what it was—the fairy cross.

"Where did you find it?" I breathed the question.

"Clever *putain*, she hid it beneath the oak tree."

Whore. He'd called Bree a whore.

I don't really remember moving, only we were standing still one second, and the next I had Louis pinned against the wall by his throat. That moment could have changed my life.

If I'd only understood all the currents that were swirling around me.

If I'd killed him then, maybe . . .

"Watch your mouth about her," I growled.

Louis laughed, though it was a rather choked sound. "Fool."

I dropped him to the ground, and he stumbled to the side, sliding down the wall. "Fool," he repeated. "She is your weakness, and Clovis knows it. Make the crucible. Her life is on the line if you take a step in a direction he does not like." He held up a hand, stopping me before I could argue. "And I do not mean he will kill her. I mean that he will hurt her, worse than she has even been hurt by you or that clown of an ex-husband. He will destroy her life and make her suffer in ways even you cannot dream of."

Louis pulled himself up and dusted himself off,

then walked to the closed door. "You know the time limit?"

I didn't move, couldn't for fear of what I might say or do. Words and actions that could hurt the one person I wanted desperately to protect . . . even from me.

"You will need the old witch," Louis said as he stepped out the door. "You will need her magic to make the crucible all we require it to be."

The door didn't even click behind the miserable fuck before I threw my sword across the room, followed by the fairy cross. The sword thunked into the far wall and stayed there, embedded and quivering as I struggled to control the rage rolling through me. The fairy cross dropped to the ground unscathed.

Time ticked by and slowly, ever so slowly, I managed to get my breathing under control. Losing myself to rage would not help anyone. I had to find a way to outsmart Clovis and the Dark Council.

I could not let Bree suffer because of my past. Because of a mistake I'd made when I was barely old enough to be called a man. Back then, I'd truly believed in what the Dark Council was offering. Or so I'd thought. Now? I was stuck.

I half expected Feish to pop out and offer to get me some tea. Of course, she was with Bree now, which was for the best. They would both be safer that way. I ran a hand over my face, wiping away the sweat, and took one step, then another, until I was at the forge.

Driving a poker into the coals, I grabbed the hand crank that pushed air into the base and spun it. Flames curled up around the black chunks, brightening to a nearly white-hot light. Too hot for what I wanted.

Backing up, I stared at the flames, wondering just what the fuck I was going to do.

"Pickle, huh?"

I whipped around, dropping into a half crouch. "Enough with the people in my damn forge!"

"Well, some days I'm not considered a person, so I don't count."

Blinking, I looked down to see a leprechaun tapping his foot. "Oster Boon."

"Ah, so you do remember me." He grinned.

"You helped swear me into the council. I would not forget you." I took a few steps back. I was not afraid of him, but I was frustrated to find myself dealing with not one but two members of the Dark Council within a matter of minutes. Only a few months before, I'd believed myself free of them forever. "What brings you to my forge, Oster Boon?"

"Just Ozzie is fine." He waved a hand at me, then climbed deftly up onto my work bench. "I came to have a chat with you. '*Ní neart go cur le chéile.*'" The Irish saying rolled off his tongue, taking me back to my childhood.

I stared at him. "Agreed, generally there is strength in unity." I didn't dislike Oster—Ozzie—but I didn't know him well. He'd always been quiet at meetings of the Dark Council, keeping his own counsel, as it were.

"I see you had a visit from Louis." Ozzie screwed up his face. "I never much liked him, to be honest."

"You knew he was in the Dark Council?" The news that Louis was working directly for Clovis had thrown me, but the reality was we didn't really know one another. Gatherings were attended in hooded cloaks so we couldn't identify one another. But some of the members, like Ozzie and myself, were somewhat . . . identifiable.

Ozzie looked up at me. "Well, something you might be interested in . . . I know almost everyone in the Dark Council."

I snorted and leaned on the other side of the table that sat in the center of the room, gripping a sharp edge until it bit into my hands. "Why would that interest me?"

His eyes were unfathomable as he stared me down. "Well, wouldn't it work in your favor if each member of the Dark Council was . . . removed?"

Was he saying what I thought he was saying?

CHAPTER
TWO
CRASH

The table groaned under my hands as I leaned forward and stared at the leprechaun. "Say it clearly, Oster Boon, so there is no mistaking exactly what you be saying."

"Ozzie, call me Ozzie." He eased himself up onto the table and walked toward me. Just like that, we were eye to eye. His smile looked as devious as his words. "I am trusting you because I saw your reaction to Louis. Because I see how you fight to protect the girl." He drew in a breath. "And because I am dying. My job was to infiltrate the Dark Council and make them believe I was one of them. To help them disappear."

Yes, my jaw dropped, and I struggled to comprehend what he was saying.

He held up a small finger. "I am not what one would expect of a spy, I know. But that is why I have been successful up until now. Clovis . . . is questioning me."

"And you want me to defect? How will that help you?"

"You already have. They control you only because of the girl. The girl my brother and I have been trying to help." He squinted an eye at me. "You know who I mean?"

"Eammon?" I shook my head, unwilling to say Bree's name out loud here in the land of the fae. Maybe it was foolish—she wasn't exactly shy about introducing herself—but I didn't want to bring more trouble to her than I already had, and every fae who did not know her name was potentially one less problem. I chose to believe it protected her a little. "Eammon has always said you're an unworthy—"

"Again, he makes a better spy than people would think. You'd never expect it from someone with sixteen-inch legs." He snorted. "But I digress. I think you are in a position where it would benefit you and the girl if you were to take them out one at a time. If Clovis does not have his council around him, he is vulnerable. And if he is vulnerable, he can be stopped."

The possibility laid out in front of me was almost too good to be true, and that made me nervous. "Do you understand what it is that he is trying to accomplish?" I asked. Not because I didn't know, but because I wanted to make sure Oster knew what we were up against.

"I do. He fears death, and so he seeks to become what does not die."

We stared at each other for a moment and sweat broke out across my face. "No. He wants the dark gift... for himself?"

"Yes. Because he is already a necromancer, he believes becoming a vampire would make him not only immortal but more powerful than any other. In some ways he is not wrong. But he does not remember the yellow fever." Ozzie made air quotes around 'yellow fever.' "That was started when a necromancer was bitten and turned in Savannah. The madness that spread from her was . . . well, it was nothing short of hell on earth."

"I was in Ireland then," I said softly. "But I heard the stories as surely as anyone else."

Ozzie shrugged. "Aye, the same was true of me, but then I came to help with the clean-up."

The forge was quiet, the air tense. "Look, I don't know how you want me to—"

"I will give you a list of all the ones I know for sure. Of the thirteen, including you and I and Louis, I have nine. Nine that if they were put down would no longer be a threat to the girl."

"Why are you so bent on protecting her?" I asked. "I know why I am, but what's your motivation?"

Ozzie sighed. "She is one of the pure souls. She gives without thinking, fights for those who need to be protected, and quite frankly I think she could do this world a favor by sticking around. But if Clovis and Louis have their way, she'll either be turned to the dark side or killed."

I raised an eyebrow. "The dark side?"

"I just finished watching Episode IV." He waved a chubby hand at me. "I'm ad libbing here. You know what I mean. They'd break her spirit, tie her in chains, and she'd never be free."

I closed my eyes. "Like me."

"Like you. Only you got some power behind you now, and they know it. If they didn't, they would have just come in here and beaten the shit outta you." Ozzie reached up and patted my cheek. "They are afraid of you, Blacksmith, and rightly so."

A frown creased my face. "And how do I know that you aren't setting me up? How do I know that you aren't bringing me about to push me down?"

He spread his hands wide. "I've been trying to help the girl. I've given her a book of spells and Celia's book. She owes me a favor, and when I call it in, it will save her life." Ozzie stepped back. "I have to go now. I suggest you follow through with what Clovis wants from you, throw him off the scent."

The leprechaun snapped his fingers, and he was gone, a glittering of faint fairy dust and sulphur smoke lingering in the air like a bad fart. I shook my head, then froze. On the table where he'd sat was a square of paper with a thick scrawl written across it.

I stared at the paper as if it were a snake ready to

rear up and sink its fangs into me, and yet . . . the pull of it was undeniable. Who was in the Dark Council with me? I truly had no guesses, beyond the obvious, and over the years had stopped trying.

I found my hand reaching for the paper and folding it in half. Into my front jeans pocket it went. I would look at it later. If I chose to believe what Oster Boon was telling me.

Because after this many years of being on the council, I was no fool. The power struggles were very, very real and incredibly dangerous. You could wake up dead just for suspecting the right person.

My hands brushed over a chunk of steel left out on the table, and I stared at it, feeling the urge to create roll through me. Without putting much thought into what I was doing, I put the steel into the forge and cranked the handle on the blower.

Picking up a pair of tongs, I set them on my anvil, left the hand crank long enough to pick out a favorite hammer and set that on the anvil too. The movements were so familiar to me, so deeply ingrained in my being, that my mind wandered.

As I bent the steel to my will, pushing and urging it to take shape, as my muscles worked to create something out of nothing, I went over my options.

Going to find the old witch—if he meant who I thought he did—would take me away from Savannah, and away from Bree. It would also bring Clovis a step closer to becoming a vampire, a thought that made me shudder. Mostly because only vampires who were born were worth acknowledging. Those who were created were a mess.

"Idiot," I whispered as I flicked my tong hand, sending a spray of sparks across the stone floor. Clovis was a fool for believing that he could or would be different than any of the others who'd been created.

But he wasn't usually a fool. Which led me to believe that there was something else at play. Something Oster hadn't figured out just yet.

The question was, what? What could Clovis be up to?

I started the fine-tune work on the item I was working on, turning it this way and that, until it began to come into focus.

It wasn't meant to be one item, but three. Three thin slivers of metal, each tipped in an arrowhead leaf. Using my tools, I etched in the veins on the leaves, then began to mark the rounded edges with a wood grain pattern.

My body went through the motions, and the tools warmed in my hands as if they were a part of me. Slowly the image of what they were meant to be pulled into view and, using a wooden hammer, I curled the thin iron into a circle.

"Not quite right," I muttered as I thought of her eyes. Digging around in my box of gems, I pulled out three tiny slivers of sapphires and set them into the steel, where the leaf met the root of the branch. I placed more and more until the 'branch' portion of the bracelet was speckled as if with tiny blue flowers.

"Better." I nodded to myself and stood up, stretching the tension in my spine. Tension that came from years of this kind of work, of forgetting that I was not young anymore. I laid my tools down and scooped up the three bracelets.

They were prepared to take something on, whether it be a spell, a curse, or . . . something else. Would she even accept them? Would Bree understand that even though I knew she and I could not be, my desire to protect her and see her happy was still there?

I found myself looking at the small plastic baggie that held the dust from my forge under Celia's house. What was in it . . . there was too much for it all to be used for what Clovis wanted.

Before I could think better of it, I took a sprinkling of the dust created from burning the feathers of the fallen angel and rubbed it over the steel bracelets. They shimmered and then took on the look of true wood—the leaves darkening to a shadowy green and the gems opening as if they were true flowers.

If I looked closely, I could see the steel, I could see the marks from my tools. But to the naked eye, they looked like well-made bracelets of wood.

I tucked the bracelets into a blue velvet bag and left the forge. Night had fallen, and I knew that I would not have much time.

Already I could feel the pull of Clovis's demands on

me. I would need to leave and find the old witch as soon as I could.

I grimaced, thinking about having to deal with her. She hadn't been seen for a very, very long time. The first witch. The biggest witch of them all. Bree would have a heyday with that.

Smiling to myself, I slid out of the forge and onto the streets of Goblin Town. They were busy, as this time of night was the hour of trade for goblins.

I returned the nods of my—people was not the right word, maybe wards would be better. The women tittered, and the men gave me nods and salutes back. They appreciated that their previous king, Derek, was gone. He'd been running them into ruin, and they could not have found their way out of it on their own.

A flash of pixy dust and wings caught my eye, and I glanced up sharply, hoping it would be Kinkly. That she could take Bree a message for me. But it was Scarlett.

Scarlett, who was one of Karissa's favorites. Best to deal with her head on. "I see you there. What do you want, Scarlett?"

She fluttered out from behind the edge of a building. "Karissa would speak with you."

I didn't roll my eyes, nor did I grunt a response. I merely nodded. "As soon as I have time."

Scarlett flipped her long hair back from her face and glared at me. "She wants to speak to you now. Perhaps sooner."

Of course she did.

"Tell her I will be along presently." That was the best I was going to give my manipulative ex-wife. She was lucky she was not on the list of the Dark Council members.

My hand went to my pocket. But what if she was? Did I have it in me to kill a woman I'd once loved, even though it had all been a farce?

Scarlett saw my hand slip to my pocket. "What do you have there? A gift for the chubby girl?"

"This is perhaps not a good day to piss me off, pixy," I snapped, letting some of my darker powers slide up with my words. The powers that gave me my connection to working iron and steel when other fae fell sick or even died when they came in contact with it.

Scarlett's eyes widened, and she flew backward. "You would not dare harm me."

"Do not push me," I said, and wondered for a moment what monster she saw in me. The blood of the old fae and . . . others . . . ran true in my veins, and moments like this reminded me of how important it was for me to keep control. There was a reason the old lines had been locked away.

Scarlett zipped away, and I knew she'd tattle on me. I sighed and picked up my pace, heading for the nearest portal that would take me out of Faerie, and into Savannah. I'd put the bracelets somewhere that Bree would find them. While I didn't know exactly what they would do for her, the angel dust I'd rubbed into them should give her a boost. Maybe even protection. She had plenty of magic of her own, so it was hard to say what might come to the surface.

I stepped out of the cool night and into the humid, heavy heat of the South. I drew a breath as I moved out of the water and turned toward Bree's home. Celia's home. And, for a stolen moment, my home too.

It was the smell of charred wood that I noticed first. The faintest whisper of charred . . . everything.

Before clearer thinking took over, I started running. I knew in my gut that it wasn't a coincidence—it was her house. What if Bree had been inside?

When I got close enough, I saw it had been reduced to nothing but smoking embers.

Bree was across the street from the wreckage, on her knees, tears streaming down her cheeks. She still wore her fighting clothes from the battle at the fort. She still had the same smears of dirt and blood, which told me less time had passed here than what I'd spent in Faerie. Which meant the magic was shifting. Normally it was the other way around.

A sob ripped out of her, and I started moving toward her, only to stagger to a stop before she could see me.

She'd think I'd done it.

Or at least had been complicit in the act. Ducking behind a tree, I drew a slow breath as I listened to her cry.

"I'm so sorry, love," I whispered as my eyes welled. Her pain struck through me, sharper than any blade I'd forged, sharper than anything I'd ever felt on my own. I shook with it, unable to reach out and hold her and tell her I would help her make it right. She did not need me to do anything for her, but what I wouldn't give to stand at her side and fix this.

All I could do was stay in that spot, a silent witness to her grief, and ensure she was safe.

Time slipped by, and she finally stopped crying. A quick look around the tree showed me her stepping away, leaving what little remained of her home. Bree paused and turned toward me. I ducked back behind the tree.

"I don't know who you are, but I'm not in the mood," she said. The fatigue was like a weight in her voice, but I had no doubt she'd fight if she had to.

Her footsteps picked up cadence again, and I waited until she was gone before I moved out from behind the tree.

As I went across the street, the smell of burnt herbs grew. All of Celia's work had been destroyed, gone a flash of smoke and flame. The heat of the embers didn't bother me, and I stepped onto the remains of the house.

The Dark Council had done this because I'd failed to find the fairy cross. They'd done this to hurt my Bree.

"Oh!"

I turned to see a young female goblin standing off to one side, a little girl holding her hand. Bridgette was the goblin's name, and the little girl was Charlotte. Neighbors.

"Hello," I said.

The little girl with dark hair and eyes looked me over. "You didn't do this, did you?"

My eyebrows shot up. "No, lass, I did not."

She bobbed her head once. "Good. 'Cause whoever did it made my friend cry. I probably hate whoever did this. Though my mom says I shouldn't say things like I hate people."

Bridgette nodded. "We heard the flames, your majesty. We called the human fire people, but they were too slow."

I bent and put a hand over the smoking rubble. "Killing fire was used."

That meant Monica, the shapeshifter, was likely responsible. She had a real hatred for Bree for some reason. Then again, Bree had managed to flip Monica upside down in front of a lot of humans. She hadn't even realized she was doing it. Monica, who'd been masquerading as human, hadn't been able to retaliate or respond in kind.

That embarrassment alone might have been enough to make her hate my girl.

"You going to find out who did this?" the young lass asked. "And kick them in the hiney?"

I stepped off the rubble and approached the pair. "I'll see what I can do."

She shook her head. "Not good enough."

Bridgette let out a sigh. "Little one, that is not—"

I went to one knee and held out a hand to Charlotte. "I swear to you on my crown that I will find who did this."

She gripped my hand, and a tingle of magic slid across my skin. Already, untrained, the power in her was strong. Her eyes were solemn. "And you'll kick them in the hiney?"

I smiled. "And I will kick them in the hiney."

CHAPTER
THREE
CRASH

Back in Faerie, I made my way to Karissa's bower with an overnight bag slung over my shoulder. I didn't plan on staying. I'd be leaving Faerie immediately after speaking with her.

Karissa's bower was not a place I wanted to be. The last time I'd willingly gone to see her she'd damn well spelled me into her bed. This time I'd taken more precautions.

I had my sword on one hip and a small pendant around my neck, tucked under my shirt. Celia had given it to me just a few days before. After I'd tried to take Bree hostage.

My guts churned at the thought and my mind shot back to the moment Bree had fled, terrified of me. I could still feel the ache of that in my gut. But Bree didn't know what had happened immediately afterward. Only three people did. Celia, me, and Sarge.

"You idiot, idiot boy!" Celia had swung a hand toward me, but it had skimmed right through my arm. Still, I'd found myself flinching. "She trusted you!"

"I had no choice! If I did not come for her, they would have sent Bruce!" Bruce of the no-face as Bree liked to call him.

Celia closed her eyes. "Fire within me, are you certain?"

"Yes. That's why . . ." I looked across at Sarge who was watching me closely.

"You might as well spill the beans now," he growled. "I don't want to have a bump on my noggin for nothing."

"If Bruce came for her, there is no telling how he'd hurt her—or you, for that matter—he's a sadist of the highest order," I said. "At least if I came, I knew that—"

"That you could give her a chance to get away?" Sarge's eyes were wide. "You know she won't trust you after this."

"I know." I rubbed a hand over my face.

Celia disappeared—literally—leaving me alone with the werewolf. "Where did Corb go?"

He blinked. "Why do you ask? Oh . . . no . . . don't try that sacrificial, *he loves her and is better for her* bit. He's a mess. She'd be better off with Robert."

"Robert is not what or who he seems to be," I said. "And while he is her friend now, that will change. He has a whole other set of issues."

Celia popped back into existence right in front of

me. "Why would it change? He's like her, a past guardian."

I stared at Celia, not sure how much I should tell her. Not because a secret would help, but because I didn't know that she'd believe me. "Just . . . do not be surprised when it happens." That was the best I could do.

The rest they would have to find out on their own.

Celia narrowed her eyes and stared hard at me. "Here. I only have two. Bree wears one, so perhaps it is fitting that you have the other." The pendant she gave me was a dragon in relief, symbols carved around the edges. "May it protect you when you can no longer protect yourself."

Now, approaching the hanging flowers and vines that covered the entrance to the bower,

my hand lifted to the pendant. Karissa's bed was littered with flower petals and covered in satin sheets that had obviously been fragranced with her perfume. A bottle of wine and two fresh chalices sat to the side.

"Karissa, I do not have time for your games." I threw my words out like a challenge.

"Oh, but they are not games if the costs and the rewards are true," she purred as she emerged from the right side of the bower.

At least she was dressed, her pale green gown floated around her on the pleasant breeze that blew through the small space. She smiled, but I did not return the gesture.

"Again, I have no time. I have a job and a journey ahead of me," I said.

"Pity. Well, I shall get right to the point." She poured herself a glass of wine, then offered me one. I shook my head and she laughed. "Almost like you don't trust me."

"Almost is not a word that belongs in that sentence." I didn't so much as shift toward her. "Speak now, or I will leave."

She lifted a hand and took a sip of her drink before she spoke. Just to make a point that she would not be rushed. Yes, I knew this game of hers well.

"I know that you have spoken with someone from the Dark Council today. I want to know what they told you."

I laughed before I could hold it in. Fuck that. I let it out completely, laughing until tears ran down my face. "Piss off, Kay."

Smarter than the average man, I didn't turn my back on her. Instead, I walked backward so I could keep my eyes on her enraged face.

The chalice in her hand cracked and crumbled until it was nothing but powder in her palm. "You defy your queen?"

I paused at the bower opening. "I defy *you*, Karissa. Because you are no one's champion. You are a goddess in your own mind and no one else's."

A hiss slid past her lips, and she dusted off her hands, lightly clapping them together. I braced myself for a blow from behind or above. The whir of pixy wings had me sidestepping as Scarlett dashed into the bower and zipped around my waist.

Before I could stop her, she shot toward my front pocket and pulled out the paper that Oster Boon had given me. The members of the Dark Council.

Scarlett was shooting back toward her queen. "Here, I saw him tuck this away. It's a love note from the fat one."

I couldn't react, I knew that. If I reacted, and Karissa understood the importance of those names, then . . . I was well and royally fucked. *Especially* if she was on it. Schooling my face, I let out a heavy sigh and put my hands on my hips. "So, you want the list of people who owe me money?"

Karissa blinked and stared at the list, frowning a little. "These people? They have all hired you at some point?"

Fighting the urge to swallow hard, I nodded. Goddess damn me for not looking at the note sooner. "And?"

"I'm . . . surprised, I suppose," she said and handed the note to Scarlett, who brought it back to me, irritation written clearly across her miniscule face.

She dropped the note, and I didn't bend to pick it up. I could not look too eager.

"Why a list?" Karissa asked.

I rolled my eyes even as sweat slid down my spine.

"I am making the rounds. And I would hate to forget someone."

"Hmm, of course." She nodded. "Strange for a pixy to owe you money is all."

Fuck.

Her eyes darted to Scarlett, and the red pixy gave a squeak. "I don't owe him money!"

"So why are you on that list?" Karissa purred, showing a glint of the jealous streak that had driven us apart. But in this case...

Before I could stop her, Karissa swung her hand at Scarlett, her fingers gripping a tiny copper dagger I'd made her. She cut the pixy in half.

Scarlett didn't even have time to scream as she fell from the sky.

I looked at my ex-wife. She looked back and smirked. "Now, tell me why those names are on that list."

"And if I don't?"

Her smile widened. "I've seen them all, and I'll warn them that you are coming to speak with them. How does that tickle your fancy?"

I glared at her, knowing she had me in a bind. "They are... members of the Dark Council." I bent and scooped up the paper, and flipped it open. Scarlett's name was there in bold, next to eight others. All eight were people I knew, people I'd trusted at one point or another. Scarlett must be able to temporarily transform herself to average human size, or I would have known there was a fairy amongst the council.

"And why do you have this list?" Karissa drew close, and her energy bounced off mine in a way it hadn't in a very long time. For once, the woman was being sincere.

I looked her in the eye. "I am going to kill them all."

Her laughter tinkled, and she gripped my arm. "Then I am coming with you, because if there is to be a true bloodbath and cleansing of our world, they must go."

Goddess in a poorly woven handbasket, I did not want to go galivanting around the globe with this woman. Yet Bree had to deal with having her ex-husband's ghost live in her handbag. Perhaps I could deal with my ex-wife. Maybe I could stuff her in a handbag too. The thought made me smile, which Karissa took the wrong way.

"Are we of an accord?" She fluttered her eyelashes up at me. "I'll help you kill the Dark Council members?"

I gave her a slow nod. "We are . . . of an accord."

Stepping back, she clapped her hands. "Wonderful! Where to first?"

I put the list into my pocket. "We go to France to find the first witch."

CHAPTER
FOUR
BREENA

I held the vial in my hand, staring at the deep red liquid shimmering and dancing, moving as if there were something inside of it—something other than the magic that would bring Robert back to life. Call me crazy, but I didn't trust Karissa and her potion, even though it felt like the only hope I had to bring my friend back. He'd been killed—truly killed—in the battle against Joseph. All we had left of him were the ashes of his finger bone.

Karissa had given me the potion to bring him back, but if I used it, there would be a cost, a high cost. I would be signing away my connection to the fae world. Including my bond with Crash. I suspected that was the real reason Karissa had given me the concoction. To keep me away from her ex-husband.

On top of that, there was a time crunch. If I didn't

make my decision quickly, the potion would be rendered useless.

Kinkly fluttered up the porch steps to where I sat at the very top. The old house was rickety, cold, and nothing like my gran's place. Nothing like my home. A safe house, set aside for the witches of Savannah, it was a place to lay our heads and fill our bellies, but that was it. Nothing more. When I thought of the home we'd lost, the pain was as hot as if I'd been stabbed with a poker out of Crash's forge. I grimaced. I did not need to be thinking about him right now. I was looking at a way to bring Robert back to life, for duck's sake! I needed to focus. Not cry over the man who'd misrepresented himself.

"I'm too ducking old for this shit, for moping about." I swirled the vial, looking it over. My body was sore all over. The fight at the fort had been hard on not just my heart, but what felt like every single muscle in my body. If I didn't get some Advil into me soon, I was going to lock up into a knot that did nothing but whimper as my muscles seized for days.

Kinkly landed on the banister, settling herself. She winced and reached up to touch her left wing—Damian, the demon ally who'd helped us foil the Dark Council's plan to set a horde of the undead on Savannah, had said she'd be sore for a week or two. The patch job that had been done was solid, the line clean and the stitches so tiny they looked like pinpricks. A demon had helped her, and her own queen had ignored her. It said a lot about how our alliances had shifted.

"You think you're too old to handle all of this? I already knew that." She scrunched up her nose and then smiled. "I'm kidding, Bree. I think you're exactly right for this role. You're perfect."

I swirled the vial again. "If I use this on Robert's ashes, he'll come back to life. He'll have knowledge about the past, we'll be able to talk and—"

"And you could kiss him," she offered.

I *could* kiss him again, that was a valid point. I shook my head. "That's not the most important aspect of this decision, Kink."

While there had been that one kiss between us, it happened while I was technically asleep (and he was technically dead). I didn't really think of Robert that way. He was my friend, first and foremost. And I wanted him by my side to help us face all the monsters that came our way.

"I think it is." She rubbed her torn wing, massaging it. "I think part of the reason you want to bring him back is because he likes you. And you like him. The two of you fit. Which is a bit weird considering he's a skeleton most of the time. But maybe he'd help you get over Crash."

I looked at her, really looked at her. "Kinkly, I'd have to give up a literal part of who I am. Maybe it's not a big portion of my bloodline, but it's not insignificant either. And that part of me has saved my roundish ass more than once."

How many times had I been able to travel to the fae realm without being trapped? Often enough that I knew I'd probably end up finding my way there again with my luck.

She didn't look up from massaging her wing. "I am still here to help you with fae matters. And we have Bridgette for any goblin stuff."

I blew out a sigh. "I know all of that. It's . . ." How did I explain this to her? How did I get her to understand that this was more than just giving up a part of my heritage? My fae blood had allowed me to connect to Altin, an ancient fae who could very well be my grandfather. He'd helped me survive the last fight. Would giving up my fae bloodline cut me off from him?

"I don't think anything will help me get over Crash," I said softly, holding out my hand in a silent invitation. "Even another man." When she stepped onto my palm, I continued. "How would you feel if your wing couldn't be fixed? If Damian hadn't been able to stitch you up? If it had been there, attached to you but you couldn't use it?"

That stopped her and she lifted her eyes to look at me. "Well, I wouldn't be able to fly. Are you saying you wouldn't be able to fly? You didn't even know you had fae blood until recently."

I nodded and set her on my shoulder. "Right, and

maybe that's why I'm struggling. What am I really giving up? Wings?"

She snorted. "You do not have wings. They would never be able to lift you." Her words slid off me, because I was already thinking about the real reason that I wasn't sure.

Maybe my hesitation to give up this part of me had everything to do with Crash. Everything to do with the blacksmith who'd made me want him. I *still* wanted him. Even though I knew it was a terrible idea. This potion was meant to push us apart as much as it was meant to bring Robert back to life. Crash had left Karissa, not the other way around, and she still wanted him. Which meant she wanted me far away from him.

"He's a terrible idea," I whispered.

Kinkly sighed. "Yeah, probably. But you still want him." She knew exactly who I was talking about. How could she not?

I cupped the vial in my hands and stared down into it. "Yeah."

Crash's touch set me on fire, my damn granny panties about melted every time he so much as brushed a finger against me. Yet he was working for the Dark Council, in complete opposition to me. He'd tried to kidnap me, he'd taken Sarge prisoner, and then he'd fought by Joseph's side against us. Sure, he seemed reluctant, but could I pretend those things hadn't happened?

Now Karissa wanted me out of his life forever. I

mean, that part wasn't really a shocker. I'd known for some time that she'd been working at getting him back in her bed. I shouldn't hesitate. He'd declared his allegiance clearly enough, but...

I closed my eyes. "Did I ever really have a chance with him, Kinkly?"

Her wings fluttered by my ears and the fact that she didn't answer right away had me second-guessing myself. Again.

"I don't know," she finally said. "He was different around you, like he was trying to be better. You made him want to be better, I think. And he didn't affect you the way he affects most other women. That probably had to do with your fae blood."

I crinkled up my nose and rubbed my face with one hand. The smell of something luscious baking in the oven had my feet moving before I could think better of it. Distractions were welcome. It would help me put off this decision a little longer.

"Time to eat some emotions," I said as I went down the stairs and wove my way through the old house to the kitchen. Musty, dark, broken tiles littered the floor. The walls were scarred, and an old burn mark curled up and around the ceiling. Despite all that, the oven worked, and Eric was bent over it. He turned toward me with a full tray of tarts, his lanky frame tied up in a too-small apron that said *Kiss me, you fool* across the front, his glasses steamed from the heat of the oven. He squinted through the glasses.

"Bree, here. I've got a mixture of things, some lemon curd butter tarts and chocolate puffs." He set the tray on the table. "Hang on, one more."

Two trays of tarts. I had half a mind to sit down and eat them all myself, trying to fill up that void inside of me with sugar and lard. I scooped up one lemon tart and hissed as the heat scorched me. "Too hot."

"Maybe Crash is like that," Kinkly said. "Tempting, but too hot. Too much."

My lips quirked as I blew across the lemon filling. "Are you saying I need to blow him?"

Kinkly laughed, and I noticed the way Eric suddenly had his back to us and started clearing his throat multiple times. I also noticed that everyone else had made themselves scarce. Everyone meaning Penny, Eammon, Suzy, Sarge, and Feish.

"Is everyone afraid to talk to me?" I took a bite of the tart. Still on the hot side, but the sweet and sour notes of the lemon curd were perfect as they slid across my tongue and down my throat. I was going to have to work on restraining myself. These were seriously some of Eric's best creations yet.

"Well, they thought it might be best if you had a chance to consider your options, then discuss them with Kinkly and me." Eric turned back to us, his face only slightly pink. He dusted off his apron, then pulled up a rickety chair and sat down.

I popped the rest of the tart in my mouth and

chewed as I considered what he was saying. "Because you're the psychologist and Kinkly would be our only connection to the fae world if I go through with this?"

Eric nodded. "You could wait. We could find Robert's grave, and then he would re-animate on his own. You know that. All you had before was a finger bone, and that worked."

I did know that. "But where is Robert's grave? You know I've walked the Hollows cemetery more than once. There's no grave with his name on it. However statistically improbable it is, there isn't even a Bob in there, never mind a Robert."

"You might never find it." Kinkly hopped off my shoulder and flew down to the table. She selected a chocolate tart that was as big as her, pulled it off the tray, and dipped a finger into the soft center. "That's why it's so tempting to use the potion. I'd bet my left wing that's why Karissa did it. She knows how hard it would be for us to find Robert's grave."

A bar stool with no back stood to the left of me. I grabbed it and dragged it close so I could sit down. My back immediately twinged, cramping up and down one side so that my ribs felt like they were being squeezed in one of Crash's vises. I reached into my hip bag and dug around until I found my bottle of Advil, pulled it out and took three out.

I started to dry swallow them when Eric got up, took a glass and filled it with water. "Here, that's bad for you. You should always take your pills with a drink."

Smothering a smile, I took the offered glass and swigged down the tepid water, washing the pills down. "Thanks, Dad."

He grinned and didn't miss a beat. "You're welcome. Someone must look out for you. You're so ready to throw yourself into danger for others, you forget to take care of yourself. And I think that is what this decision comes down to. Not what's good for everyone else, not what's good for Crash or even for Robert. What's good for you? What do you want, Bree? You should consider what you're *willing* to give up, not what you think you have to give up."

His words started a definite tickle behind my eyes. I bowed my head and pressed the heels of my hands into the traitorous orbs. I did not want to cry. I was still covered in smoke and blood and sweat from the fight, from Gran's house burning down, from running all over the damn place. I needed to be strong.

"I don't know what I want," I answered honestly. "A few months ago, I would have said there was something special building between me and Corb. And even just a week ago, I would have told you it was Crash who held all the cards. And now Robert—"

Eric held up his hand. "You're missing the point, my friend. What do you, Breena O'Rylee, want? It doesn't have to be which man you want, but what you want. Fae, or not fae, Robert or no Robert . . . I've watched you these last months. Part of the job, you might say," he adjusted his bowtie and smiled down at me, "and what I see is a girl trying to fix everyone else's problems. You're trying to be everything to everyone. Even if you bring Robert back to life, you are not obligated to be anything more than his friend. And he is not obligated to be anything more than a friend to you. What you need to do is ask yourself some hard questions."

I blinked up at him. "Like what I want out of life, and not just at this particular moment?"

His smile softened. "Now you're onto it. You won't figure it out all at once, but I think you should be asking yourself that question. You spent a long time with one man, who told you a lot of lies. Those lies need to be unravelled, and you need to find yourself in more ways than one."

I hadn't expected him to ask me to do any self-analysis, not when I was already struggling with an ultimatum. Worse, we were running out of time.

"Kinkly, how long before the spell expires?" I asked.

"You have another hour," she said as she dipped her fingers into the chocolate tart again. "An hour before it's as dead as Robert."

Eric tsked at her. "That's not nice."

"But it *is* funny," she whispered back. "Morbidly funny."

I pushed to my feet. "I'm going to go get cleaned up. Thank you. Both of you."

With the lingering taste of the lemon tart on my tongue, I made my way through the house to the only working bathroom. My remaining friends were all in the front room where Penny had brewed up our shapeshifting potions prior to the big showdown at the fort with Joseph and the zombies. And Crash. Couldn't forget that man even when I wanted to.

Penny, Eammon, Suzy, Sarge, and Feish all looked at me, concern etched into their faces. Of course, Gran was there too. She moved toward me first and I waved her off. "Not right now, Gran."

"Child." She still came after me. "I've let the bigfoot discuss matters with you, but now I want to have my say. It is no small thing to bring someone back from the dead. You have a power in your hands that you perhaps don't realize the magnitude of."

I didn't doubt her. I just kept on walking, moving away from Gran. Wanting to stay oblivious to whatever she was trying to tell me.

Don't worry, I'd kick myself for that later. Give it a hot minute.

Penny stopped me at the bathroom door with a hand on my arm. "I have everything ready, should you choose to go forward with this."

"Do you think it's real?" I asked her. "Will this spell really bring him back to life?" Let's be honest, Karissa had not exactly been straight with me in the past. I could see her fooling me into using a potion that wasn't what she'd said it was.

Penny held out her hand and I gave her the vial. She swirled it up in front of her face, close enough that she could peer into it. "It be a life giving potion for sure. I've only seen one before, but this looks and acts the same."

She handed me the vial back and I clutched it in one hand. "Thanks, Penny. I'll . . . I'll have a decision when I come out."

Her smile was gentle. "You will make the right choice, I'm sure of it."

The bathroom was small, with several missing tiles in the floor. I stripped and got into the shower and scrubbed my skin until it stung all over. The Advil was slowly kicking in—I really should have chased it with whiskey— and I was feeling the heavy fatigue that came with everything I'd done in the last twenty-four hours.

Towel drying, I winced as I rubbed across new bruises and sore muscles that even the Advil couldn't touch. The whole time I scrubbed, the question Eric had asked of me rumbled through my head. What did I want? I wasn't sure that I'd ever asked myself that. Not really. I'd come back to Savannah hoping to regain ownership of Gran's house, which was supposed to belong to me.

I'd fallen into Corb's life.

Fallen into the job with the Hollows.

Fallen into Crash's bed and arms.

But none of those had really been choices, not in

the way Eric meant. "Jaysus." I pulled on clean undies and then my work leathers, silently thanking whichever of my friends had thought to grab a few of my things out of Gran's house after we went into hiding from Joseph. Everything else I'd owned had been destroyed in the house fire.

Almost everything.

I touched the dragon pendant that hung around my neck. It was a gift from my grandmother, meant for protection. Yet I seemed to keep finding trouble.

A soft tap landed on the door. "Fifteen minutes," Kinkly said. "Just so you know."

Fifteen minutes and the gift would be all used up. Was there even a choice? I was being given the chance to save a friend. Truly save him. To be honest, I didn't really question what I should do. Mostly I was just sad at what I was going to lose. I'd needed time to come to terms with that. To grieve the certainty that whatever was between Crash and me was sliding even further out of my grasp. My fingers slipped from the pendant around my neck, and I scooped up the red vial of liquid magic Karissa had left as a temptation.

For the life of a friend, I'd give up a part of myself.

"What has the fae part gotten me anyway?" I whispered aloud.

No sooner had I said the words than I got my answer. The remembered sensation of hands brushing across my skin, lips burning their way down my throat to the sensitive hollow . . . The rush of his touch was like a living thing, as if Crash stood right there behind me, reminding me of exactly what I was about to give up. I struggled to stand, hell, I even crossed my legs and squeezed tightly as I breathed through the onslaught of visceral need and heat.

"I can't do that anymore," I whispered as if Crash could hear me. "I have to let you go. We are on different sides, and I can't . . . I can't risk my heart on a man who would betray me. On a man who can't put me first. I lived that life for too long."

I stumbled as I took my first couple of steps. Then I gripped the banister as I made my way down to the main floor. I walked across the room without a word, moving between my friends to the work bench that Penny had set up.

"Girly, you make a decision?" Penny asked, concern etched into her face. Gran stood to the left of her.

"I'm sure she will make the right choice." Gran smiled, echoing what Penny had said earlier.

I smiled back. "I am too. The life of someone I care about means more than a piece of my bloodline."

Robert's ashes sat in a bowl on the table.

I uncorked the red vial and, without ceremony, poured it over the ashes of the finger bone. "Welcome back, Robert."

CHAPTER
FIVE

"Oh, for duck's sake!" Gran exploded as the vial dripped out the last few drops onto Robert's ashes. No, no she did not actually say duck. Which was even more shocking as the f-bomb reverberated through the room. I wasn't sure I'd ever heard her say it before. Ever.

My eyes shot to her, jaw dropping simultaneously, and I spluttered, "What? What? Is something wrong?"

Yup, I was that thick. Or maybe just that tired. Or a lot of things. Gran threw her hands into the air and, well, I would have said stomped off if she weren't a ghost. There wasn't a lot of noise, but she did float angrily out of the room, her arms swinging and her skirts swirling about her legs as she muttered to herself. There were several more ducks involved thrown out in her stomp-away exit.

I looked at Penny. "What is she so peeved about?"

Penny sighed, but we were interrupted by a poof of smoke from Robert's ashes.

The smoke was red like the liquid in the vial, and it curled up and up until it touched the ceiling in a long, thin curving line, turning in on itself as it spooled back down to the bowl of ashes. I took a step back.

Color me cautious, but magic tended to bite at times, and I was all done with the biting for the day, thank you very much.

The smoke thinned out further, sinking back into the ashes, and then, with a little burp that sent up a tiny poof of what was left of Robert, it disappeared altogether.

The others drew close, everyone peering over the desk. Probably thinking the same thing that I was. Ducking Karissa had screwed me again.

"Well, that's disappointing," Feish burbled. "I thought it was going to be a big bang, beautiful smoke show. Like fireworks." She put her webbed hands to her hips and glared at the pot of now soupy, red-stained ashes.

Kinkly fluttered across the table and peeked into the bowl. "I think maybe he just needs time? Or do we have to do something else, like bake it?"

Eric cleared his throat. "I don't think baking a Robert cake is a good idea."

I snorted. "Or Karissa deliberately ducked it up. So I'd use it, it wouldn't work, and I'd still lose my connection to the fae realm, because a deal is a deal." I rubbed a hand over my face. Gawd above, had I really let her dupe me again?

Gran came stomping back into the room, her face tight even in its transparent state. "It needs a drop of your blood to finish it up. I suggest you do it quickly, or the spell *will* die and you won't get your *friend* back." Her eyes were narrowed, arms folded, and her face hard. Okay, so she was still pissed.

I had no idea why she was so upset, but I believed her about the spell. My one remaining knife would have worked, but Penny had a pin cushion full of needles on the table that was more convenient. And clean. My knife was not clean.

Strike that, she had a doll full of needles. I raised my eyebrows at her. "Can I use one, or am I going to ruin something for you?"

Penny smiled. "He'll appreciate it if you take one out."

I didn't ask again, just pulled one of the needles free, ran it through the candle flame, and pricked my finger. Wincing, I massaged the tip of my finger until the blood welled and then held it over the bowl.

"Sure hope this does something," I said as the drop held for a second and then let go, plopping into the bowl.

I was expecting something.

I was not expecting an explosion.

The second the drop of blood hit the soupy ashes, a concussive force blew out of the bowl, shattering the earthenware and throwing every person in the room back to the closest wall.

Bodies hit hard, the sound of heads bouncing, and then my friends all slid down to the floor, unconscious or close to it. I, on the other hand, hadn't been thrown away at all. If anything, my feet felt glued to the floor as I stared at the man crouched on the worktable, his back curved as he flexed his fingers against the wood. Dark head bowed, he was completely naked, his skin glistening, his muscles flicking and shivering. His back was littered with tattoos, strange marks that I couldn't quite make out. His breath came in wind-sucking gasps.

The smell of sulphur filled the room, like a giant matchstick had been lit, and I snorted.

His head snapped up.

Sharp, brilliant blue eyes locked on mine. "Bree? Is this real?"

Before I could speak, someone else spoke for me.

"Hey, Robert. You aren't dead anymore," Feish said from her spot against one of the walls. "Say thank you."

Robert didn't move from his crouch but instead looked down his body. "A blanket would be nice."

Sarge was the first one to approach him, a blanket in one hand, the other pressed to the lump forming on his forehead. "Here you go, man."

Robert took it and slid it around his waist before coming out of the crouch. He slid his butt off the table, planting his feet to the floor. "What happened? I remember Joseph—"

"And you getting killed." Feish dusted herself off. "That's what happened. You were *dead*-dead, and now you are alive because of Bree. Say *thank you*."

I just kept staring at him, partially because he was there—he was *real*—but also because he looked a little different than when he'd been solid before. He was . . . edgier. It was less of a coherent thought than a feeling. Something was off, but I couldn't put my finger on it. "You okay?"

He didn't look away from me, didn't move, didn't say thank you as Feish suggested. He went straight to the heart of it. "What did you have to give up? What was the deal you made to bring me back?"

I shrugged. "It doesn't matter. I wasn't using it anyway."

His eyebrows shot up. "Surely not your . . ." He waved his hand at my stomach and then seemed to think better of the question.

"She's too old to give up her childbearing ability, you nignog." Kinkly snapped her wings and fluttered across the room to my shoulder. "Yes, that is typically what would be asked of her, but Karissa no doubt knew it would be more painful for her to give up something else."

I leaned hard to one side so I could look at Kinkly. She didn't seem any different to me now that I'd lost my connection to the fae. "Or she knew that I can't bear children, so it wouldn't have been a good deal on her part."

Robert's face fell. "Bree, I'm sorry. You should not have brought me back."

Well, that was not the response I'd expected.

I could have been truly hurt, could have started crying. Nope, not today.

I frowned up at him, then pressed a finger into his very solid, very trim chest, right against a tattoo over his heart. "You're welcome, you ungrateful prick."

He pulled back. "Don't touch me, Bree."

Don't touch him?

He shook his head and tried to step away from me, bumping into the table in his haste to get away.

How was this the same guy? In my dream that wasn't just a dream, he'd kissed me, and now he couldn't stand a simple touch. I don't care what anyone says, men are the flakier gender.

"Just don't." He pulled his blanket tighter around himself.

As if I were... what? Diseased? Not good enough?

Double nope.

"Fine. Whatever your issues are, you deal with them. I have my own. We have to figure out what to do to prevent a possible resurgence of vampires." I turned and stomped out of the room with a tight throat. Here I'd thought we were going to be a team, that he'd still be my friend once he had flesh on his bones.

Had he been using me all along? Duck me upside

down, I just couldn't believe it. He'd saved my life more than once as Robert the Skeleton. Which meant something else was going on with him. I called over my shoulder, "When you're ready to tell me what bee is up your tight ass, you let me know."

We had other problems—pressing problems—and if Robert was going to be like this, then I was not going to stick around and wait for him to talk. There was literally no time. "I'm going down to Death Row if anyone wants to come. I need supplies. Robert, why don't you get yourself reacquainted with being alive."

Feish slid up next to me. "Of course I'm coming. You can't go by yourself."

Sarge grunted and fell in with us. "I'll come too."

Fine by me. They were my friends, and I loved them, and they were obviously worried I'd get into trouble on my own. As much as I hated to admit it, they probably weren't wrong.

The humidity of Savannah hit me hard as we stepped out of the house, and I started sweating right away. "We could take my bike?" Sarge offered, obviously forgetting that both Feish and I would not fit on it. I shook my head, feeling the need to move my body. It was aching, the Advil working at half speed, but I needed to move.

"No, I think walking would be good." Because I was all twisted up inside. Robert had not only acted ungrateful, he'd been . . . distant. Damn it, he'd all but flinched from my touch, which wasn't exactly how I'd seen it playing out. I mean, I'd thought he would at the very least hug me.

After everything I'd lost, I figured this one thing would be okay, that I'd have my friend back.

Even that had turned out to be a fantasy.

"My belief in men is questionable," I whispered.

Sarge laughed. "You and me both, sister." He held out a fist, and I bumped it with my own.

"Well, I think you need to read more," Feish burbled. "There are many, many good ones out there if those books are right. Every book, the woman finds a perfect man. Maybe he doesn't look it, but he's there. Usually by chapter two or three."

Sarge and I looked at Feish. "Those the romance books you've been reading?" I asked.

"Romance education books." She bobbed her head. "Like the ones you suggested."

I'd suggested she read a few Denise Grover Swank books. As in fictional books, not non-fiction self-help books.

I looked at Sarge for help, and he just shrugged. "Shit, maybe she's right. Maybe we'll both find the perfect man."

I shot him what I hoped was a withering stare—that comment didn't even deserve a response—and picked up speed as I strode in the direction of Death Row. Well, I took a few steps in that direction anyway... which was when it struck me. I had a check worth a million dollars in my bag. Payment from Roderick for dealing with his brother, Joseph. I should really put that in the bank. "Change of plans, let's go to the bank first."

"You getting forgetful in your old age?" Feish asked as we crossed the street and headed toward the bank, crossing Orleans Square. "I didn't think you were that old."

I glared at her. "I'm not, Feish."

She winked at me. "I'm teasing, friend. I know you are only middle-aged and not old-old."

I sighed, and on my other side, Sarge sighed heavily, mimicking me. "What's the next step?"

Wasn't that the question of the day? "Deposit said check, give my friends what they're owed, and go shopping."

Sarge slowed. "Really?"

"Retail therapy is probably my best bet other than therapy from Eric, be it his advice or his cooking," I said. "I mean, unless I want to eat my feelings?" I shook my head. "No thanks. Shopping it is."

"No, I mean . . . you're giving the rest of us money?" Sarge seemed shocked.

"That was the deal," I said. "Wasn't it?"

He nodded. "Yeah. But you keep my portion. I don't need it."

I looked over at him. "What do you mean you don't need it?"

"Long story, but I'm loaded. I do all this stuff for fun, not because I need the money." He grinned at me.

I stopped in my tracks and stared hard at him. "You're...loaded, and you do this for fun."

He shrugged and looked up at the trees above us. "Werewolves are driven to find excitement and danger. I might as well do something kind of good with that drive, you know? The local pack won't have me because I'm mostly gay, so this is the next best thing, having a group of friends who put up with me and get into trouble all the time."

"Well, shit. You learn something new every day, that's what Gran always said," I said and then stopped dead in my tracks. Gran.

Yup, the penny dropped.

"Oh my Gawd." I struggled to breathe. "I could have brought Gran back to life. Her ashes . . . she was cremated. I could have brought her back instead of Robert."

Feish patted me on my back as I went to my knees. She was talking, but I couldn't hear her over the white noise buzzing in my ears.

That's why Gran was so pissed with me. She should have just said it! Because as much as the idea of Robert was amazing, I would have picked my gran over him a thousand times.

I struggled to breathe through the horror, finally gulping a big breath. "Duck me, she is never going to let me forget this." And I would never forget it either. "Wait, maybe I could get another spell!"

Sarge and Feish both just looked at me. I looked

back. "What, you don't think Karissa would want to take away another part of me?"

"I think this spell took a lot out of her," Feish said. "To get you away from Crash, she would do anything. But she doesn't like you. She won't help you get your gran back."

I thought about my first interaction with Karissa in the women's bathroom, how she'd helped me do my makeup. Of course, she hadn't known about the connection between me and Crash yet.

"And that spell wouldn't have worked on your gran," Sarge said. "At least I don't think it would have."

I looked up at him and then Feish, hoping they were right. "Why not?"

"Because the whole reason Karissa borrowed Robert a while back was because she needed something from him in order to make the spell—at least that's what Penny said." Sarge helped me back to my feet. "You think that's why Celia was being pissy? Because she didn't know the spell was geared toward him?"

He'd noticed it too. "Yeah. But wouldn't she have realized what you just told me?"

"Maybe she's getting old too." Feish clucked her tongue. "Do ghosts go through menopause? Do they lose their minds and memories? I read that somewhere."

I didn't feel like pointing out that Gran was far past the stage of menopause, even if she'd been alive.

Mostly because I was too busy staring at the person striding across the square, headed our way from the direction we'd come.

Robert looked good in modern clothes—dark blue jeans and a slightly too tight light blue T-shirt. His hair was a bit on the wild side, but as he walked toward us, he pulled it back into a low ponytail.

"You want a moment of privacy with him?" Sarge asked.

"Yeah, so he can say thank you?" Feish said, loudly enough that there was no way Robert didn't hear her.

He stopped just in front of us. "I'd like to speak to Bree alone, please."

Sarge and Feish looked at me, and I gave them a nod. "Yeah, it's fine. He has some grovelling to do."

Feish snort-laughed, and Sarge gave me a wink. "Get him on his knees, that's a good place for a man."

Jaysus. My face flushed all hot and probably went bright red like a flaming light bulb. Feish and Sarge moved off, giving Robert and me some privacy.

Robert took a step closer and brought his hands up to grab hold of my upper arms. His blue eyes were serious as he closed the distance between us.

"Bree."

"Robert."

His hands tightened, and he leaned his head in, his eyes dipping to my mouth. I closed my eyes, feeling the tension between us. This was a terrible idea. I did not want a rebound with Robert. Nope. No. Not happening.

Lips brushed against my earlobe, sending a shiver down my spine.

"We are in danger." And he yanked me hard to the left as something shot past us both, something hard and metallic by the sound of it.

Not even one day since our last fight, and we were being attacked again. This was getting tiresome.

CHAPTER
SIX

Robert's yank on my arms snapped us both to the ground as several projectiles shot over our heads.

"Hurry! More are coming!" He kept his grip on my arm as he started crawling across the ground on his belly as if we were back in the Hollows being trained. I followed, though I cursed that I was back to this army-crawling business.

"What the hell is happening? What is that?"

He kept on dragging me, and I managed to get my body moving. The Advil had fully kicked in, but I was still sore, and so very ducking tired, so I was slow. Or maybe I just wasn't in as good shape as I'd thought—that was a distinct possibility. With a grunt I got moving, dragging my body across the grass, but let me be honest, I was *ridiculously* slow. And moving like maybe an inch with each grunt.

An inch was not going to get me out of danger any time soon. I pushed to my hands and knees, crawling far faster like that even though it hurt like a son of a . . . something dropped across my body in lines, like rope. I twisted around. Check that, it *was* rope.

I rolled away, but the rope twisted around me as if it were alive. "Ah, crap!" I reached for my bag, but my arms were clamped tight to my sides so fast that they slapped my leather pants. "Really?" I stopped struggling and let out a slow breath. Fighting my way out of this was not going to work.

I wiggled my fingers and bellowed for my friends. "Feish! Sarge!"

"Yeah, nope!" Sarge yelled back. "We got roped too!"

I didn't squirm. Damn, this would have been the perfect time for Robert to pop out of my bag, and bite through the ropes. But by the sounds of it . . . "Robert, you caught too?"

"Yes," he growled. Oh, someone was cranky this early in being alive.

I worked my hand toward my bag. I had a knife in there—the one Crash had left for me to replace the two I'd lost. My fingers flipped open the leather flap, and I kept right on wiggling them until they brushed up against the smooth handle. "There we go." See, as much as having your friends around was good, sometimes you needed to save yourself. I gripped the handle and rolled my wrist just so. The blade popped out and cut through one of the ropes.

The rope screamed.

Yup, screamed. High-pitched, ear-piercing, making all the birds in the region fly away, screamed.

Thrashing and shrieking, the ropes slithered off me, and I rolled to my hands and knees and sat up. Robert was fighting for all he was worth, and it looked like the ropes were just digging in harder. Feish was calmly lying on the grass, and even Sarge seemed to have figured out that the more he fought, the tighter the ropes got. Like some sort of Chinese finger trap.

I went to Robert first. When I cut the ropes, they shrieked, and he came up swinging, his fist snapping out toward one of the ropes. It had no interest in him once it was injured. He spun and nearly caught me in the chin with a fist.

I stepped out of the way, but just barely.

His eyes were wild, his hair all mussed up, and for a moment it was like he was not there . . . "Chill out, Robert." I patted his shoulder, and he turned his face toward my hand. Mouth open.

Teeth bared.

Teeth bared?

I jerked my hand back. Took a few steps back and stared down at him. "Robert?"

"Something's . . . wrong," he whispered and shook his head, stepping away from me. "Bree, this is not good."

I reached a hand to him, and he took it. "You're new at this living thing. You probably just feel weird."

He squeezed my fingers and then let me go. "Help them."

I spun and hurried over to Feish and Sarge, setting them free with a quick slash to each set of ropes, though I use that term lightly. Whoever had sent the ropes hadn't sent anyone to gather us up, at least not with any sort of urgency. The other people—humans milling around in the park—glanced at us but didn't flinch. They couldn't see the ropes. Didn't hear the screeching as they were cut off my friends.

"Weirdos! Get out of here!" a man yelled as he crossed, passing close enough to see Feish and Sarge lying on the ground, and Robert still vibrating. He'd probably seen us army crawling across the square.

I flipped him off. "We're practicing for a play, douche!"

He cursed at me.

"Go away, you are not important in this story!" Feish yelled as I cut into the rope.

Feish sat up and rubbed at her arms. "That was terrible. Just terrible. Like being caught in the nets again."

I helped her stand up. "The nets?"

"Yeah, when Karissa first caught me." She shivered, and her gills flicked open and shut more than usual. "Terrible. They did a similar thing, wrapping tighter and tighter the more you fought."

I offered my hand to Sarge, and he waved me off. I noticed the tiny spider sitting on his shoulder. Jinx waved at me, and I glared at her and pointed a finger. "You could have helped!"

Sarge grunted as if I'd punched him. "I was tied up too, remember?"

"Not you, your freeloader friend there on your shoulder."

Jinx ducked down his back before he could see her, but she wasn't fooling anyone. "Jinx!" Sarge snapped. "I told you to leave off! I'm not interested! I like men, not androgynous spiders!"

"Which is why I didn't help." Her voice was loud for someone in such a tiny body. "And you said it yourself, you're mostly gay."

"I should have said all the way gay," he growled.

"Let's get back to the house," I said. "Maybe we won't get attacked there?" It didn't sound convincing, but at least there we'd have Penny and the others to help against anyone wanting to harm us. The theory was as sound as any.

Robert was on his knees, staring at the ground with his chin to his chest. I gave Feish and Sarge a 'wait for me' move with my hands.

They shrugged in unison, though I could see that Feish was paler than usual. The ropes had stressed her out. Fair enough. She'd experienced them before, so this had to trigger some PTSD for her. Just one more reason to hate on Karissa. Did that mean Karissa had sent the ropes? If so, why?

Also . . . if Feish was captured by Karissa, how had she come to live with Crash? Had he taken her under his wing to keep her away from Karissa? She'd been an indentured servant to him, too, but she was loyal to him by choice, anyone could see that.

"Lawd help me, I do not need to give him a reason to be a hero." I spoke under my breath, mostly to myself. Sarge grunted though. Of course he'd heard me with his wolfy ears.

I went to Robert and crouched beside him, but he flinched away from me. "Something is wrong, Bree. I can feel it in my body. I'm not myself. And I don't want to hurt you. Of all the people in this world, you are the one I want to protect. The only one I need to protect."

Gotta be honest, it took a lot for me to reach out and put my hand on his shoulder again. But I did it, and I gave him a little squeeze. "Maybe it's just like vertigo. You've got to get used to being alive again, right?"

"Like getting your sailor's legs!" Feish offered. Apparently she had good ears too.

He lifted his head, eyes on mine, face distraught. "I wanted to bite you, Bree. And I don't mean in a sexual way. I wanted to bite on you and make you bleed."

"Like, you wanted to hurt me?"

There was a hiss in the air that turned me around

in time to see something flying through the big Spanish oak trees. More nets.

I yanked him to his feet, and the four of us were running back toward the house as fast as we could go. Robert gripped my hand, and I held on to him too. Because we'd face whatever was going on with him as a team.

We had to.

The four of us—five if you counted Jinx—ran all the way back to the house, with the sound of slithering ropes following us. I didn't look back. Sarge did at one point.

"Yeah, not good! Keep running!"

Like I was going to sit down and have a break right there. Okay, I wanted to—my breath was coming in sharp blasts and my heart felt like it was going to explode. More training was needed, obviously, if I was going to be put on the run like this on the regular.

Who was I kidding? It was already happening on the regular.

We blasted through the front door of the house, I tripped over the ledge, and we all went crashing to the floor in a pile. I landed on Robert, and his arms went around me, and we found ourselves nose to nose for the second time in like fifteen minutes. He stared at me, and one hand slid up my back to the side of my face and brushed across my skin as he mouthed my name. As if he were tasting it.

"What in hell is going on here?" Penny barked, and I stiffened like I'd been caught as a teenager with a boy.

"Someone came after us," I said as I carefully pushed off Robert and got to my feet with only a little bit of a wobble. Feish and Sarge were dusting themselves off, and Robert got to his feet last, slowest.

"Who?" Suzy poked her head out of the kitchen area. Her blond hair was swept up into a high bun, and wisps had curled out around her face. She was wearing an apron—baking lessons with Eric, no doubt. Eric leaned around her and rested his head on top of hers.

"I think maybe Karissa. Feish said she'd seen nets like that before, but it doesn't make sense. You guys have any idea?" I turned to Sarge, Feish, and Robert.

Robert was the one who nodded. "I think it was one of the council members. He's worked with the queen of the fae before. Since she's the one who gave you the spell that"—he gestured to his body—"it fits."

I scrunched up my face and tipped my head back. "Seriously?" My guts gurgled with discomfort at the thought. The council had been less than helpful, to say the least, and I knew some of them also served on the Dark Council. Unfortunately, we weren't certain which of them were pulling double duty.

In general, they really didn't like me, being that they were a group of old-school, misogynistic dink holes and I was a strong, gaining-my-confidence-back woman in her middle years. It kind of set us to locking horns about basic decency.

So yeah, I wasn't too keen on the idea of the council coming after me, or us, for any reason.

I bent at the waist, and my lack of oxygen from running caught up with me, a mighty stitch forming in my side that had me grimacing and limping toward the kitchen. "What the hell could they want with us now?"

"Probably not us," Feish pointed out. "Just you. We in the way. You are the one with all the trouble around her."

I slid into one of the kitchen chairs that I'd so recently vacated, keeping one hand jammed into my side to help with the stitch.

"Keep walking it off," Sarge said. "It'll fade faster."

I pushed to my feet and circled the kitchen. Eric put out a tray of muffins that looked a tad overcooked. Okay, they were black. "Look, Suze made these," he said proudly. "Her own flavor profile! They aren't burnt. Everyone take one and have a bite. See what you think."

He was obviously trying to lower the tension in the room, and everyone dutifully took a muffin. We bit into them at the same time. Which meant we all spat it out at the same time, spewing chunks of . . . well, I'd say muffin, only it tasted nothing like any muffin I'd ever had. Well, not quite all of us spat it out.

"Squid ink muffins," Feish moaned. "These are amazing! Did you make them for me?"

Suzy smiled. "I did think you'd like them; you haven't been eating the ones Eric made. The waterborn truly have a different palate than the rest of the world." She winked.

Robert slapped a hand on the table, and I noticed that he hadn't taken a muffin. I mean, I got it. I'd only tried the black muffins out of loyalty. Then again, wasn't he hungry? There were other treats on the table, right within reach, and he hadn't eaten anything. "Wonderful, wonderful. Can we get back to the point at hand? Someone just tried to kidnap Bree. Again."

I sighed. He wasn't wrong. "We'll get there, Robert. Or they'll come here. I mean, we don't know who tried it. It might not have been the council. Maybe it was Karissa just being a stinky muff again."

He ground his teeth loudly enough that everyone went still. "I *know* who it was. Lucas Brave. He has been on the council a long time. A warlock with great power and great pull within the council."

I frowned. "How do you know it was him?"

"Because that flying rope trick is his signature move. I saw them coming, but I didn't realize what they were until I was right on top of you." He breathed out a heavy sigh. "I was too slow."

Feish snickered. "I bet you want to be right on top of her, but no! That is *not* your place."

Lawdy gawd in heaven, I did not need her to start shipping me and Crash again. "Feish, ease off. It's been a rough morning for Robert."

She bit into her muffin and mumbled something around it. Something about me putting dicks before chicks, and I did not want to know where she'd picked that up from.

"I am not." I pointed at her, then turned to Robert. His face was tight, and I couldn't tell if it was from pain or concern. "Robert, any idea why he might have tried to net us all?"

He closed his eyes. "Because you just brought me back from the dead."

I pursed my lips. "I didn't use any magic; it was Karissa's spell."

Robert's jaw ticked. "I'm just guessing here, but what if Karissa slipped him a note suggesting it was your ability that rose me from the dead, not hers. Now Lucas thinks you know how to raise the dead back to true life." He paused. "Your connection to the shinigami and Mori would only further cement this belief."

Dr. Mori was a newer friend. He and the shinigami had a connection to the dead, just like I did, and he'd offered to start training me in like a week. I was looking forward to it, if I were being honest. Up until now, I'd only used my connection to the dead accidentally, or by experimentation driven by desperation. The possibility that I could learn how to harness it was alluring to say the least. But flexing my *power over the dead* muscles obviously had some drawbacks. Or at least some associated problems.

Basically, if Robert was right, this Lucas thought I could raise the dead and wanted that power for himself. Not good. I cleared my throat, and a knock on the door had us all turning our heads.

"All your trouble always comes in through the front door," Penny muttered. "At least it doesn't try to disguise itself as something else."

Nobody moved toward the door.

I mean, there was a chance it was just a salesman. Maybe a real estate developer. Someone other than Lucas Brave of the Savannah council. But let's be real. We all knew it was trouble—Lucas, Karissa, or someone else intent on giving me grief.

The stitch in my side was easing, so I went toward the door. The scramble of feet behind me made me smile. Sure, my friends didn't want to answer the door either, but they weren't going to let me answer it on my own.

I held my hand out toward the doorknob and waited, feeling the pulse of energy coming off the steel. The pendant around my neck heated against my skin. I held up a hand to stop my friends. "The door is unlocked; you can open it." I wasn't dumb enough to invite him in, not when I'd just learned that vampires were a real issue and not monsters who were polite enough to ask for an invitation inside before chowing down on you.

I took a step back. There was a muttered curse from the other side of the door, and I glanced at Robert. "That sound like your friend?"

"Not friend," he growled, sounding just like his more skeletal self.

I smiled. "Okay, not friend."

The doorknob turned, and we all took another step back, as if were in a damn musical together and the big bad wolf was about to blow the door down. Maybe not a bad analogy, all things considered.

The large door swung inward, and in the framed doorway stood a rather nondescript man. He was wearing a sweater vest over a long, checked shirt, khaki pants, and knee-high black rubber boots. His light-colored hair was a mess, but it was jammed under an orange baseball cap from Hooters, so you couldn't see all of it. Just the ends sticking out in every direction.

"Who the hell are you?" I blurted out. "Because I'd have remembered you from the council chamber."

He cleared his throat. "If you must know, I have to dress in accordance with the rules when I am in the council chambers. But I can dress as I like when I am outside of those walls."

"And this is what you like?" Suzy whispered. "Wow. I mean, that's some serious balls."

He smiled as if she'd given him a compliment. "Yes, wow indeed. But let's continue to the matters at hand. The council wants to speak with you."

I startled. "What?"

He leaned forward but did not cross the threshold of the door as he repeated himself, this time at a much higher volume. "The. Council. Requests. Your. Presence. Immediately."

I grimaced. "Louder won't make me say 'what' any less. You have *actually* got to be kidding me. They don't like me. I don't like them. There really is no good reason for me to go to talk to them. They don't even believe me when I am trying to help. We all recall me trying to tell them just *YESTERDAY* that Joseph was an issue, correct? Right. So, goodbye."

I touched the bottom edge of the door with my boot and started to shut it. "Time for you to go, Mr. Brave, and take your damn rope-a-dope spell with you."

He pushed the door open, which wasn't hard to do with just my toe stopping him. "No. You must come. They have something—or should I say someone—that you will want to see."

"Bad idea," Robert said. "All your friends are here."

Were they though? Yes, my closest friends were present, but there were other people in my life who could be hurt. Other people whom the council could use against me. Bridgette. Charlotte. Crash.

My jaw ticked. "When do they want me to come by for tea?"

Penny grabbed at my arm and squeezed. I agreed with her concern, but I didn't know what else to do. I mean . . . it was the council. They could hurt someone I loved. It could even be . . .

I looked at Sarge. He locked eyes with me, and I

knew we were thinking the same thing. Corb worked for the council. He'd disappeared after I'd shut him down. My gut twinged, and I knew that I was right.

Damn it, it really could be Corb.

We were at odds, but he was still someone I cared about.

Which meant there was no choice but to go.

CHAPTER
SEVEN

Knowing that Corb or one of my other friends could be in the council's custody was the only thing that made me agree to speak with them. Mind you, my friends were not going to let me go alone, not after everything that had gone down in the last couple of days.

Not after the council had poo-pooed me trying to get them to help me go up against Joseph and his zombies.

Penny stood at my side on my left, Robert on my right, and Suzy, Eric, Feish, Sarge, and Jinx (though the council couldn't see her) ranged out behind us. Eammon claimed that he had a few errands to run, but Penny whispered the truth to me as we stood in front of the council.

"His brother, Oster Boon, is likely here. Apparently, they've been fighting." Her dark eyes swept the room as she spoke from the corner of her mouth. I did the same, but there was no sign of the smaller figure of Oster Boon.

"Brought quite the entourage today?" Roderick said from his seat near the front of the council room. He shook his head ever so slightly, his eyes worried. And then he locked eyes with Robert.

They shared a moment, one that had Roderick narrowing his eyes at my friend. For his part, Robert gave the slightest tip of his head toward the council member. They'd been friends once, but Skeletal Robert hadn't liked Roderick. Was it because he'd known Roderick was a vampire and had no way to tell me? Or was it something else?

My mind skipped to Roderick. He'd given me that check hours before. Why hadn't he said anything about the council wanting to speak to me? His eyes swept left and right, and then I got it. His small head shake said it all.

He hadn't known about this.

Either that or something had happened in the few hours between his visit with me and now. Also a distinct possibility.

"Well, you know how it is when you want to crash a party. Best to bring everyone. That and I didn't feel like being wrapped up in screaming ropes again." I shrugged as if that was nothing but took note of the looks the council members exchanged.

"Lucas." Roderick's voice went gravelly.

Lucas had swapped his casual outfit for a long black trench coat, black pants, and shirt. The Hooters hat was nowhere to be seen. He looked familiar now, in this place and dressed relatively normally. He bowed at the waist. "You said she would need to be convinced to come speak with us. I did not think there was a great deal of time, so I made a decision. My ropes could have brought her here quickly if she hadn't cut through them. Which, I should point out, she should not have been able to do."

Roderick looked to me. "She has a habit of surprising people. Get used to it."

The compliment made me feel better than it should have. Especially coming from a vampire. Unlike his brother Joseph, though, Roderick seemed to want to stop the whole *rising of the vampire army* business.

I took note that the oldest council member, Stark, sat in his usual chair, seemingly asleep, his head resting against the back of the chair. I say seemingly because the old fart wasn't as mute and over the hill as he liked to pretend. He'd given me advice when no one was looking before. The council seemed to think he was a nincompoop, but their mistake had worked in my favor.

"You going to tell her what the hell has happened or not?" A strident, ear-piercing voice crackled out of the darkness. The old guy snorted and slumped further into his seat at the sound of that voice.

A voice I knew all too well.

Of all the people I'd thought might be there, Missy hadn't made the list. Missy, my gran's ex-best friend, the lying witch who'd sided with Joseph, stolen my gran's book, and . . . "What the actual duck is she doing here? Why is she not locked up somewhere? Or dead?" The words flowed out of me as I stepped forward. My hand reached for my knife before I thought better of it.

Roderick held up a hand. "Missy has been working for this council for many years, but quietly. She infiltrated the Dark Council and has brought us information that we can use to stop what they are planning."

His eyes locked on mine, and I felt my insides turn sloppy, sloshing around. He was talking about the vampire army that the Dark Council was working to raise, something so much worse than the zombie infestation they'd created using Joseph's skill set. "Are you sure she isn't fooling you? Because she's pretty good at that."

Roderick shook his head. "After you and I had our discussion this morning, I . . . spoke at length with Missy. She is not lying. She corroborated what you and your team have deciphered. That the Dark Council is indeed trying to bring about a new age of vampires."

The council members all shifted uncomfortably.

Missy huffed and put her hands on her hips.

Penny drummed her cane on the ground, drawing everyone's eyes to her. "That one cannot be trusted, but I will agree with the rest."

"This from the witch who taught Homer and Marge their voodoo magic," Missy sniffed.

I didn't look at Penny, but I'll admit the shock was real. Maybe it shouldn't have been, though. Hadn't I just seen her with a voodoo doll? Yes, yes, I had. Then again, Marge herself wasn't a bad person, more of a trickster. She went where the money led.

Penny sighed. "That was a long time ago, Missy. And it's a mistake I'll own. More than you'll ever own yours." She drummed her cane again. "What information has she brought?"

I was glad Penny was speaking, because it gave me the chance to study the council members.

She and the council members went back and forth while I looked around.

There were eight of them, which meant they'd lost a few. Roderick, Lucas, Stark. Jacob the necromancer was also present. The other four were not familiar to me. But I was looking for one person in particular. No-face Bruce. Where was he? I'd seen him with Roderick a few times, and he'd given me the damn willies. The guy was literally hard to look at. His features morphed and danced, making it impossible to actually see what and who he was. Everyone else was talking and I . . . well, I let my feet move me. I stopped in front of the first council member I didn't know and stuck out my hand.

If they were going to screw me over, then I wanted to know their names. "And you are?"

The old white guy snorted. "I will not touch your hand."

"Your name," I said.

"No."

"Okay, No. Nice to meet you. I'm going to call you Fred."

I moved on down the line and was greeted with 'I think not,' 'Go away' and, my personal favorite, 'Bitch.'

Well, that rounded out the crew nicely. "Are you listening to any of this?" Roderick asked as I passed him.

I returned to my spot at the front of the council room. Dredged up the words that had been said.

"Missy thinks they're still working on the spell. They stole the fairy cross, which I already knew, and suddenly she wants to help us. That about sum it up?" I raised my eyebrows and scrunched my nose.

Roderick dipped his head, and Missy let out a long, low hiss.

"You have no idea what you're dealing with, girl."

I rolled my eyes. "Really? You think I don't at this point? Clovis wants to raise an army of vampires. You think I don't realize we're racing against a clock that we can't see the hands of? We don't even know who's really on our side, and who isn't? Like *you*."

Even as I said it, a memory flashed through my mind. "You know what? That last bit isn't true. You were on the dark side of Dr. Mori's table."

I could feel the confusion rolling through the room.

Of course, they didn't know that Dr. Mori had a magic freaking table that showed where people stood in Savannah. In the shadows or the light.

"What table would that be?" Roderick tipped his head, and I waved at him.

"Never mind. I know Missy. She might say she's trying to help you, but she's just doing it to save her skin. Which means she's worried for some reason. Maybe she lost clout with the Dark Council when Joseph died? Are they hunting for you now, Missy?"

Her face paled and I nodded. "Thought so. Basically, unless you have some magical way of assessing whether she's speaking the truth, I wouldn't trust a thing she says." I glared at the old witch, who glared right back at me, her moment of shock already buried under her hatred of me. When Roderick looked away . . . I stuck my tongue out at her.

Robert grunted, holding back a laugh. The first noise he'd made since we'd come in.

Roderick heaved a heavy sigh, but it was Stark who stood and drew everyone's attention.

"One element of the spell that would raise the vampires from the grave is more difficult to attain than the others. Once it is secured, the others will be more easily obtained."

"Stark, no!" Lucas yelled.

Stark snapped his fingers on his right hand, and Lucas sat down like a marionette whose strings had been cut. Everyone stared at the man who had been silent for years. I grinned at him.

Stark's eyes crinkled at the edges. "You've inspired me to make a change, Breena O'Rylee. The others would tell you that the one they wish you to bring back to Savannah has done a great wrong. That they wish to put her on trial. But that is not the case. You must bring her back so we can keep her safe."

"Safe?"

He gave a slow nod. "Safe. If the Dark Council gains her soul, they will be one step closer to creating their spell. One of the biggest steps, for the soul of a witch, particularly *that* witch, is not easily obtained."

I stared at Stark. "The spell. The spell to raise the vampires."

The words of the spell hummed inside my head.

Of demon skin and angel wing
Of stolen cross and healing spring
Blood of a ghost, and an unmarked grave
Soul of a witch, and a siren's cave.
Bound swiftly neath the darkest night
Those of the blood shall have their sight
Of death and power, of magic and pain
That which comes shall find those slain
Raised anew and given life
A warning once, this call is strife
One last line to lock this spell
A soul whose blood has tasted hell.

Thus shall the ambrosia be brewed and given life to death.

Soul of a witch.

"Can't it just be any witch? Why didn't they just take ole Missy here? She was already ripe for the taking." I smiled at Missy. She glowered at me.

"Because she's not strong enough," Penny said. "That's what I'm betting, yes?"

Roderick nodded, his eyes sweeping reluctantly away from Stark. The old bugger had really thrown a wrench in whatever they were planning. "Correct. In order for the spell to work, they must have the soul of the oldest witch alive. She is always the most powerful of all witches, and they need that level of power to push the spell into existence."

My back ached from standing on the concrete floor, and I reached back to rub at it. The council all leaned back as if . . . as if they were afraid of me. Maybe they were? I kept my hand there, massaging my lower back.

"Do not pull a weapon," Lucas said.

I laughed. "My back is sore. I'm not going to stop rubbing it, thanks."

"We are leaving the track we need to be on." Stark's voice echoed through the room. "Breena O'Rylee, we need you to go and find the first witch. We need you to bring her back here for safekeeping. And we need you to leave post haste. You will start in Paris. You will have to face three challenges to reach the first witch. Fossette was ever so clever and wrapped a spell of protection around herself using other supernaturals as her dupes. They might even believe that she cares for them, but that is not the case. They are used, as surely as any tool." He paused. "With each challenge, you will find a new clue that will take you closer to Fossette. It's said that if you prove yourself worthy, she will award you with a boon. If that's true, when you get to that point, ask her to come back to Savannah with you."

"How many people have seen their way through all the challenges?" Sarge asked.

Stark looked over at my friend. "None that we are aware of."

Penny drew in a long, slow breath. "Why would you send the girl? Why not your own delegation? Unless . . ." She swept her hand to encompass the room. The missing members suddenly made sense.

Feish finished her thought. "Unless they already messed up the bedroom."

"You mean shit the bed?" I turned to her, and she smiled and wiggled her webbed fingers at me. I turned back to Roderick. "You shit the bed already? That's why there are council members missing? No one could bring her in. No one could get through the challenges."

Roderick nodded. Stark nodded. The whole damn room nodded.

"That is where Corb went," Roderick said. "He took the mission when it was offered to him."

So my gut feeling was right. Corb was involved in this mess. He'd stormed off in a snit, and the council had sent him on a jaunt. A very dangerous jaunt by the sounds of it.

Behind me my friends muttered, Sarge cursed under his breath and Kinkly tightened her hold on my ear.

"Your friend, Corb, was sent to her first. As a male siren, we thought—" Jacob shook his head slowly. "We thought he would be able to charm her. We lost contact with him and then we lost contact with our second delegation of council members a few days ago. We do not know if they are dead or defected."

Jaysus lawd in heaven, this was a mess. And they wanted *me* to clean it up. Again. Which of course I would do, because Corb was involved, and even if he'd been a bit of a dick, he was still sort of my friend. I didn't want him to be hurt. Also, to state the obvious, I didn't want the Dark Council to win. It wouldn't be good for anyone if an army of vampires started running amok all over Savannah and then the world. But I wasn't going to tell them that right away.

I held up both hands, palms out, high above my head as if I'd suddenly gone to church and seen the light. "Let me get this straight. You sent Corb and a few of your council members to gather this first witch. They are missing, and we can safely assume she's killed or otherwise harmed them, and now you want to send me?" Again, I had every intention of going, but that didn't mean I didn't want them to sweat a little.

"You will go," Stark said. "And you will bring her

back. And, if you are lucky, your friend will still be alive."

The rest of my friends bristled around me, but none more so than Robert. He stepped out just in front of me. "You are sending her to a woman who is a known dark arts practitioner, one who fornicates with demons." Kinkly giggled in my ear and whispered, "Sounds fun," but Robert was just picking up steam. "A witch who hasn't been seen since the last vampire uprising. Wisely so, since her predecessor was killed, her soul trapped for eternity. Corb—if he found her—is dead."

Everyone was staring at Robert now. Other than Roderick, who'd spotted him immediately, they seemed to truly be seeing him for the first time. His words cut into me, making my breath come in little gasps. Corb, dead? He couldn't be. I felt like I would have known. I glanced over my shoulder at Sarge, who shook his head.

"And just who are you?" Lucas asked.

Roderick's jaw clenched. "He is an old friend of mine actually. From the first uprising."

"I am not an old friend of yours, jackass," Robert snapped out. "Robert. That is my name, and I am Bree's friend. Not yours."

My friend.

Funny how that one word could make my heart swell ten sizes and tighten up my throat. Yup, just a little bit squishy there. Or maybe totally exhausted and needing a good swig of caffeine. Or whiskey. Preferably both.

Stark stared at Robert. "You look familiar, though the name is different from the one I know. Fine. Go with Bree, Robert. Be her *friend* and help her with this task, because despite her objections, I know she will go. Her sense of justice and devotion to protecting the town she loves are too ingrained in her for her to do otherwise."

I wanted to argue with him, but he was right. If nothing else, Corb was out there, likely hurt and in need of rescue. I refused to think that he was dead. "Fine. But I'll take whoever I want with me."

"I'm going," Kinkly said.

"Me too." Feish put a hand on my shoulder.

Missy sniffed. "Neither I nor Penny can go. The first witch would smell us out, and she could steal our souls from miles away."

I smiled at her. "Then you would be the perfect person to go."

Missy was dumb enough to ask, "Why? So she can capture me? Because you hate me?"

"No soul to steal. Like zombies going after brains. Come to think of it, half the council here would be safe." I winked.

Penny snorted. Missy's eyes widened and then narrowed as her mouth pursed. A few council members muttered.

"You little—"

"Enough." Roderick's one word bounced through the chamber, and there was some solid power behind it. In fact, everyone seemed to slump—everyone except for Robert, Stark, and me. When I narrowed my eyes, I saw a slight light emanating from Roderick, like a pale mist out of his fingertips. It circled around the room, covering everyone's eyes.

Roderick stared at me. "Bree, this is an incredibly dangerous thing that they ask of you. The first witch . . . she is not to be trifled with. Even for Corb. Robert is right, there is a high probability that he has been killed."

My guts twisted up. "Nope, his story isn't ending like that. Sure, he's a dick, but he's family too. Besides, I like trifle." I smiled, but my smile slipped as he continued to stare at me. "That bad, really?"

"I did not want to ask you," he said. "I think she will kill you on sight, even should you make it through all three challenges."

Robert stiffened beside me. "Then tell them to fu—"

"I do not run the council, Robert," Roderick snapped. "Listen, if you will. I have a moment to explain this to you, no more or less. If you go, go with the utmost caution. She is beyond cagey. She will have traps and spells lying in wait for any who would find her. Are we clear? If you must run to save yourself, then do it. I would rather have you here than dead. There are other things we can do to try and stop the spell."

I nodded slowly. "Is there a time limit?"

Roderick spread his hands wide. "You have to find her before the Dark Council does. They have sent two parties that Missy knows of. One is Bruce and another companion of his kind."

Gross. I wanted to groan but managed to keep my mouth shut. How was I not surprised that I was in a race with No-face Bruce? "I thought you were buddies. He hung out with you!"

"I was keeping tabs on him," Roderick said. "Not very well, obviously." The fatigue in the vampire's voice was heavy.

"And the other team?" Robert asked, pulling us back on track.

"They have sent the blacksmith. He is charming enough that they believe she might fall for his fae abilities. Which is exactly what our council thought about Corb. Obviously, it did not work."

My guts churned. The Dark Council had sent Crash to find the first witch. I'd be pitted against him again.

"Let me guess. They are already ahead of us?" I put my hands on my hips.

"They are. I suggest you find your way to Paris as expediently as possible. Death Row is on notice that you may purchase anything you like, and the council will cover the bill." He paused and produced a piece of paper. "One of my homes is on the Seine. Stay here, as there are protections in place that you will not find elsewhere." He shoved the piece of paper into my hands, then clapped his hands together. Everyone else pulled out of their stupor. I wondered if they'd noticed.

Most had not. But some had. Penny knew for sure. And Sarge bristled at my back.

"I don't like this," he grumbled. I reached back and he took my hand. "Bree, I am coming with you."

I looked at my friends, knowing that we were going to have to leave most of them behind. I mean, how in the world could I get passports for everyone?

CHAPTER
EIGHT

Death Row was quiet, with most of the vendors not even open. I went straight to Gerry, grateful that she at least was there. She was a master of leather clothing that acted as protective gear, and I knew I wouldn't have survived a lot of what I'd been through without her skill set. Penny walked beside me. The others had stayed at the house, arguing about who was going to Paris with me.

"Had an undead alligator bite down on my leg," I said as I reached Gerry.

Yes, that was the first thing I said to her. Not hello, not how are you. But check out my war wounds.

Gerry's eyes went wide. "And the pants?"

"Not a single tear. I still got bruised up, but it was a hell of a lot better than it should have been." I showed her the faded bruises. "And a zombie gnawed on my shoulder." I touched the short shoulder bolster that

Gerry had given me on my last trip through Death Row.

She touched the spot. "Excellent."

"You can bill the council for anything you give me today." I smiled. "So maybe mark things up some."

She laughed. "I don't have much left to give you from my stash. Where are you headed? On a job for them?"

I nodded. "Paris. On the hunt for the first witch."

Gerry didn't slow. "Dangerous stuff, that. Not the first person lately to go looking for her."

Penny looked through Gerry's wares and then through the tiny snuff boxes that Bob-John had on a rickety table next to her. "A few of these might be good, but you need to pick them, Bree." Her hands trembled as she pointed to the boxes. She had been exceptionally quiet for such an outspoken old lady. I knew she'd come with me to Death Row so she could tell me what she knew about the first witch. So she could help me prepare to face down yet another monster from the shadow world.

I put a hand gently on her shoulder. "Okay. I'll pick some."

Gerry rummaged through her leather stuff. "I think a pair of forearm bracers would go well with the gloves I gave you last time. They'll deflect a lot of spells and, like the rest of your gear, they'll adjust to fit you."

She held out a pair of leather cuffs, and I slid them onto my forearms. Soft as butter, they hardened as they settled over my arms. I pulled my gloves out. They were thicker leather on top, thinner across my palms. Everything Gerry made was smart, very smart. "I love these."

"You can still use your cell phone too." Gerry winked. "And here, take an extra pair of pants. Different color, and it's nice to have clean ones."

These leathers were a smoky black. I held them up, and as they hit the light, they kind of . . . shimmered. "Camouflage?"

"Yes, something like that." Gerry tossed me a slithery velvet bundle. "If you need to hide, use that with them."

The velvet bundle turned out to be a long cloak with a deep hood and cutouts for my arms to go through. Even though it was velvet, it had the same look as the pants. "Amazing. How am I ever going to go back to jeans after this?"

"Yes, my most expensive items. You've pretty much cleaned me out." Gerry laughed. "But I could go on vacation now. Maybe I will after the council pays me."

I grinned at her. "You should. Take a break, go to Mexico." On impulse, I gave her a hug. "Be safe, okay? Wherever you go, be safe."

Startled, she took a beat before she hugged me back. "Okay. You too. Maybe you more than me if you're going after the first witch."

Penny pointed at the snuff boxes, and I scooped up three that looked interesting. Bob-John shrugged and said nothing—no pointers from him today. The three boxes that had drawn my eye were simply made rectangular boxes about the size of a pack of gum. One red, one blue, and one shimmering white. I tucked them into my hip bag. "Wish me luck."

He sneezed and shivered. "You need all the luck, crazy girl. First witch is bad mojo."

Close enough. The rest of Death Row was simple. A few small knives that I tucked inside my boots from Tweedle Dee and Tweedle Dum, the blond twins, and then...

At the very end of the row was a familiar face. He hadn't been at the council meeting earlier, or if he'd gone, he'd stayed hidden.

"Oster Boon." I strode toward the leprechaun who sat on a stool, precariously balanced on a stack of books, a massive tome splayed open on his lap. He lifted his bright eyes to me, a definite twinkle in them, his hands gripping the edges of the huge book.

"Ah, Ms. O'Rylee. Fancy to be meeting you here on this lovely day." He smiled and, with some effort, closed the book. His seat wobbled, but he didn't fall over.

"Oster Boon, are you ever going to call in your favor?" I looked at the few books scattered around the pint-sized book seller.

He shrugged. "Perhaps. One day, when you least expect it and when I need it the most, I'll call in me favor." With a spry hop, he jumped off his precarious stool and landed at my feet. "But you're here for something? A new spell book? Something to read before bed?"

I shook my head and started to turn away. "No, not really."

Penny tapped a smaller book that lay at Oster Boon's feet. Red leather cover, tightly bound with a metal clasp. It was the size of a Harlequin novel, not big at all. "This one. I think you should take this one."

The leprechaun grinned and shook his head, then pushed the book Penny had suggested aside. "Nah, that one be a dime a dozen. Now this one, this one here comes with something extra."

He nudged his toe under another book, then kicked up so it landed neatly in the palm of his hand. He held the small book out to me, and I took it from him. He flipped the book open, and a bracelet sat inside of it. Made of what looked like real wood, etched with leaves and a few brilliant blue blossoms, it was stunning. I ran my fingers over it. Three bracelets actually, woven together. "Why would I need these?"

"Call it a hunch." He winked at me. I slid the bracelet on, and it sat between the gloves and the forearm bracer—a perfect fit.

"Charge it to the council, they're covering my costs today," I said.

He rubbed his hands together. "Yes, I know, I heard that through the grapevine. Of course, I'll charge them double then."

"Why weren't you there? Or did you just hide in the shadows?" Penny asked him.

"Thought me brother might come with you. Didn't much feel like seeing him." Oster Boon shrugged. Then, barking a laugh at something only he found funny, he turned away and snapped the fingers on one hand. The remaining books floated up and around him, shrunk in size, and flew into his hands. "Best way to pack." He winked and touched his nose.

I looked at the tiny books, wishing I could do that. "Is it?"

"You get to take everything you want with you if your things are no bigger than a thimble."

Penny snorted and then grabbed my arm, fingers digging in hard. I winced. "Penny?"

"We have to go. Right now. I've just thought of something!"

Which was how we ended up racing all the way back to the house where everyone else waited.

And by racing I mean we took a cab and got ourselves there almost as quickly as if Penny were driving. Penny all but ran up the stairs, impressive with her cane and age, leaving me to pay the driver, which was fine. I followed more slowly. Something had gotten her knickers in a twist, but what? Was it what Oster Boon had said, or what he'd done with the books?

By the time I got into the house, Penny was at her

work desk, herbs scenting the air, a fire lit under one of her spelling pots. "Penny, what are you—?"

"Oster Boon reminded me of something," she said as she threw a vial of pale yellow liquid into the pot. "You heard him. If you make things small enough, you can take them with you anywhere. That's something you need. Most of your friends don't have passports, but we all bring you different strengths. I have a spell that can make us small. For a time. We can all come."

I wasn't so sure that my other friends would want to get shrunken down, just to go with me. Besides, I remembered how the shapeshifting spell had turned out, and how its effects had faded at a most inopportune time. What if they all popped back to normal size mid-flight? How would we explain that away? "Penny, I don't think—"

"No, they want to go with you, Bree. They know how dangerous this is. They were already discussing booking a private flight. Easier to magic our way around the passport problem that way. But those arrangements will take time, and leaving you alone in Paris for even a couple of days is—"

"It's fine." I put my hand over the spell pot, stopping her from throwing in the brown chunk of muck dripping through her fingers. "Penny, it's fine. I'm going to take Kinkly. And I was going to ask Jinx if she wanted to come too. No one will see them."

Of course, if Robert had still been able to change into a single finger bone that would have meant I got to take four friends. I sighed. "Sarge will come with me. He's got a nose on him that could help us track the first witch." Plus he, at least, had a passport. He stepped into the room as I said his name, an undeniable look of relief sliding across his face. "Kinkly can hide under my hair, and if Jinx comes in her spider form, she can ride along with Sarge."

I'd already pulled out my phone to look up flights. The next one was soon. We were going to have to make some moves quickly. I was back scrolling through the options when Robert, who'd been sitting quietly in the far corner of the room, seemingly asleep, roused at my words. He sat up, his face tight with worry. "You can't just leave us all behind."

I noted that he was being careful with his mouth. As if he didn't want to show off his teeth. No, my imagination was running away with me. Whatever was wrong with Robert, it had nothing to do with vampires. Even if he'd wanted to bite me. More than likely, he was just hungry. He hadn't eaten anything in a long time, after all. Or maybe the whole being risen from the dead thing had scrambled his mind.

I shook my head, bending to the phone again. My finger hovered over the final purchase. Damn it. I clicked the button and the autofill put my information in. I quickly filled in Sarge's info. "I have the check that Roderick gave me. You cash it and get flights for whoever else wants to come help in Paris."

He snorted. "Whoever else? You mean all of us? No one's going to willingly stay behind."

I took note that Eammon had shown back up. "You too, old man?"

The leprechaun pointed a finger at me. "You need all the help you can get. I've been to Paris. I know it like the back of my hands!"

Penny snorted. "And I will come too."

"What about the witch?" I asked. "I don't care if she takes Missy's soul, but I rather like yours where it is."

Penny smiled. "I won't go hunting for her with you. I'll hold down the fort. I will stay near Roderick's house as much as possible, and keep a low profile. I can help if there are injuries or questions."

"And where will that be, exactly? Our future fort, that is." Suze came into the room, dusting her hands. Kinkly fluttered around her head. Her flight pattern was still a little off after the damage done to her wing.

I reached into my bag and pulled out the piece of paper Roderick had given me. "I have the address." I showed it to the others. "563 Rue Merce, Paris."

Eammon gave a grunt. "I know that area. That's just outside the city, near the river like Penny said. Good situation, close enough to get to things, far enough out for privacy. River runs along that area too, so if we're lucky it will back onto the property. Very good."

Sarge gave me a look. "You think it's safe to stay at Roderick's house?"

I stared at the paper. "I don't think he'd hurt me. Not intentionally. And he wants to stop the Dark Council as much as we do. He stopped his own brother, didn't he?" I looked at the clock. "Damn it. I have to get to the airport. Kinkly, will you come with me?"

She shot over to my shoulder as quickly as she could. "Of course! I have cousins in Paris. I'll look them up, and they can help us."

Then I looked at Sarge. "Jinx. Will you come?"

She scuttled up over Sarge's shoulder. "You would . . . trust me?"

"Look, I know you can be a trickster, I get it, but you've saved my bacon more than once. And you're part of the group now whether you like it or not." I shrugged. Whether any of us liked it or not. "So, yes, I would like you to come. Just don't turn into an elephant on the plane."

She waved her tiny legs in the air.

I deliberately didn't look at Robert. He was my friend, but he was being . . . weird. "We'll call when we get there."

A quiet burbling cry in the corner drew everyone's eyes to Feish. Yeah, this was going to be tough.

"Feish, don't cry."

"You don't want me there!" She covered her face with her hands. "I thought we were friends!"

"Girls gotta look out for their bitches' cats, right?" I said.

She lifted her head. "Yeah."

"And I still need you to do that." I smiled. "You and Penny are going to take the money and get flights. A private one if you have to, then you will come with everyone else."

She huffed. "I could swim faster than a flight!"

My eyebrows shot up. "You . . . really?"

"Well, yeah!"

I looked to Suzy for confirmation. "She could," the blond siren said. "I can't, but because she's a river maid, she can use the currents and propel herself across the ocean in a matter of . . . well, I'm not sure how long."

Feish lifted her chin. "I bet I beat the plane to Paris."

I grabbed her and hugged her tightly. "The river runs not too far away from Roderick's house, that's what Eammon said. You'd better get going if you're going to beat us there."

She gave a burbling squeal and took off running.

"I still think I could have shrunk you all down," Penny muttered.

Eammon put a hand over his belly. "No. That cat spell was enough to leave me guts rumbling and angry for days, thank you very much."

I nodded. "And the last thing we need is for them all to return to normal size in the middle of the flight.

Maybe another time, Penny. Who knows when we might need to be all teeny tiny? You could make the spell just in case."

Penny must have realized I was just humoring her because she huffed and then slumped into her chair, waving her cane at me. "You'd better go. We'll be there as soon as we can. Try not to get into trouble before we arrive."

A round of hugs for my friends, and Sarge and I got on his bike, without a single piece of luggage. Then again, most of my things had burned up in the fire.

I gripped his waist as we whipped around corners and the bike drifted across lanes. It was still better than Penny's driving. Jinx, perched on his shoulder, screamed *wheee!* as he used his bike to maneuver through traffic. Kinkly clung to the back of my neck, hanging onto my pendant chain.

As we approached the terminal, Sarge slowed. "Problem, Bree."

I looked over at where he pointed.

"Are you ducking kidding me?"

Why she didn't pick a different form, I don't know. But there was Monica—who was also working for the Dark Council—strutting around the entrance to the terminal. "Kinkly, can you sneak in, see what's going on?"

"Me too!" Jinx leapt off Sarge's shoulder and took on the form of a seriously ugly pixy. She looked like a miniature goblin with wings. Her craggy face still had huge fangs, and her flight pattern was more bat than pixy.

Kinkly shot away, and Jinx followed her. Sarge parked the bike just to the side of a big tour bus. "Why would she be here?" he grumbled.

"To stop us?"

"How do they even know you're coming?" Sarge asked.

The only people who should know were on the council. The only other person we'd told was Gerry, and I didn't think for a second that it was her. That could only mean one thing. "No-face Bruce isn't the only traitor. Someone else in the council works for the other side," I said. "That has to be it."

We didn't have to wait long. Kinkly came back first, Jinx close behind.

"Go, go!" Kinkly was screeching. Sarge got the bike started back up, and as soon as Jinx landed on his shoulder, we were off.

"What is it?" I yelled into the wind.

"Monica is guarding the terminal. There is a spell, too, and it almost got us! It's not snagging humans, but I think it grabbed another fairy."

"I saw it first!" Jinx yelled. "It's stretched across the opening like a spider web. If any of us had gone in, we would have been immobilized. It's keyed to supernaturals."

"Good job!" Sarge barked and Jinx wiggled happily on his shoulder, a tiny spider once more.

Well duck me up and down on a pogo stick. Just like that, our plans had crumbled. Sure, we could try another airport, but how many would be rigged up like this one? Probably more than we wanted.

"There has to be another way," Sarge said over his shoulder. "We'll just take a private plane with the others. Might take us a day but..."

"A day could be too long," I yelled back. "By then... they could have found Fossette."

Kinkly cleared her throat. "There is another way... but . . ." She pulled herself closer to my ear. "It's through a darker path. The path of the demon fae."

CHAPTER NINE

"I'm sorry, what did you just say?" I repeated back to Kinkly, because the words she'd spoken sounded so foreign, so ridiculous that I honestly wasn't sure I'd heard her right.

She cleared her throat and shouted into the wind. "Demon fae, different than the dark fae. There is a path through their realm. It has stops in major cities around the world. London. New York. Sydney. Paris. Cairo. Vancouver. Every continent has at least one doorway. Usually more, I think."

"Yeah, that's what I thought you said, but then I thought no, no she didn't say that. I must be losing my hearing." I cupped a hand to my one ear. "You did not say demon fae."

Kinkly laughed as if I'd spun a great joke. "Ha! You are old! That's why you thought you didn't hear me right!" She winked and then nodded. Sarge slowed down once we were a good distance from the airport. "Yes, yes, demon fae. So little is known about them, even among our kind, that they are like a ghost story, a legend. But even if they are not real, the pathway is. It's blocked, though, and it's in the goblin city somewhere. That's all I know."

I tapped Sarge on the waist. "Do you know anything about..." I swallowed hard. "...demon fae?"

He shook his head. "No. I mean, I know about demons. You think your new friend might know anything?"

I shrugged. It was possible that Damian or one of the other demons who'd helped us crush the zombie scourge might know, but my feeling was that if Kinkly didn't think it was common knowledge, then it was likely the demons didn't know about it. "Maybe, but we honestly don't have time. We're chasing our tails here." I rubbed both hands over my face and then turned to my other friend. "Jinx? Do you know anything about demon fae?"

She gave a slow nod from Sarge's shoulder. "I've had only two dealings with them. They are uncommon. Many were killed out or absorbed into the other fae. They are far more bloodthirsty and prone to violence. I kinda like them, to be honest."

Killed or . . . absorbed. I scrunched my eyes shut. "Kinkly. How dangerous is it? Even if you don't know much about them . . ." Only, now that I thought about it, I wasn't so sure that part was true. I'd noticed that some supernaturals seemed bound by rules of their people. Maybe Kinkly knew more but couldn't tell us more. That felt like what was happening, the way she wouldn't look at me, the way her wings stuttered more than usual.

She flew around our heads and then back to my shoulder, her wings brushing against my cheek. "We've faced worse. And I can say no more."

I snort-laughed and turned so I could look at her. "That is not comforting."

She lifted her hands up and shrugged. "It's the truth. The path will be dangerous, but more so because we must go through Karissa's realm to get to it. The entrance to the demon fae pathway is in the goblin city, like I said. After that, I'm honestly not sure what we will face. The tales I know are just that—tales. Maybe Bridgette could help?"

The goblin city, where Crash ruled as the new king. Where I'd had to face down a rather large monstrous goblin.

"Sarge, you got your phone?"

He handed me his cell. I dialled Roderick's number. The vampire picked up before the first ring was even done.

"Yes?"

"Monica is holding the airport terminal hostage. Kinkly is suggesting we use the pathway of the demon fae to get to Paris. You got a better option? Something, oh, I don't know, less ducking dangerous?" I asked my question and then literally held my breath.

Roderick was quiet. "Let me check something."

There was a click. "I think the bastard put me on hold!" I grumbled. Then again, said bastard was, in his own way, trying to help.

I looked at Sarge. "Any other ideas? I mean, we can't swim like Feish."

"She's going to be pissed if she gets there before we do." He smirked. I laughed.

"No, she'll be incredibly proud of herself for beating us." I sighed. "We could drive out of state, to another airport?"

Roderick clicked back on. "Bree. The council is in agreement. The pathway of the demon fae is viable. Missy said that's the route Crash would have taken, and since the magic in Faerie is changing, the time differential should work in your favor."

He'd said a lot of words that I wasn't fully sure I was comprehending. Maybe I was just tired. Maybe I was slow. "They want us to use that path?"

"They agree, as do I, that time is of the essence. Use the route that Crash has opened. Be swift, take a guide, and do not linger. I must go, there is unrest here." Roderick hung up on me before I could ask about driving to another state.

I sighed, not seeing any other option. "Okay, time is of the essence, as Roddy put it. Unless there are major objections, I think that's our best option. Kinkly, lead the way."

And all of that is why our entire contingent wound up standing in front of the fountain in Forsyth Park with our neighbor goblin, Bridgette, as our guide. She'd confirmed there was indeed a path—a *locked* path. Sure, Roderick said Crash had opened it. But Bridgette seemed wary. The goblin's big eyes kept sweeping over the group of us, all with at least one backpack, her mouth moving as she counted us again. Penny, Suzy, Eric, Sarge, Robert, Eammon and, of course, me. Eight if you counted Bridgette and chose not to count Kinkly and Jinx.

"Oh dear, this is a lot," Bridgette whispered as she wrung her hands. "I don't know how we are going to get past all the goblins."

"You sure you want to come with us? You could just give us directions," I asked her again. Because I didn't want to force her hand.

"You need me." Bridgette blinked up at me. "You won't be able to get back through the tunnels of the demon fae without me. The inscriptions are what take you to different places, but you have to know what you're doing . . . and you have to be able to read goblin."

"We also need at least one more person with a connection to fae in order to get this many people through safely," Kinkly said, pointedly not looking at me. Me, who'd given up that ability to bring Robert back. "Kind of like a sandwich. Everyone who doesn't belong, stuck between a couple of fae. That's doable. And Bridgette leans to the darker side of things, so that's helpful too. You know, being able to read goblin and all."

I pulled myself back to the moment.

The splashing of the fountain was lulling, and I found myself breathing in the smells of the park, as if... well, as if I weren't going to be coming back to my home in Savannah for a good long time. That's what it felt like—an unexpected goodbye. I wasn't sure whether there was anything to it.

"Gran," I said. "You with us?"

My bag moved, but there was no answer. Gran was still pissed at me for not bringing her back to life.

Penny swung her cane at me, which I dodged easily. "She's in your hip bag, and you know it. Asking her ten times won't change that!" Yup, she was jittery too. We all were.

I put a hand to my bag. I hated that she'd gone in there, yet at least she'd come. Having my gran with me meant the world. She bumped under my hand but still wouldn't answer me. "Stop fussing, girl. Just move quick."

Kinkly fluttered around our heads. "I'll go first. Bridgette will bring up the rear until we get to the tunnels."

Without another word, she dove through the splashing water, and my friends followed her. Feish was going to be pissed to find out we'd all traveled together after all, and she could have come with us. I smiled at the thought, mostly because I missed her.

Everyone went through, with the exceptions of Robert, Bridgette, and me. Robert held his hand out to me, and I took it.

"I'm sorry," he said softly. He'd barely spoken to me, almost as if he'd gone back to his skeletal form. "You lost this part of yourself to bring me back. I'm so sorry."

I shrugged. "I wasn't using it anyway. Though I kind of wished she'd just asked for my ovaries. They're out of date."

His lips twitched. "Expired already?"

"Completely past their best before." I tightened my grip on his hand. "My friends are worth fighting for, Robert. And you're one of my best friends. Cross my heart."

His eyes searched my face, as if he wasn't sure I was telling the truth.

Bridgette cleared her throat. "We should go."

I tugged Robert along with me. We needed a chance to talk, to really . . . I mean, we should probably address that not-quite-a-dream kiss. Maybe it hadn't meant anything to him, beyond the need for connection after being alone for so many years. In truth, that would make me happy. I needed a good friend. One that I could trust.

We jumped through the fountain together and landed in the land of the fae.

I took a breath, and the world kind of... fuzzed.

The beauty of the world—the smells, the way the air felt against my skin—everything was so heightened that I struggled to breathe and see through it. We stood in a field filled with flowers and grass that brushed against the middle of my thighs. Each blossom had its own glittering color that ran the spectrum of the rainbow. I took a breath, and I swear the flowers actually dipped toward me, a breeze pushing their scents my way and up my nose. Lilac, vanilla, rose, lily, and wisteria. They were like a drug, and I drew in the smells hard enough that my brain rattled and my legs tried to buckle. The only thing that kept me on my feet was my hold on Robert, who didn't seem to be as deeply affected.

Damn it, was this what everyone else felt like here? A quick look at my friends, and I could see that they were also being hit with the sensations of this place—well, those who did not have fae blood anyway. I swallowed and shook my head to clear my thoughts.

"Let's go." I pulled it together, though I sounded like I'd had one too many pulls on the whiskey bottle. "Post haste, as Stark would say."

Kinkly fluttered around. "Yes, let's go. Karissa's spies will be watching. We must hurry."

As before, Bridgette stayed back with me and Robert, kind of herding us along.

In order to keep myself from losing it completely, lying down in the field of flowers and just letting the fae world take me, I dove right into the hard questions. Topics that would keep us both occupied.

"Who is Eleanor?" That was the name of the woman whose grave he'd always hung around in the cemetery where I'd found him. He'd called her a friend. But seeing as that was one of the only words he had in his skeletal vocabulary, it could mean a lot of things.

Robert didn't exactly pull his hand away from me. But he relaxed his grip as if he wanted to.

"She . . . was my wife."

Okay. About on par with what I'd suspected.

"And did you like her? I mean. I was married, and look at what that got me." I smiled to soften the words. Because I really wanted Robert to open up so we could get to know each other on a deeper level. I mean, did he want to bring her back from the dead? Was she walking around the way he used to, someone else's skeletal helper?

Robert glanced at me, then looked away. "Bree. It was a marriage of convenience. She was a guardian, like me. It made us stronger to be together. She was my friend."

Friend.

Like I was his friend.

"Huh." Yup, that was my initial response, because the ever-present pit in my stomach opened up a bit wider. I didn't want anything but friendship from him.

I wasn't about to get hitched for a power boost. "Interesting."

Robert tightened his hand on mine and smiled. "Not like that, Bree. Not like . . . why are you asking?"

"Because she was obviously special to you. And it's not like we've been able to have conversations beyond the *look out, that monster's going to eat your soul* variety prior to now." I sighed and a tall stalk of dandelion fluff blew away. Okay, it literally flew away. They must've been tiny bugs or something. I squinted. No, just fluff.

Maybe I was seeing things differently here now that I'd lost my connection to the fae world? No, not lost. Given up.

"Are you sad?" Robert squeezed my hand gently, pulling my attention back to him.

"I'm just trying to work out where your head's at." I squeezed his hand. "I need a friend. That's it, Robert."

He laced his fingers with mine. "I'm here, Bree. I am your friend, and hopefully I will be able to help you through the challenges you seem to draw to you." He smiled. "And maybe, once the challenges are gone, perhaps . . . then there could be something more for us."

I forced a smile. Because I didn't want something more with him. No matter that his kiss had been good. No matter that he was a handsome man . . . he didn't call to me. Not even as a rebound from Crash. I . . . was I even looking for a relationship at all? I rather liked not being beholden to anyone.

I pulled my hand away. "Okay. Perhaps. Let's see how this goes." Then I motioned for him to go ahead of me. "You have good instincts. Why don't you walk up there with Kinkly? I'll keep the back spot."

Robert's jaw ticked and one eyebrow went up in a perfect arch that mine could never duplicate. "You're dismissing me?"

I shrugged and then smiled as I raised both eyebrows. "Perhaps."

His lips twitched upward, the frown gone in a flash, and I knew then we'd be okay. Gut feelings were my jam lately. Regardless of what role he filled—friend or friend with benefits, if that was what he was into—Robert was with me on this journey. He leaned in and kissed my cheek, then jogged toward Kinkly's position at the front of the group.

I fell back a little more, and Bridgette kept stride with me, her big eyes very definitely on my face.

"What about Crash?" she asked, her voice low.

I sighed and brushed a finger through a stalk of velvety flower petals. "He's working for the Dark Council, Bridgette. He's the one we are racing against to find the first witch. There is nothing else between us."

There couldn't be. No matter how much I wanted it.

Bridgette looked over her shoulder and sucked in a sharp breath. "Someone's coming."

I followed her gaze in time to see a group of fae

men racing through the meadow toward us. Even at a distance I could make out their shining hair and bright green and blue armor. Each one carried a long, shining piece of . . . I squinted. Shit, they were each carrying long swords. "Can we make it to Goblin Town ahead of them?"

Bridgette shot me a look and pushed me forward, smacking her hand against my leather pants. "We have to. Those are Karissa's executioners."

CHAPTER
TEN

Karissa's executioners were damn fast, even carrying their oversized weapons. "Eric, pick up Penny!"

"Do not!" Penny snapped and she flung her hand out around us, a dusting of something sparkly hitting the group. Kinkly shot high into the air, dodging it. Robert grabbed me and dove to the left.

As if he knew what it was. Maybe he did?

Oh . . . crap. We hit the ground and lay there as the others gulped and yelped. "Thanks."

He smiled down at me, winked and nodded. "You do not have to thank me. It's my job to look out for you. While I can."

While he could? I wanted to ask just what the hell that meant, but we didn't have time to discuss it. Bridgette was looking at us. "Um, there's a new problem now."

We sat up together. "The dust hit them all—Penny, Eric, Eammon, Sarge and Suzy," Kinkly squealed, "and they just disappeared. Gone!" She was freaking out, and I didn't blame her. What had Penny just done?

"Robert, what are you doing?"

He was moving around on his hands and knees, as if he'd dropped a contact. "I've got Eammon and Penny!" he yelled as he stood with his hands cupped. It looked as though a very angry cockroach was jumping up and down in his palm. Holy crap, Penny had made the shrinking potion! On the plus side, it clearly worked.

I hurried over to where Eric, Suzy, Sarge and Penny had been standing, careful of where I planted my feet.

Sarge waved up at me, no bigger than my pinky finger. I scooped him, Eric, and a very confused Suzy into my hands and then tucked them into my hip bag. Robert dumped Penny and Eammon into my bag, which set off a string of high-pitched yelling.

An arrow thudded into the ground at my feet, making me jump, the bag bounce, and my friends inside it holler.

"Sorry!" I said.

"You are trespassing!" the executioner closest to us snarled. "And your apology means little to us!"

I grabbed Bridgette's hand and took off running. I threw my words over my shoulder. "Wasn't apologizing to you, tit face!"

Kinkly landed on Robert's shoulder, and the two of them quickly surpassed me and led the way.

Despite her size, Bridgette was keeping up easily. I couldn't say that Penny had made a bad decision, to be honest—she and Eammon would have slowed us down, between her age and his short legs.

But I could hear him cursing from my bag. I mean, he was really letting fly with the stream of f-bombs. Another time I would have been giggling my ass off at the high-pitched ducks.

As it was, the pair of fae at our back were shooting arrows in a near continual stream, and I didn't have any extra breath. I kept dodging left and right as if that would help. Actually, since I didn't get shot, I guess it may have helped. I'm sure a fart slid out of me, but over the cacophony of thudding feet, zinging arrows, and heavy breathing, no one else heard. I guess that's the blessings of being attacked.

I offered Bridgette a hand, and she took it. Together we ran, me half dragging her along. She yelped out as we slid down a sudden embankment, flowers and tiny bugs shooting up all around our group.

We hit the bottom of the embankment, rolled through thick mud, and then we were jostling out the other side.

The high-pitched hollering from my bag intensified, but there was nothing I could do about them.

"Busy running for our lives!" I gulped out.

On Robert's shoulder danced someone I hoped was

truly on our team. "Jinx, can you slow them down? Please!"

How she'd missed getting hit by Penny's magic, I had no idea. Maybe it didn't affect her because of her ability to shapeshift.

Jinx leapt off Robert's shoulder and as she did, she shifted into her much larger spider form. The one I'd first met. "I'll do what I can!"

An arrow sung past my head, clipping my right ear. The pain was . . . intense. "Duck off!" I yelled back at the group of fae even while I clamped a hand over the wound. Tiny, it was so tiny, and yet . . . my legs wobbled on the next stride. "Oh, no."

Robert was at my side in a flash, helping me run. "We're almost there, we can see the outskirts of the city."

"Skeletor," I whispered the horse's name as my knees kept buckling. Poison or sedative, I couldn't say which one the arrow had been dosed with. Either way, it was working pretty damn fast, and I could hear more arrows thudding into the path and greenery around us. The executioners screamed, signaling that Jinx had intercepted them. "I'm about to delete you out of this story!" she bellowed at them, and there were a few screams in response.

"Editors all be the same," I whispered. "Always trying to take out extraneous characters."

But even though she was buying us some time, I

knew that some of them would get around her. Jinx couldn't stop that many fae.

The ground just in front of me heaved, and the big black horse I'd summoned threw himself out of the dirt, faster than he'd ever managed before. I grabbed his mane when he was still low to the ground, and Robert shoved me up onto his back, leaping up behind me, one arm going around my middle and pinning me to his chest.

"Can't outrun Bridgette," I mumbled as my head bobbled forward.

"I'm here," Bridgette said. "Just go now, as fast as you can, horse!"

I pressed my face to Skeletor's neck and breathed him in. He didn't smell dead; he didn't even feel dead anymore. He was warm, and the pulse of a heartbeat thrummed under my cheek. Whatever magic had brought him to me the first time seemed to be making him more and more whole. I grabbed at his mane, just managing to stay on as Robert's arm left me. Maybe he was pulling Bridgette on with us?

Skeletor leapt forward, and in moments the sound of his hoofbeats shifted from the thud of dirt to the ping of cobblestones under us.

"We're sort of safe." Kinkly fluttered around, her wings fanning my face. I struggled to focus. I looked over my shoulder to see flashes of Bridgette's worried face behind Robert. That was good. She was with us still.

"I feel like I'm going to puke," I mumbled.

"We stay on the horse, Kinkly, you stay between his ears." Robert's voice was solid, even though the rest of my world most definitely was not. I managed to sit up, and again, Robert's arm went tight around my middle and held me to him, though I'll admit the squeeze on my belly was not welcome. I belched and groaned.

"Go there," Bridgette said. For a moment, we were riding down the main street, which seemed unwise, but Skeletor followed Bridgette's directions and quickly took a left-hand turn down a narrow alley.

I opened my mouth, and nothing but a stream of wickedly strange words came out. What I wanted to ask was if I was going to be okay. Or maybe do we need to find someone who can help. What came out was: "Penis wrinkle." I tried again. "Titty bobber." Nope. No, that was definitely not what I wanted to say. It felt like Robert might be laughing if the shaking behind me was any indication.

"Here," Bridgette said, and then I was being pulled off Skeletor's back. The knock of knuckles on a wooden door. "Leland, it's Bridgette. I need the pills for the executioner's poison! Don't argue with me, now!"

I'd never heard Bridgette sound so authoritative. I smiled. Mumbled something that was supposed to be badass. "Blubberbutt." I hiccupped. Maybe it was just a sedative. "Donkey licker."

Robert rolled me in his arms so he had one arm behind my shoulders and the other under my legs. Like he was going to carry me across the threshold on our wedding night. "If you weren't dying, I'd say this was damn funny as hell." He grabbed my jaw and popped my mouth open.

A hard, smooth object dropped into my mouth. Like a gobstopper, only smaller. More like a metal bead. Tangy and metallic, it tasted exactly like I would have thought a metal bead would taste. I mean, if I was into eating beads.

"Keep it under your tongue. It'll melt that way," Bridgette said. Her hand was on my ankle and she gripped me tightly. As if she were worried I'd slip away.

"Snakepiss," I muttered. "Slapmyass." Yeah, none of this made sense. But the hard pill in my mouth was dissolving, and I blinked up at Robert, who was still grinning.

"Slap your ass?"

I tried to speak normally. "Only in the sack."

His eyebrows shot up. "It's not working. She's still muttering gibberish. Can we give her another one?"

I scrunched my face. "No, that was me. I'm coming around." I reached up and touched my ear. The tip had been completely taken off, leaving a divot there. "Damn."

Bridgette scrambled back up onto Skeletor's back. "We go now. The executioners are still behind us. The horse bought us some time."

I looked over my shoulder and saw a taller than average goblin with spiky white hair waving at us as we took off. He grinned and winked at me, like he knew me. But I didn't know him. Did I?

Robert drummed Skeletor's sides with his heels, and the sort-of-dead horse shot forward. The motion threw me backward into his chest, and he held on tight.

Maybe this wasn't so bad.

We raced down the alley, and Bridgette had us weaving through the goblin city at top speed. Kinkly clung to the tips of Skeletor's ears, her wings spreading out behind her. This path we were on felt exactly like a maze, which matched my impression of Goblin Town when we'd first come here, not long before. We cranked hard around corners again and again, until finally there was nowhere left to go. Literally, no more turns. It still felt like a maze, a labyrinth all its own.

We were at a dead end of sorts. If you didn't count the massively thick iron doors that were secured shut with a chain and a single lock, we had nowhere to go if the executioners caught up to us.

The doors were covered with spray-painted messages.

Nothing to see here.
Turn around by order of the king.
Not your place.
Go back or have your balls eaten.

"Subtle," I whispered. Yes, whispered. Because the gate we'd slid to a stop in front of had the feeling of being... dark. Evil, even. The area around the gate was dim. Trees were rooted into the top of the wall beyond the doors, and their branches and the Spanish moss that clung to them hung over the dead end, creating a moving mass of shadows. I tried to shake off my reaction. I didn't want to think that the doorway and path we were on were inherently evil, seeing as we were planning on going farther in.

"You sure about this?" Robert asked.

I looked at Kinkly and then Bridgette. They both nodded, and I trusted them. "Yes."

The three of us slid off Skeletor. I patted his back. "You coming with us to Paris, my friend?"

He blew out a long hot breath and then collapsed in front of me, not unlike the way Robert used to. All that was left was a tiny, boat-shaped bone, porous looking with tiny holes all over it. I scooped it up and tucked it carefully into my bag. Maybe he couldn't just appear on soil on another continent? That was my only guess. I could call him up here, whenever I wanted, but the ocean between us was too much.

My friends stared up at me. Eric waved, his voice weirdly deep and high-pitched at the same time. "We're good! A little bruised, but good!"

"Tell me if you feel funny," I said. Robert had deposited Eammon and Penny into my bag. "'Cause if you're going to get big all of a sudden, I'd like to know." While my bag seemed to be bottomless, I didn't want to test the limits of its capacity as a bunch of people became full size within it.

Basically, I didn't want to wreck my bag, thank you very much.

Eammon screeched something, but it was so high-pitched I couldn't decipher it. He was really working himself up into a state if I couldn't understand him now.

"Good, that's great!" I grimaced out a grin. Eammon was going to kill me. As if this was my fault and not Penny's doing.

My gran huffed and turned, showing me the row of buttons down the back of her shirt, and I tried not to think about the fact that she was still pissed at me for not bringing her back to life, even though it hadn't actually been possible. Or at least I thought that's why she was pissed. I sighed. Nothing was going right.

"Is it Monday?" I asked as I walked up to the big doors. "Sure feels like a ducking Monday."

"The better question would be how are we getting through these?" Robert touched one of the chains. "Roderick said Crash had been through here first. He seemed to think it would be open, but . . ." He flicked the chains. "Not so much."

I looked at him and he grimaced. "And hurry. I think Karissa's friends are getting close." He looked over his shoulder, blue eyes pensive as if he could see the executioners.

"I have a key," I said.

"You do?" Bridgette gasped.

I pulled my knife from the sheath on my thigh and

grinned at her as I put the point into the lock holding the chains on the central part of the door. One big breath and I pushed, using all my weight as I wiggled the tip.

Get your mind out of the gutter.

The metal screeched, and Robert, Kinkly, and Bridgette clapped their hands over their ears. I had no such luxury and just gritted my teeth and kept on pushing. I was banking on the knife that Crash had made getting me through.

The knife tip began to glow a deep red, and the chains it was touching vibrated, humming with a deep thrum that made my bones ache and my teeth grind. The door fought back with a pulse of energy that had me bracing my legs until my boots skidded across the cobblestones. I managed to get a toe in a cobblestone crack and use it as leverage, but I was still shoved back some.

"Help!" I yelped the word over the crackling of the metal.

"Here." Robert wrapped his arms around me and put his hands on mine, helping me push the knife into the lock.

The added weight forced the blade deeper into the lock. Robert's hands gripped mine, and I couldn't help but notice . . . that he was rather happy to be tucked in tight behind me.

"Really? I thought we were just friends!" To be fair, the whole leaning forward, pushing for all you were worth into the lock thing kind of . . . well, it begged to be sexual.

"It's been a long time, Bree," he gritted out, "since I've had any sort of physical contact with a woman. I can't help it. Don't take it that way."

I twisted my hands on the knife handle, trying to force the lock open. I laughed at him. "So you'd react to just any old warm body? Nice. Good to know. I'll be sure to tell Jinx that. She's looking for love."

"No, of course not!" He tightened his hands further and leaned with me. He huffed, and I realized he was laughing at me.

I snorted. "Or Missy? Maybe she's a bitch because she's just lonely!"

We were both laughing now. "Well, if we're going to matchmake me, then I pick Eric. He can cook at least. And I'll bet he'd be plenty warm."

Okay, have you ever had a fit of giggles when there is danger? Yeah, that was us two idiots. We were giggling away, throwing out all sorts of options for Robert's nonexistent love life, each one more ridiculous than the next.

"Corb. He'd have a go at you," I offered as I tried again to wiggle the tip into the right position. "He likes pretty men."

"God in heaven, a siren? No offense, Suzy!" Robert grunted as we lost traction again. The door flexed in front of us, like it was Schwarzenegger trying to prove he still had the muscles.

From my bag Suzy yelled something.

"Stop talking and push!" Bridgette yelled and smacked the side of my leg with the flat of her hand.

"On three," I yelped. "One. Two. Three!"

Robert and I shoved together, and this time the knife slid right through the big lock. The steel mechanism shattered, cracking like glass, and the fissures spiderwebbed up through all the chains that held the door shut.

Chains that Crash had put on the door after he went through? I had no idea how he would have managed that. Unless someone had locked him in? Hard to say, but I was guessing he found a way to lock it behind him, seeing as he was the only fae I knew who handled iron.

Bridgette shoved the door inward, and I stumbled after her, putting my knife away, and shoved aside my thoughts about Crash too.

Robert grabbed at my hand just as the big doors shut behind us, taking the light with them. Well, that wasn't good.

"You close those?" I asked, instinctively tightening my hold on him. What the hell, did we have self-closing doors now?

"No, I did," Bridgette whispered in the dark. The sound of a match striking followed her words, and then a lantern bloomed, held by the goblin. "Come on. Karissa's men won't follow us in. They might not even realize there were chains on the doors." She gave a shuddering sigh. "I hope."

With a grimace, I put myself right behind Bridgette.

Kinkly landed lightly on my shoulder, shivering. "It's cold in here."

I actually didn't mind the temperature change. My skin was flushed from the exertion and probably as a side effect of either the poison or its cure. But if I didn't know better it felt like I was still heating up, my skin getting incrementally warmer with each step. I frowned. "You think it's cold?"

"Quite," Robert said. "And that's from the guy who's been walking around in rags for a couple hundred years."

There he was, the Robert I knew. I squeezed his hand tighter. "I like this temperature. My skin is too hot."

Bridgette held the light up a little higher. "Don't humans get something like fire ass?"

"Fire . . . ass?" I'll admit, I stumbled over that one a bit. "What is that?"

Kinkly answered. "Goblins go through the life changes too, you know. When they are closing in on triple digits, they get fire ass."

Fire ass.

Hot flashes.

I blew out a breath because I wasn't sure if I should laugh or cry. Duck it. I started to laugh. "Fire ass sounds a helluva a lot more impressive than 'hot flash.'"

"Well, to be fair, they can actually catch fire." Bridgette shuddered as we paused at an intersection, holding the light up to read some inscription etched into the stone. She nodded to herself, then took a left-hand turn. "So maybe you've got the better deal."

"At least you aren't part goblin," Kinkly whispered.

We went on like that for some time, pausing at intersections, waiting for Bridgette to direct us to whichever tunnel she thought was good. The air was cold on my hot skin, the path was quiet and dark. But otherwise, the tunnels were easy. No demon fae, and Karissa's executioners hadn't followed us in.

A win for us across the board.

"We aren't far now," Bridgette said. "A couple more turns, and we can leave through the Paris exit."

Kinkly shuddered. "Good, I'm freezing my feet off."

We started down the tunnel, the light bouncing a little. A click on the stone in front of us stopped us all. Like a pebble falling maybe. Or maybe a drop of water. Nothing serious, right?

Bridgette held up a hand. "Wait. I hear something."

We all held perfectly still, the silence of the drilled-out rock tunnels beating against us. All I could hear was my own heartbeat. Kinkly gave a low moan. "Oh no."

Bridgette began to shake, so hard that the lantern light flickered. I let go of her hand and grabbed the light, holding it up high. "I don't hear anything." Just that one pebble falling. If the beastie had dislodged a single pebble, how big and bad could it really be?

I turned to the left, nothing. But to the right . . . well, to the right was a problem.

CHAPTER
ELEVEN

"Snicken," Kinkly whispered in my ear and the . . . thing . . . twisted its head toward her. Which meant it looked right at me. And I use the word head loosely, because this creature was ducking weird.

The 'snicken,' if that's what it was, looked like a cross between a chicken and a snake, if such a thing could possibly exist. Yes, I was looking right at it, and even though I didn't remember eating any half moldy cheese, it seemed more reasonable to assume I was having a food-induced hallucination than that this thing *actually* existed. Maybe the poison from the arrow was still working through me. The snicken stood over seven feet tall, and most of its body was covered in feathers, though the color was hard to see in the lantern light. Maybe black. Maybe dark brown. The head was elongated with massive fangs lining the top and bottom of a jaw that looked like it had been borrowed from an alligator, yet a long, forked tongue flipped out from between the fangs, tasting the air. The long neck was covered in feathers even as it spread wide like the hood of a damn cobra. Body of a chicken, clawed talons, and a long featherless, scaled tail spooled out from behind it, flipping lazily back and forth from one tunnel wall to the other.

Six months before, I would have passed out, pooped my pants, or flat out screamed. But I was no spring chicken—see what I did there?—and I was too damn tired to run. I also had no shits left to give.

"You a guardian or something?" I held the lantern up higher, forcing the snicken's head back a bit. Bridgette gave a whimper, and Robert tugged on my arm.

"You can't make friends with this one," Kinkly whispered.

"Not trying to make friends." I shoved the lantern closer yet, and the snicken squinted its chicken eyes at me, not liking the light. A low hiss began in its throat as the neck feathers bristled. Yup, definitely cobra stuff going on there. "I saw a documentary on snake charming. Once. Let's try it."

I swayed the lantern from left to right, and the snicken followed the glow.

I kept the swaying up, back and forth, as I shoved Bridgette lightly with my other hand. "Start walking slowly. I'll keep it distracted. Someone keep hold of me so we don't lose each other."

Bridgette squeaked, but she did as I said, and then we were doing this weird parade where we continued walking slowly backward with the snicken following us.

"They are venomous," Kinkly whispered. "One bite and you're done. Nothing can heal their bite."

"Lovely," I whispered back, sweating now. Maybe I *was* part goblin, because there was so much heat rolling off my skin, it felt like my ass *was* on fire. I'd love to say it was just nerves, but this felt like I had hot embers inside my clothing, burning through everything.

Of all the times to get my true first hot flash, this was probably the worst. And yet, here we were. Having a hot flash while a monster stared us down. Just perfect. Just another day in the exciting life of Bree O'Rylee.

"You're doing great." Robert was helping me walk backward, keeping me from falling over. "How's the arm?"

I swayed the lantern back and forth easily, but I could feel the strain starting from keeping it up so high. "As long as we aren't in here for like another hour, we should be good."

Bridgette squeaked from the front of our group. "Bigger problem."

I didn't dare look. "Seriously?"

"These tunnels lead to the land of the demon fae. They're like a highway," she said. "And they are full of guardians. We've been lucky so far. Maybe because the king went ahead of us."

Lucky so far. "Crash could have cleared the path?" Maybe that's why the council had agreed this was a good idea.

Bridgette bobbed her head. "It's likely."

Of course, no one had mentioned that before we came in here. "How bad could the guardians be?"

A beastie roared in front of her in answer and then something slammed into my back, throwing me and the lantern directly at the snicken.

The world slowed down, so I got to watch as the snicken's eyes widened along with its mouth.

I ended up slamming into the long-necked monster and grabbing it around the neck, giving it a hug and clamping its flaring neck flaps down. Could it bite me from this position? I wasn't sure. I was pretty high up on its neck.

Kinkly squealed right in my ear, Robert was yelling, and Bridgette was screaming in a pitch that only dogs should be able to hear. The snicken thrashed its neck, trying to dislodge me, but I was so far up that it couldn't do much more than shake. I squeezed a little tighter and tried to dredge up what I knew about catching snakes.

Not much.

"What's the other monster?" I hollered. I couldn't see anything, thrashing around with a snicken, the lantern bobbing in my hand, my face all but buried in its neck feathers.

"Wendigo!" Robert yelled back.

Oh, that one I knew from Gran's earlier teachings. Built kind of like a man, but tall, slim, and with a voracious appetite. They'd eat your body *and* your soul given the chance.

Bridgette's screaming suddenly cut off, and the snicken began to slump under me, sliding to the ground, head tipping forward. I hit the tunnel floor but kept my grip on it.

"I think you choked it out," Kinkly yelped.

I wasn't about to let go and find out the thing was faking. I lifted my head out of the feathers, though, and could see what was happening with my friends.

Robert had put himself between the wendigo and Bridgette, and they were pinned against a wall. The wendigo had mottled gray and white skin that kind of glowed in the semi-darkness, and its limbs moved at a speed that my eyes had a hard time tracking. No eyes, no nose, just a mouth filled with tiny silver teeth. Those did catch the light, quite well actually.

"Kinkly, is this thing out?"

She moved gingerly up its neck, dancing across the feathers. "Huh. You really did choke it out cold! I didn't think you were that strong with those weak old lady arms—"

"Not now." I didn't know for sure that I could do what my brain said I needed to do. But I wasn't going to question it. Robert and Bridgette were in trouble. I set the lantern down and kept hanging onto the snicken.

Call me crazy, but I thought the big bird snake thing was faking it. Still holding its neck in one arm, I reached for my knife. Pulling it free, I took a breath. I would have one throw, and one throw only.

My view of the wendigo was blocked by Robert. "When I say drop, you drop!" I yelled. Robert didn't answer. "Kinkly, make sure he knows!"

She took off, her flying slightly ragged because of her stitched-up wing. She landed on his shoulder, and I adjusted my hold on the snicken.

"Winner, winner," I whispered. "Chicken dinner."

I gripped the knife in my hand and took a steadying breath. Then, with as much speed as I could muster, I sat up. "Duck!"

"You said drop!" Kinkly yelled back.

Drop, duck, whatever! Robert went down and I threw the knife, fully releasing the snicken's neck so I could make the move.

The beast was a total faker.

The elongated face shot back toward me, and I rolled to the side, dodging the open mouth and taking the lantern with me. I'd like to say I shot to my feet and ran to my friends.

Nope, stumbled, landed back on my ass, and ended up holding the lantern in front of me as my only protection against the snicken.

The wendigo's screams lit the air and then it rushed in our direction. I saw my knife sticking out of its chest.

"That's mine!" I yelled as I leapt up, grabbed the knife, and yanked it free. I wasn't about to lose another knife. The wendigo spun to face me. I mean, it had no face, but you catch my drift.

I grimaced. "Bad placement. Look behind you."

The wendigo whipped around just as the snicken launched a full attack, mouth wide open, eyes narrowed. The two monsters went to the ground, writhing and screeching, hissing and biting. I pushed back across the floor on my butt until I was against a wall, barely dodging a flip of the snicken's barbed tail. Barbed? Damn, I hadn't seen that before! I kicked it away. Hands helped me up, and then the three of us were running through the tunnels, Kinkly sobbing as she clung to Robert's earlobe.

There was no pretense of being quiet now. We disturbed a bunch of other guardians, but I think they were as surprised to see us as the first two had been.

"There, that's the way out!" Bridgette yelped as the tunnel brightened around us. A way out that was open? It seemed too good to be true. Far too good to be true. Crash must have left it open. Or maybe the people on this side didn't worry about monsters coming into Paris?

The light continued to get stronger, illuminating the space around us so I could see the walls, the scores that ran down them as if claws or weapons had been dragged across the surface. The uneven ground we ran across, covered in bones. The fear on Bridgette's face. The tension in Robert's. The way Kinkly sobbed as she clung to Robert's ear.

Me? I was fine. Weirdly fine and not freaking out, and *that* kind of freaked me out. Why was I not melting down? Was something wrong with me? Strike that. There were a number of things wrong with me. But was I that far out of ducks to give that even this deep, dark place that led to the demon fae didn't scare me?

"I can't," Robert said suddenly. "I can't do it."

Now I was more confused than ever. Bridgette slid to a stop, and I all but ran over top of her. "What are you talking about?"

Robert was shaking as though someone had grabbed his shoulders and was snapping him back and forth. "It's too much. She's calling to me. But how?"

"What's too much?" I didn't understand.

"The darkness," Bridgette said. "The demons are calling to us. Can't you feel it?"

I blinked and looked around. "No." If I was the only one unaffected, then I had to get us the rest of the way out of here. "Everyone take hold of me. Just close your eyes and let me lead."

Bridgette and Kinkly did as they were told, but Robert stepped away. "I don't want to hurt you, Bree. Something is calling to me, a woman. A voice. She wants you dead."

Oh, for duck's sake. "For right now, Robert, I need you to trust me. Just hang onto my hand for the moment and let me get us out of here before that weird-ass bird snake thing comes for us again!"

Yelling, I was yelling—let's just say a little suppressed rage was finally coming to the surface. Or maybe it was a bit of fear, because if Robert was hearing a voice calling to him, ordering him to hurt me . . . who could that be? Was it possible that the first witch was already on to us?

My voice echoed through the tunnels and something roared in response, the smell of its breath coming up through the shafts. I dropped the lantern, clamped down on Robert's hand, and all but dragged him and Bridgette the last twenty feet.

Whatever had roared deep within the tunnels was coming up fast, and I leaned into the effort of getting them out. Bridgette leaned away from me, and Robert literally dragged his feet. It was like some external force was making them resist me.

"Kinkly, get out the door!"

She, at least, was able to resist the pull of the demon fae.

Why, though? And why could I? My connection to the fae had supposedly been severed. Well, no time to consider it right then. One problem at a time.

We got to the opening, the light beckoning; I shoved Bridgette to safety first so I could turn and grab Robert with both hands. "Come on!"

"I . . . friend," he whispered, and his body shimmered.

Crap on toast, was he going back to being a skeleton?

What else could possibly go wrong?

No, don't answer that.

CHAPTER
TWELVE

That question 'what else could go wrong' never even left my mouth, yet the universe still decided to show me up. *Hold my beer*, it said. *Watch what I can do.*

Robert's eyes rolled and he shook his head violently as I did my best to drag him to the door. Bridgette and Kinkly had already escaped the demon fae tunnels, and here I was with Robert, stuck.

"Robert, please. Stop fighting me!"

A snarl ripped out of him. "You will never find me! You will die on the first challenge!" Laughter poured out of him, feminine cackling laughter. The first witch, it had to be her.

How the hell was this happening? "Fossette, I'm trying to help you!" I yelled.

All the resistance that had been in Robert's body suddenly eased up as he leapt *toward* me.

"That's not what I meant!" I yelped as we went down in a tangle. Robert pinned me to the ground with the full length of his body, a growl shuddering through him that I felt in my own body.

His lips peeled back and . . . no. Just that one word was all I could think. This could not be happening. Fangs, he had *fangs*. All my earlier fears came rushing back. Vampire. Somehow Robert was . . . a vampire?

The confusion almost got me killed.

I got my forearm between us at the last second as his mouth came toward me. His teeth sunk into my arm, between the bracers and the upper jacket—the one vulnerable spot—and a scream ripped out of me. "This is not the way it's supposed to be, Robert!"

His growls reverberated on my arm like a damn tuning fork. The roars deep in the cave were getting closer. We were sitting ducks, and if I couldn't get Robert off me, we were both dead. Well, dead again for him.

I was stuck. Well and truly stuck. Robert's other hand reached around and scrabbled at my corset, but the leather held against his efforts.

The power in my gut, the magic that had so interested Dr. Mori of the shinigami, rolled through me. The power over the dead. I wasn't sure it would work, but I sure as shit wasn't going to just let him chew my damn arm off without trying. He'd been dead up until recently, and he seemed to be some variety of undead now, so I was hoping to hell this worked. "Release me!"

Robert's jaw popped open, his eyes lost the glazed look, and he went semi-limp. I grabbed him by the ear and dragged him upward with me.

With one good shove, I got him out of the opening, out of the tunnels.

I stumbled, arm bleeding and aching, and fell through the opening on the other side. The warmth of the late morning sun was heaven on my face, and I just lay there, soaking it in. "That . . . I don't want to go back that way. I'll swim the Atlantic before I go back in there."

The bag on my hip rumbled, and teeny tiny voices began to shout at me. I flipped open the bag and dumped the contents out as my friends all regained their original sizes. The stench was something else.

"Damn it, Penny!" Eammon roared, his fury coming out his back end too. I crinkled up my nose as he let out a massive fart that sounded like thunder and smelled like a backed-up toilet. Suzy and Sarge both clutched at their bellies.

The four of them immediately started fighting. Eric, of course, was trying to calm things down. I just lay there, breathing in the sort-of fresh air. Glad to be out of the tunnels.

Propping myself up on my elbows, I caught Bridgette's eye. Bridgette and Kinkly were staring at me, eyes and mouths perfect circles, faces pale. I touched my face and patted down my body, looking for whatever it was that had them so agitated.

Only when I really thought about it did I realize how cold my left foot was compared to the rest of my body. I looked over my shoulder.

"Oh, duck me."

My left foot was still in the tunnel.

Something cold and slimy wrapped around my left ankle and yanked me hard back into the darkness. None of my friends even had a chance to reach for me.

"I do not have time for this shit!" I hollered as I sped through the darkness. Probably straight toward an open maw filled with teeth, spit, and venom. I mean, let's be honest, that was a pretty good guess at this point.

I should have been more afraid. Should have been ducking terrified.

But I found myself feeling weirdly irritated about the whole thing. Like all my ducks had flown the coop, and I had none left to give. Yes, I know that ducks don't have a coop—don't get all semantic on me.

Whatever had me around the ankle was yanking me through tunnel after tunnel at a speed that wasn't worth arguing with, so I stopped fighting it.

"I'm saving my strength to kick your ass in person!" I snapped as the speed of my descent slowed. I was revving myself up to see the monster in all its glory, and hopefully kick its ass, but as its sharp-toothed maw and huge glowing eyes came into view, it flung me down a tunnel *away* from it.

I rolled, grunted, cursed, and came to a tumbling stop.

Lights blinked on all around me, giving me a good view of a dark field stretched out ahead of me. I was sitting in an archway, a cobblestone-studded path under me, looking into . . . a different exit out of the tunnels. If I were to guess, I'd say I was looking at the path that would take me straight to the actual realm of the demon fae. Whatever creature had seen fit to drag me down here was nowhere to be found. Had it been convinced to bring me here? I pushed slowly to my feet, my thighs, calves, and lower back protesting every move. As I stood there, staring out into a land that had a very different kind of beauty to it than the fae lands Karissa ruled, my heart fluttered.

In the darkness, light still thrived.

Specks of it danced through the air, only they were dark reds and oranges, more like tiny flames than miniature suns. Tall, slender figures moved gracefully, walking with purpose to the left and right of me, too far away for me to see if they were male or female. They could have passed for human in shape. The call of night birds filled the air, and a cool breeze that blew through the grassy fields, bending the stalks of the long grasses around me. I didn't realize I'd stepped out into the field, following the path, that I'd bent to grab hold of something, until a soft voice whispered in my ear.

My name on the wind. One of the figures stopped

and turned to me. Male, that one was male. He didn't move forward. Just stood there looking at me, and me at him.

This place called to me on a deep level. Far more than the fae lands ever had. Was that good? Bad? Or just because I was a weirdo with mixed-up DNA? I held out a hand to one of the tiny fire lights, and it flickered closer.

Flames danced around a creature that was no bigger than a firefly, but it was no bug. The flaming bird flitted closer and closer to my palm. Warmth rolled off it and to my skin. It waved at me. Smiled. I smiled back.

"Do not move, Lass." Crash's voice, right behind me.

A shiver ran through me, from my head straight to my lady bits. I closed my eyes and just breathed in. Wait. No. I was not feeling anything for him! I couldn't, not again.

I threw an elbow back into his gut, driving the air out of him in a whoosh that bent him in half. Probably I should have thought that through, but I was done being careful around Crash. I had to be. Whatever spell the place had on me faded as my anger at the man who'd caused me so much heartache filled me up and burned away all the other emotions.

I spun and headed back the way I'd come, then realized in a flash of irritation that there was no way I'd find my way back through the tunnels. I couldn't read goblin, and I certainly didn't remember all the turns I'd been dragged around. Preservation won out over pride. I had to get to my friends. Maybe along the way I'd find a way to slow down his search for the first witch.

"You know the way out?"

He grunted what was likely a yes.

"Let's go then." I didn't touch him. I wanted to, but I didn't. Okay, maybe I reached out for him and accidently touched his ass. I mean, he was bent over, and I jumped away quickly. As if it were an accident. As if I hadn't just grabbed his butt. Yeah, it was a grab, not just a touch. Bad, bad me. It was almost as if I couldn't help it.

I looked back into the field, and that one figure was still watching us. Unmoving. Head tipping to the side.

Crash rubbed at his stomach and motioned for me to go ahead of him, touching a finger to his lips. My eyes tracked the movement, and gawd damn if I couldn't help myself from licking my own lips.

Something was seriously wrong with me. I needed help. Therapy. A freaking intervention. The man was an addiction I couldn't seem to get out of my system. Though, to be fair, he and I had been not even truly broken up (were we ever *really* together?) for a very short time.

Biting the inside of my cheeks, ignoring the way Crash's eyes slid over me, I made my feet move.

We left the dark meadow as more of the other figures noticed us and turned our way. They drew closer, their eyes glowing a strange green. Crash put a hand to my lower back and propelled me forward, pushing me into a jog as soon as we were out of sight of the meadow and the demon fae.

"What is that place? Were those the demon fae?" I asked as we traversed the tunnels. There was a fine glow of something on the walls, just enough that you didn't need a light to find your way. How had we not noticed it before?

"It is a place you should never go, ever again." His voice was a low rumble. I had to stop and lean against the wall as the reverberation went straight to my hoo-haw. Lady bits. My cat, as Feish would say.

A shudder rippled through me that I struggled to contain. Nope. Not containing it.

"Bree?" His voice was closer, the sound caressing my ears, and I closed my eyes. Tried to think of anything but him.

Cleaning toilets.

Newspaper stains on my hands.

Being sick after too much whiskey.

He breathed too close, and the warm air brushed across my cheek. I struggled not to come right there.

"Jaysus, don't speak to me." I hissed out the words, knees clamped together as I fought whatever hellfire magic was happening. He clearly wasn't affected by it.

Then his eyes widened, and he put a hand to his head. "Goddess. She said she had a way to block your connection to the fae. But that's impossible. It shouldn't have worked. I thought she was just . . . full of shit like usual."

He seemed to be talking more to himself than me. Either way, it was driving me crazy.

"Stop. Talking." I bent at the waist as waves of building pressure had me clamping my knees together. I kept a hand against the wall, barely managing to stay upright. "Just. Lead."

Now you'd think that would be better. It was not.

Here I was, staring at the perfect ass I'd just groped, my body aching and panting for air as if I'd just sprinted a half mile. Remembering every hot, seductive moment I'd ever shared with him, from the feel of his hands to the taste of his lips, to the pressure of his body against mine.

You try walking up a steady slope with your knees together and your lady bits pulsing with every step you take. *"Every move you make,"* I whispered. *"I'll be watching you."*

Crash turned around and looked at me. I shrugged. "I'll take songs of the eighties for a thousand, Alex."

I don't know how long it took us to get out of the tunnels. Too long.

I was covered in sweat by the time we got to the exit. I stumbled through, and Eric caught me.

"Bree, are you okay? Injured?"

That reminded me. I lifted my arm. The blood had crusted where Robert had gnawed on me, and the bites were tender, but I wasn't about to bleed to death.

"I'll be okay. Where is Robert? He was . . ." I didn't want to say possessed. But that was the best description I had for what had happened to him.

Looks were shared. Eammon cleared his throat. "He took off running. Screamed that we'd never find him, and he'd kill us all if we tried." Eammon shook his head. "Sounded an awful lot like a woman to me."

Gran floated at the back of the group, and her sniff was loud enough for all of the ghost-seers to hear her loud and clear. Penny held up her hand and pointed to the man at my side. "He's not our friend any longer. I suggest that we discuss nothing else while he stands here."

She wasn't wrong. I looked over at Crash and then turned my back on him as the heat rose through my body in a wave that had all my parts tingling mightily. "I don't know what happened, or why I'm reacting this way, but I don't want to talk to you. I think you should go."

He sighed, and even that subtle sound had my body perking up. I closed my eyes, but I could still see him in my mind's eye buck naked, wrapped in a sheet, or soaking wet in my shower, all slippery and soapy. I groaned and went to my knees, grateful for the soft grass under them.

"You could tone it down," Suzy snapped, and there was a sound like a slap. "You are capable, fae king. Or do you wish to torture her?"

Tone it down?

"I am used to being myself with her." Crash sounded . . . sad, but his voice didn't strum the hormones in my body into an orchestra headed straight for orgasm. I peeked with one eye and looked over my shoulder. He was still the way I'd always seen him, handsome and drool-worthy. "Better?" he asked.

No pings in my lady parts. I nodded. "This was part of the cost. It's . . . it is what it is." Of course, I hadn't understood what exactly it would mean to give up the fae side of me. But obviously part of it was this heightened sensitivity to fae magic. Like how the land of Faerie had affected me. How Crash affected me.

"No." Eammon stepped between us, vibrating like a pissed-off chihuahua facing off a wolf. "Get out of here, Crash. You work for the Dark Council. We do not."

Crash gave a stiff, stilted bow from the waist. "I will say one final thing. You brought Robert back to life, to the moments before he died the first time. If you do not find a way to cure him, he will die again in the same manner. Which . . . as you can see by the bites on Bree's arm, will be death by vampirism."

I spluttered and got to my feet, only to immediately stumble and grab for the person closest to me. Eric held out a big hand, and I clung to him. "Wait, what?"

Crash just shut the double doors leading to the tunnels, sliding a padlock between the handles and closing it with a click. Still, he didn't say a single word—he just turned his back on us and strode away. He'd said his "final thing" and not a word more. Damn his literal ass.

I looked at my friends and Penny just shook her head. "To the house that waits for us. Then we will discuss everything."

Limping and stumbling along, my friends led the way, Penny and Eammon arguing, Eric and Suzy holding hands. Sarge right at my side, his eyes worried as he sniffed the air. Bridgette was at the back, and I let myself drift back to join her. Kinkly flew from her smaller shoulder up to mine. "The gates . . . they were open on this side," I said.

She flinched and looked straight ahead. "I'd . . . hoped they would be. With Crash going ahead of us, like you said . . ."

"But you didn't know for sure."

Her shoulders hunched. "Leland said the king had come this way, confirming what Roderick had guessed. Once I knew that, I figured our way would be safer because he'd gone ahead of us."

I looked over my shoulder at the now closed gates, feeling like we'd forgotten something. Something important, like not turning off the oven before we left home, but what was it?

CHAPTER
THIRTEEN

The house that belonged to Roderick backed onto a winding section of the Seine River. Actually, it was less of a house and more of a small castle. A vineyard spilled out on the western slope of the field around the house, the river peeked out on the northern edge, and there were stables to the south and bare fields to the east with waving stands of grain.

All in all, if we weren't there to work, I would have loved to explore the area. This would have been a hell of a vacation spot. Of course, there was no chance we were going get a break.

Our group sat around a big table in the main dining hall of the castle, a butler serving us food while a pair of maids prepped our rooms. The only one not with us was Bridgette, who'd insisted on searching for her cousins right away. I couldn't stop her, and she'd left within minutes of making sure we were settled safe and sound.

"Is this for real?" Suzy asked. "I mean, I like it and all, but are they spying on us? And by they I *do* mean you and the maids," she said to the butler—Pierre, who jerked as if she'd pinched his ass.

"I think not, mademoiselle." His accent was not too thick. He was easy to understand.

She looked him over. He stared back, totally unintimidated.

Sarge stood and leaned toward him. "What she means is, we need some privacy. So scat, Pepe."

Pierre sniffed and turned stiffly, his heels clicking across the tile floor before he slammed the door shut behind him, sealing off the dining hall for a little privacy.

"He didn't like that much," Kinkly said through a yawn.

Penny rapped her cane on the floor. "We have limited time. We know Crash is here hunting for the first witch, though at least he isn't far ahead of us. We also know she's dangerous and has likely taken other hunters into her custody or killed them. We can't dilly-dally at this point."

"And Robert," I said. "He bit me, and Crash said . . ."

"Vampirism," Eammon growled. "It's possible. A dirty trick to bring a person back to life, still infected with whatever killed them!"

"Gawd, what I wouldn't give to stick some spiny

cactus in her shorts and make her sit on it for a week. And then add some itching powder for good measure," I muttered.

"Karissa?" Kinkly asked, and I nodded.

Sarge touched the wounds on my arm. We'd wrapped them, but they weren't bothering me much, to be honest. "Maybe he was afraid he'd hurt you again? The bite marks were deep."

I grimaced. "I was able to get him off me."

"How?" Penny asked quietly. "I don't mean to belittle you, Bree, but he must be physically stronger than you."

I shrugged. "I used my connection to the dead. I figured it was a solid bet."

"But he isn't dead anymore," Kinkly mumbled in my ear.

I nodded. "But he's recently dead. And when I realized there was some sort of vampire thing going on, I figured close enough. That's a thing, isn't it? Almost dead?"

My friends didn't look so sure, even if it made sense to me. Penny's deeply lined face was troubled. "Does anyone know how Robert died? To be sure. Not that I doubt you." Of course, she hadn't seen Robert's fangs. Or felt them in her arm. "What I heard was Fossette coming out of his mouth. That is of concern. She was so focused on Robert, she did not see me."

Ducking hell, I hadn't even thought of that. "Penny, we should fly you home."

She waved her cane. "It will be fine. I will be careful. Now, who would know exactly how Robert died? We need to be sure."

Everyone looked at me. "Roderick would," I said. "They knew each other before."

Which is how I ended up calling him. It was the middle of the night at home, but he didn't sound tired.

What was I thinking? Of course he didn't sleep. He was, after all, a vampire himself.

"Bree?" Roderick's voice was clipped. "You're already there? Faerie must be changing faster than I thought. Interesting." He paused. "Have you per chance found the witch already?"

I stared at the phone in my hand and wished it were Roderick's neck so I could strangle him. Interesting was not the word I'd use. "I just came through hell and . . . never mind. Look, do you know how Robert died?"

The silence was heavy and lasted far longer than it should have. "Why do you wish to know that?"

I banged the old-school phone on the table, wishing it were Roderick's head, before I pressed it back to my ear. "Because he's alive, as you saw in the council chamber. Karissa made an elixir that restored him, but I guess it brought him back to the way he was just before he died. Crash said we need to find a way to help him. He said it was a vampire who took him, and we need to be sure."

Silence again. "Say that one more time. I want to

make sure I am not hearing you wrong." His voice was careful, monotone. I didn't like it. I repeated my words.

"Karissa gave me an elixir to bring Robert back to life. It brought him back to his state of being just before he died the last time." I turned to my friends. They looked as bewildered as I felt.

Roderick swallowed so loudly I could hear it through the phone. "Crash is correct. He was bitten by a vampire, Bree. He killed his wife, and then he ended up dying because his body could not handle the transition. His remains were locked in a crypt. You called him up when you first visited the Hollows' cemetery those many months ago."

I almost asked *him* to say it again. I had been hoping that Crash was wrong. That my own eyes were wrong. There were not enough ducks for this truth. I wanted my friend to be okay, but Robert was in serious trouble.

Sarge took the phone. "How much time do we have?"

"Maybe a week," Roderick said. "It will depend on how much blood he takes from others. The last time this happened the blood-letting was unwilling on his part. He essentially killed himself so he would not harm others after he killed Eleanor."

Which fit with Robert's sense of guardianship and honor. And it explained why he'd been acting weird.

"Find Fossette, she is your priority," Roderick said.

"It will not matter if you save Robert, if we are overrun with the undead."

"Says the vampire," muttered Kinkly.

Roderick went on. "Bree, are you hearing me? It's not that Robert isn't important. He was a good man then, and he is a good man now, even though he hates me. But the first witch must be your target. Find her quickly, and then find Robert."

He hung up on me before I could get all my spluttering done, before I could tell him that Robert was likely with Fossette.

The urge to throw the phone across the room hit me, and then I thought about all the muscles I might end up pulling if I did it. Probably would throw my back out at the rate I was going. I set the phone down and leaned on the table.

"How could Fossette take Robert?" I looked at Penny as I asked the question. "How?"

Penny shook her head. "I don't know. Because he is a guardian perhaps? Or she may have the ability to sense the undead."

I closed my eyes and took a breath, let it out, and then looked at my friends.

"No matter how we look at this, we have to find the first witch. We *have* to find her, and when we find her, we find Robert. The question is how?"

· · ·

We decided to go out in teams of two or three to see what leads we could drum up in the shadow world here in the mean streets of grand ole Paris. Bridgette and Feish were out: Bridgette was not back yet, and by Suzy's calculations, Feish would get to the house around dinnertime. Penny, Kinkly, and I were Team One. Eammon and Sarge, Team Two. Suzy and Eric, Team Three. And yes, Eammon said it was necessary to name our teams so we could avoid using our real names over the short-wave walkie-talkies we'd found at Roderick's house.

Eammon and Sarge headed out into the countryside, to use Sarge's nose to see if they could pull up any leads. Suzy and Eric went into Paris to speak to a list of potential leads Penny had given them.

Team One, aka Penny, Kinkly, and I, had yet to leave the house; we stood in the front entrance. We couldn't seem to agree on a plan . . . mostly because I was worried Fossette would sense Penny's magic and come for her. "It'll be fine." She just waved her cane at me and I had to dodge her. "Trust me, Bree. Fossette isn't looking for another witch."

Kinkly curled herself into a ball in the palm of my hand. "I'm exhausted with all this bickering. Can I sleep in your bag for a bit?"

I opened the flap, and she slid down into the bottomless bag just as Gran stepped out from around the door to the dining hall, smoothing her skirts as if there was a wrinkle in her ghostly clothes. I knew the move. She was prepping herself for a lecture. My gran looked at me and then sighed. "I forgive you, Bree."

My eyebrows shot up so high, I'm shocked they didn't fly off my damn face. I couldn't help it, I laughed. "Gran! The spell was keyed to Robert! If I'd tried to use it for you, it would have been wasted."

Her eyes narrowed. "That's *not* how the spell works. Only one person could have made it for Karissa, and there's no way they would have been able to key it solely to Robert. She just wanted you to believe that. To see if you'd do it. To see who you loved best."

Penny tapped her cane. "That's not true, Celia. And would you have had the girl waste the offering?"

Gran huffed as she flowed along next to the table. "I know of what I speak. But no one wanted to listen to a dead woman."

I held up both hands to my gran. "Stop. I'm sorry. If what you're saying is true, I would have chosen to bring you back, a thousand times over. Gran, I love you. I hope you know that?"

She sighed and crossed her arms before looking me in the eye. "Yes, my girl, I know. Karissa is a tricky one, and she pulled a fast one on you this time."

Yes, that tricky bitch surely had pulled one over on me. And I'd been exhausted, heartsick, and desperate enough to cling to the first hopeful thing I came across. In this case, the possibility of bringing one of my friends back.

Now, if I wanted to save him, I had to find the first

witch *and* a cure for vampirism? Was that even possible? "Where do you think we should start?" I asked Penny.

"I've never been to Paris before." Penny tapped her cane on the ground then, swung it toward Gran. "But Celia has."

My gran bobbed her head. "Let's go to Maison Magique. It's the equivalent of Death Row back home. Much more French, of course." With a silent swish of her skirts, she led the way. My eyes swept over the streets, the people, the architecture of the city, but I was numb to the beauty and history. I wished I could take the time and brain bandwidth to appreciate it, but I had a job to do, and I wanted to get it done as soon as possible so that I could find Robert. Of course, finding Robert would offer its own set of problems. "Gran, how far?"

"Twenty-minute walk," she said. "Why?"

"Time for twenty questions. What happens when we find Robert? How do we stop him from, you know, becoming a vampire?" I asked.

Penny and my gran exchanged a look that I really did not like. My guts tightened, a sudden ache flared in my back, and the world kind of fuzzed. Because they didn't need to say it out loud for me to understand. "That can't be the only answer," I whispered. "You can't mean that the only way to save him—"

Penny looped an arm through mine. I wasn't sure if she needed the support, or she thought I did. Her grip tightened on me. Yup, she thought I needed the support.

"He has two options. Either he becomes a vampire, or he dies. There is no turning back now for him, or for you."

CHAPTER
FOURTEEN

Penny's words haunted me all the way to Maison Magique—the French equivalent to our Death Row back in Savannah.

Robert would either turn fully into a vampire, or he would die. Was that even a choice? I mean, both of those options meant a certain kind of death. If the beauty of Paris had been lost on me before, it was even more so for the next twenty minutes as we wove our way through the streets, following my gran.

"Here, this is the entrance." Gran stopped in front of a bakery. "We go through to the back hall where the toilets are, but there is a wall on your left. Press the middle of it, right where the menu is stuck to the wall."

Penny tugged me along. "Come on, Bree, you can't let Robert's fate stop you. The easiest way to find him is to find Fossette."

She wasn't wrong. I knew that. But damn, it was

hard to think past the problem that had been shoved in my face. I wasn't upset, per se—okay, yes I was upset, but that wasn't my driving emotion. I was determined to think of a way around Robert's predicament. I'd been given a puzzle, a problem, and I'd be damned if I didn't solve it.

There had to be a way to save Robert. Again.

We stepped into the bakery, and the smell kicked me in the salivary glands, reminding me that we'd barely eaten for the last day. "Penny, tell me you have some euros on you?"

With a twist of her lips, she went to the front and purchased something for the both of us. All I saw was flaky pastry, and when I bit into it, the rush of chocolate was unexpected. I didn't care what it was—except that Eric was going to have to learn how to make it. Immediately.

"Amazing," I mumbled around buttery pastry flaking down from my mouth and the sweet chocolate coating the interior. "Makes the day better."

"*La journée ne peut être que meilleure lorsque vous rencontrez une belle femme qui aime autant que vous la patisserie.*"

Both Penny and I turned, because even though I didn't speak French, I knew enough to know he was talking to me.

He was . . . stunning. Yup, that was the word. He looked like some crazy-hot hybrid of Corb and Crash.

Salivary glands were nowhere near activated

before. Now I was struggling not to let my mouth drop open and drool run down my chin. I managed a pithy, "Wha-att?"

He smiled, showing off just the slightest hint of dimples. Square jaw, full lips, and eyes that were a deep, dark green stared right back at me. His dark brown hair was shoulder length but swept back. "Excuse me, I did not realize you were American. I said simply that the day can only be better when you meet a beautiful woman who loves pastry as much as you do."

He held out his hand, and the cashier—who was also staring as if she'd been hit with the same stick as me—gave him the same flaky pastry.

And then we all watched him take a bite of it. With a silent laugh, he shook his head. "May your day be as good as your pastry."

I managed to pull myself together. Okay, okay, he was good looking. He was. But the more I looked at him, the more I could see that while he was handsome, he really was gorgeous—he wasn't as drop dead gorgeous as I'd first thought. Some strange scars sliced across his collarbones, and one even cut through the hair in his left eyebrow. He had dirt smeared across one cheek, or was that blood? I blinked, and my perception of his face wavered between top-notch model and bad boy who'd been rolling around in the dirt.

I frowned. Was he changing even as I looked at him?

He was staring at me, waiting for me to acknowledge his response, so I did.

"Flaky, chewed up, swallowed and eventually pooped out?" I shook my head as I forcefully pulled my eyes from him. "No thanks. Penny, let's go. He's wearing a glamour of some sort."

He was no No-face Bruce, but he was trying to hide his scars. I could both respect that, and still think that it suggested he was trouble.

I tucked my arm through hers and started toward the front of the pastry shop. She dug her heels in. "No, no, we go to the back, remember?"

Of course. We hadn't come just for sweets. Penny directed us to the back, passing one more glance over her shoulder. "That is a handsome man."

"Glamour, remember? He's hiding who he really is."

Penny startled. "No doubt he is headed to Maison Magique, the same as us then. He is trying to hide what he truly looks like, and you can see through it."

I grimaced. I'd had enough of all these hot supernatural men ducking up my life. Not that I thought this particular man was going to be in my life. More like the universe was just messing with me.

"You are going to Maison Magique?" The words, spoken in a French accent by a very pleasant, husky voice, followed us. I quickened my pace, all but dragging Penny to keep her moving. We shoved ourselves into the small bathroom. Gran was already there, pointing at the menu.

"Press it," she said.

I did as she instructed and the wall shimmered, showing off a narrow door.

So narrow I was going to have to go through it sideways. I grabbed the doorknob. Penny put her hand over mine and had me twist the knob hard to the left. "That opens it up," she said. "Turn it the other way, well, you don't want to do that."

Note to self, don't turn the knob to the right. I almost giggled—yes, my mind went straight into the gutter, thinking about knobs and turning them left and right. I snorted and opened the door. The hallway—if it could be called that—was narrow and smelled strongly of straight alcohol. My eyes watered, and I coughed. "What are they doing down there?"

"Distilling liquor," the not-my-friend hot guy said. "A magic brew that will make you feel as though you have wings!" He laughed, and his laugh had me throwing an elbow at him because he was too damn close. He was all but breathing in my ear, damn it!

"Ease off, bucko."

My elbow missed, and I stumbled back while he continued to laugh. "You will need to be faster than that, *Cherie*."

"Duck your *cherie* shit," I snapped, flushed and irritated. Maybe it was another hot flash.

"Focus," Penny said. "Bree, focus."

"Bree?"

Damn it, now he had my name. I shuffled along, breathing shallowly until we hit a nice sloping ramp that curved downward. Huge sconces were bracketed to the wall every few feet, lighting up the space and dispersing any shadows. If you didn't count the massive open space to our right that went straight down into complete darkness. No railing.

"No stairs. And lights!" I said, ignoring the obvious danger that could come if you got in a scuffle and were thrown off to the side. "At least they are civil."

Penny snorted. "We have to come back up this ramp, fool girl." Gran was ahead of her, acting for all the world like she wasn't already dead, clutching at the wall for all she was as she moved downward. I hadn't realized she was afraid of heights.

Still, all and all, it wasn't worse than stairs. We shuffled at Penny's speed down the ramp. I kept a hand on the wall because the other side was just that empty space straight down. "Kink, you want to shoot ahead?"

I flipped open my hip bag, and she peered up at me. "What?"

"Want to go ahead? We're headed down into the Maison Magique."

She was up in a flash, her sparkles catching the light. "YES!" She shot up, spun three times, and then zipped down through the open space to my right, moving past the multi-leveled ramps we were using to get down.

"Make good choices!" I yelled after her. A grunt from behind us, and I held up a hand without looking over my shoulder. "No comments from the peanut gallery."

"I think it interesting that you keep a fairy in your bag, is all," he said, completely ignoring me.

I sighed. "Penny, men will be the death of me. Because I'll tell them to swim when they are drowning, and they will have nothing but one breath of air, and they'll use it to tell me that they are not drowning and they don't have to listen to me."

She laughed. "There might be a few who would listen. You just seem to draw in the ones who want to test you, girl. At least right now. What does that tell you?"

I frowned and shuffled down the curving ramp. "That the universe hates me? Or that I have terrible taste in men?"

"That the goddess is preparing you to be more than you ever thought you could be," the man behind us said, his voice softer this time. "My apologies. I will keep my thoughts to myself from here on out."

Nope, I was not turning around and looking at him again.

By the time we got to the bottom of the ramp, there were no thoughts of speaking—at least not from me. My thighs were fully cramping, and I was dreaming of having a cane like Penny. Maybe I could cover it in rhinestones, really bling that shit up.

"They're worse than stairs," I whispered, wincing as my right thigh spasmed.

Penny sighed and leaned against the wall. "I wish they'd put in an elevator."

The man behind us slipped past with a nod but not a single word. I knew I'd regret this but . . . "Do you have a name?"

Seeing as he knew mine, it was only fair.

He paused and looked over his shoulder in a fair attempt at a smolder—strike that, it was a full-on smolder. "Remy."

I would not swallow, would not gulp. "Good luck with your shopping," I managed to squeak out.

His smolder turned into a smile. "And you with yours. Bree."

He left me and Penny, and she fanned herself. "Damn it, I wish you'd been around when I was younger. You seem to draw the best-looking men to you!"

"They also tend to be trouble," I pointed out. "All of them are trouble."

A sparkle and flutter of wings, and Kinkly was making her way back to me. She was still a bit gimpy with her flying, but it was getting better. "You are not going to believe who is here!"

I did swallow then. "Crash?"

She crinkled her nose. "Yes, but it gets worse. He has someone with him." Kinkly landed on my shoulder. "You're going to want to brace yourself, after what she did to poor Robert."

Duck me, it just had to be Karissa, didn't it? I did not want to go bracing myself for anything. I swiped a hand over my sweaty face, tucked a few strands of hair behind my ears, and took a deep breath.

"Fixing your hair won't help, you won't be able to look good next to her even if you had all day to prep," Kinkly whispered. "You'd need magic to achieve that."

A soft footstep, and Remy stepped out from the shadows. "Crash? Is he an . . . enemy of yours?"

I rolled my eyes. Obviously he'd been listening in. "Why, is he an enemy of yours?"

Remy's smile was wide. "We go way back. If I am correct, it might bother him to see you on my arm?"

My lips twitched. "You want to piss him off? Aren't you afraid of him? Him being a fae king and all that."

Remy laughed without any reservation. "Gods no, but I would rather like to see him flustered. And I have a feeling that you might just fluster him."

I looked at Penny, and she shrugged. "Could be worse than to show up on that one's arm."

Could be worse. Oh, I wasn't so sure about that. But hell, in for a penny, in for a pound.

I held out a hand and he scooped it up and kissed the back of it. "Let's get to flustering then."

CHAPTER
FIFTEEN

Yup, I wasn't sure who was more flustered. Me or . . . me. Yes, the answer was me. Remy's kiss on the back of my hand had been a sweet gesture, nothing sexual about it, yet there was a zing of electricity that had our eyes locking.

"Damn." Kinkly let out a low whistle. "Whatever mojo you got, I need. You could bottle it up and sell it for millions, girl."

Remy seemed suddenly unsure of himself. His eyes lifted to my face, searching for something. I knew I wasn't that stunning. I was average. I grinned. "Rattled?"

"Completely. Now," he tucked my arm through his, "let's go shopping, new friend. See if we can make that blacksmith sweat half as much as you make me sweat."

I wasn't here to shop. But maybe this would be a good ruse to cover up our real purpose for being here. I looked back at Penny, and she waved at me with her cane. "Go on, I'll keep an eye on things. See what you can find out."

In other words, we'd both learn what we could.

The smell of alcohol faded, replaced by herbal scents. Mint, lavender, honeysuckle, sage, basil. I drew them in and tried to push away all of my worries and fears. Worry about Robert. Corb. The first witch. Crash. Yup, Crash was at the front of the list now.

I breathed out and felt some of the tension leave me. The Maison Magique was an underground street, surrounded by buildings with multiple floors shooting upward. Unlike on Death Row, the wares were sold inside stores. A few people walked down the cobblestones, pausing every now and then to peer into storefronts. Lamp posts lit the way, flickering with different-colored lights. The stone walls were mostly dark, and different types of plants crawled up them, which explained the rush of herbaceous scents.

"Here, this is where we need to start. I will speak to this one." Remy tugged me gently toward the building on our right.

He opened the door and motioned for me to go ahead of him. As I stepped over the threshold, the air changed from cool and damp to a breathtaking heat that had me sweating in a split second. The sound of a bellows filled the air, and the crackle of flames said it all.

Remy had brought us directly into the line of fire,

so to speak, though I doubted he'd known for sure that Crash would be there. It had been a good guess, though, and it had paid off.

Crash's back was to us—a small blessing—but it was most definitely him, and the woman next to him, with the intricately braided blond hair that fell to her perfect ass, was equally unmistakable. Karissa was here in Paris with him, just like Kinkly had said. With her hand on his lower back, her fingers gently digging into him, massaging him.

They were speaking quietly with a man who had to be the owner of the shop, another blacksmith if the leather apron and bulging arm muscles were any indication. I overheard 'witch' and 'find,' and that was it.

Crash was here looking for information about the first witch's location. Karissa's hand slid over his ass cheek, and I sucked in a sharp breath.

I should not feel this jealous, I should not. He was never truly mine. He'd been her husband.

Of course Karissa was with him. Why had I ever thought I was saving him from her?

"Holy Dinah," I whispered through the strange pain in my heart, and Kinkly squeaked.

Remy stepped around so that he was in my line of sight. "*Ma cherie.*" He said it nice and loud and the laughter on his face said it all. This was a game to him.

He was going to enjoy making Crash squirm. Though I wasn't so sure he would squirm—he was obviously back with Karissa.

"Too hot in here. It makes me want to take all my clothes off," I said.

A grunt from Crash confirmed that he'd heard me. That's the problem with being so tied to someone. You knew they were there, even when they barely whispered.

Remy pulled me in close, one arm around my back and the other cupping my face, and Kinkly stayed where she was on my shoulder, pointing a finger at him even as he wrapped my arms around his very firm middle until I was pressed hard against him.

"This is not helping me accomplish anything," I muttered.

He dipped his head until his mouth was level with my ear. "What will drive him wild?"

It was a question that I wasn't sure I had the answer to. And then it hit me in a flash. "Tell me that you know where she is, and you're taking me to her."

Remy pulled back, his eyebrows high and the confusion obvious. "But of course I will take you to her. You had only to ask, my beauty. Shall we go now? Or would you rather wait until the morning, after I have kissed every inch of your satiny skin? After I have drawn every cry from your lips, until exhaustion overcomes us both." He winked, slid his arm around my shoulder, and turned us both to face Crash and Karissa.

Crash looked as if he were made of stone. Perfect, perfect stone, except for the pain in his eyes. Oh, that did terrible things to my belly.

Karissa had her hands on her hips, and she full-on glared at me. The owner scuttled out of the main room, eyes down. Apparently he'd seen her anger before.

"*You* know where she is?" Karissa blurted out. "Impossible!"

Remy tightened his hold on me. "I know much more than you think, you self-indulgent sun rider. What are you doing here, in my country?"

Sun rider, that was new to me. And his country? France did not belong to Remy. Even I knew that much.

She huffed and stormed out past us, trying to push into our space. Remy tugged me just out of her way, so she stumbled when she went to hip check me—far from her usual graceful self. The door slammed behind her, and then I was looking at Crash again.

Why did it feel like it had been weeks since I'd last seen him, rather than hours? He was not good for me, I knew it. *He* knew it. And we were on opposite sides yet again. Before I could speak, Crash gave a slow nod. "If you have him as a guide, be careful he does not lead you down a dark path, Bree."

Irritation rubbed up against my hurt. "Again with the sage advice. Don't go after Robert. Don't follow Remy. Maybe you just don't want me with other men?"

Crash's eyes locked on mine, and there was a moment of understanding. Just a glimmer. He was jealous, but he knew he'd ducked up and didn't have a leg to stand on. But that didn't mean he wasn't going to try and keep me away from other men.

Messed up, that's what that was.

"Men are dumb," Kinkly whispered in my ear. I didn't disagree.

Remy laughed, and Crash shifted his attention to him. "As though you wouldn't have done the same? You will see, Remy. She is not to be trifled with, and once you tangle your heart with hers, there is no untangling it."

There was a clatter out on the street.

Kinkly tugged on my ear and pointed out the front window. Karissa was talking to two very large men. Judging by the armor they wore and the swords they held, they were guards of some sort. Then she pointed to the smithy. And her knee. And when she turned her face, she had the perfect crying face going on.

"She's framing us," I whispered. I let go of Remy and took off deeper into the shop, past Crash and the bellowing forge. "Kinkly, help me find a way out!"

"Upstairs!" Remy was there behind me, shoving me along.

"What about Penny?" Kinkly yelped.

"She's better off not being a part of this jaunt," I muttered.

I couldn't help but glance back one last time as Remy rushed past me up the stairs. Crash stood there, looking up at me. He mouthed something, two words.

"Be safe."

I gave him a smile, my heart twisting. "You too."

He grinned and winked and then Remy was back,

grabbing my hand. "I have a way out, you good with heights?"

"Maybe?" I yelped, but what choice did I have? I was already in trouble.

We climbed the stairs up to an opening in the roof, which let out just beneath the overhanging ceiling of the caves this place was built in. The space was not very large, and we had to crouch as we moved.

"Here!" Remy snapped a hand up, and something spilled from his fingertips. Magic, but it spiraled and danced like liquid. Deep red, it shot away from him and wove itself around my waist and squeezed tightly. "Hang on!"

"To what?" I put my hands against the tightly wound magic and then snatched them away. It had seared my skin.

Remy grinned and leapt off the building.

"Lawd in heaven," I whispered, and then the magic rope tightened. And yanked me straight off the edge of the roof.

Kinkly grabbed hold of my hair. "You're too big, I can't slow you!"

Remy hit the ground just ahead of us, landing on his feet, and spun quicker than a cat and caught me. I knocked the wind out of him, and our combined weight sent him tumbling backward until he was up against the building.

"Put me down!" I shoved at him until he did as I asked.

"They were not chasing you, *ma cherie*." He took my hand and kissed it again. "But they *are* looking for me. I bid you adieu. It was lovely meeting you."

He spun on his heel and walked crisply down the street. I stared after him. "What the hell was that all about?"

I found myself patting my body down, checking my handbag to see if he'd snatched something. But everything was there. Right down to my new bracelet.

The clatter of running guards reached my ears, and I stepped back as they ran after Remy. Huh. He hadn't been lying when he'd said they were after him. So, he and Karissa had a bad relationship?

I smiled. Sometimes you had to take pleasure in the small things in life, like other people disliking people you also disliked.

The guards disappeared, somewhere beyond the beaming lights.

"Kinkly? What was that all about?"

"No idea. Handsome devil though, isn't he?" She purred and then sighed, leaning into my shoulder. "Didn't help us much though, did he?"

She was right, he hadn't. He'd made my heart beat a little faster, though, and it had been nice to see Crash jealous. "There are probably easier ways to find the first witch."

"Okay, but how?"

I looked around the space, checking out the different shops and trying to decipher what each one said. "Seems to me everyone is being sneaky about this—the council sent Corb in to seduce the witch. The Dark Council sent Crash with the same objective. Why not just come right out and ask for her help? Maybe she doesn't want to be seduced."

I mean, look at what being seduced had done for me: a chipped-up heart and a healthy distrust for handsome men.

Kinkly tugged on my ear. "It could get us killed?"

"She already knows we are looking for her. She said so through Robert's mouth," I pointed out. "Acting like we aren't makes us look sneaky. We want her to trust us, right? So let's come right out and say that we're trying to help."

I wrinkled up my nose and headed for a shop with a spattering of herbs across its sign. Then I paused, because next to it was a shop that smelled like fresh leather. I touched the clothing that Gerry had made for me.

Gerry always had good info. People respected her and trusted her with what they knew. A tingle in my belly said it could be the same here. I followed the pull toward the shop. Something about it felt right, and I wasn't going to ignore the sensation.

A half step to the left, and I was inside the armorer's shop. It was not a woman at the desk as I'd half-hoped.

A grizzled old man with one good eye and an eye patch on the other barely glanced up at me from the counter. "You not from around here." He was stitching two pieces of leather together with a large golden needle. His accent was not French, but more Gallic. Scotsman maybe?

"I am not. How did you know?"

"That's Gerry's work you're wearing. And she only sells in Savannah." I watched as he pushed the needle carefully through the layers of leather, not at all put off by someone watching. "What do you need? Not repairs, she never has a problem with her wear and tear."

I took a deep breath, thinking that maybe this was a terrible ducking idea, and maybe I was damn brilliant. We'd find out soon enough. "I'm looking for the first witch, and I need the starting point for the first challenge." He froze as if I'd put on Medusa's head and turned him to stone. I cleared my throat and dove right into the deep end. "I figure lots of people go sneaking around, pretending like they aren't looking for her, and in doing so they probably get their asses handed to them. I'm trying to help her, but I must find her first. There are others looking for her, too, and they aren't in it for tea and cookies. They will kill her and steal her soul if they can."

His needle didn't move. His one good eye slowly lifted to my face, then darted to the windows. "You . . . want to find the first witch. Why would you ask me, of all people?"

I stared hard at him, taking in the way his good eye

dilated and his skin flushed. I smiled slowly, seeing it written all over his face. Brilliant, I was damn brilliant, and I took a final gamble that I'd chosen wisely by following my trust in Gerry and my gut. "Because you know where I need to go. Don't you?"

Kinkly squeaked and fluttered but otherwise remained still—or as still as she could remain.

The leather worker lowered his needle and the piece he was working on. He slid off a stool, and it was then that I saw he was not quite as tall as me. He walked to the door, slid the bolt, and then went to the windows and pulled the shutters down until we were in semi-darkness.

"Crima-nitley, woman, are you trying to get us both kilt?" Kilt? He had to mean killed.

"No, but you know what I see?" I put my elbow on his work bench and leaned on it. "Too many people thinking they're smarter than an old witch who probably has more smarts than all of the people looking for her combined. She wouldn't have lasted this long otherwise."

His one eye just kept on staring. "Crazy. I'll let you know where to start. I can give you that. And only because you are wearing Gerry's gear. She won't sell to people she doesn't believe in." A heavy sigh slid out of him. "Mercy on us both. Me for sending you into the depths, and you because you're going to need it.

Kinkly kept on fluttering, and then she whispered, "Crash is close. Karissa is close."

"Hurry," I said to the armorer. "Please."

A knock on the door that was almost the booming of a fist, and the armorer shook his head and pulled out a piece of leather. He took a marker and scribbled something on it. "Go there. That's the starting point. She likes games, this one. So be prepared to play for your life."

I took the leather scrap and tucked it into my bag. "Thank you. And don't tell them." I tipped my head at the door as it rattled again.

"Clansman, open the door," Crash yelled.

His one eye closed, and he shook his head again. "Don't thank me. Never thank me for sending you there."

"A way out." Kinkly fluttered and danced in the air between us.

"Out back." The armorer slumped back to his seat. "I won't tell them. I see you for who you are, Guardian. Be careful."

My feet didn't want to move, but Kinkly grabbed my lip and yanked. "We have to go now!"

The front door rattled harder, and the press of Crash's magic on it had my skin tingling. She was right, we had to go. Before I threw my panties and the leather scrap at Crash just for looking at me.

CHAPTER
SIXTEEN

Kinkly led the way through the shop and out the back door, which emptied into a tiny alley that I had to turn sideways in just to fit. Even then, my boobs brushed one side and my butt brushed the other.

"Hurry," Kinkly said. I didn't pick up what she was putting out, but I hurried, shuffling sideways, bumping along until I stepped out onto the main street. I slid to the side so anyone looking down that narrow alley—aka Crash—wouldn't see me.

"Where is Penny?" I searched the street but didn't see her or her cane. Or Gran. There was nothing for it—I had to take a guess. I turned left and hurried down the street, peeking into shops, startling all sorts of people. We had the starting point to find the first witch, and I wanted to get going. Because Robert . . . no, I wouldn't think about Robert turning into a damn vampire! I gritted my teeth and swallowed all the anger that spilled up. He could have just said what was happening. He could have told us right from the beginning, but no, he'd decided he had to go it alone.

"Are you losing your marbles?" Kinkly shot around my head. "What are you muttering about?"

"Stupid men," I spat out and then paused. The shop I'd just peeped into showcased a bunch of tiny sticks—wands, I was guessing—and Penny was in it. I opened the door and let myself in as a series of chimes rippled through the air. The shopkeeper was a perfectly round woman in a dark green dress, with a perfectly round face and spectacles to match.

The place smelled like freshly shaved pine and cedar, and some other woodsy scents I couldn't quite pinpoint. I took a deep breath, trying to slow my racing heart.

"Heather, this is my friend," Penny said. "Bree, this is Heather, one of the foremost wandmakers in Europe and even in—"

"We have to go." I took hold of Penny's hand and gave it what I hoped was a meaningful squeeze. "Right now."

Her dark eyes shot to mine. "That was quick."

"Where's Gran?"

Her eyes flicked to the back of the shop. Ah, Gran was snooping then. "She went home after we parted ways. Said she wasn't feeling well."

Heather made a cooing noise. "I 'ave some 'erbs to settle the belly should you think..."

Gran busted out of the back of the shop, muttering under her breath about messy cauldrons making poor wands. "Nothing but a ridiculous number of cobwebs. She's not keeping her stock clean!"

"Thank you, but no." Penny gave a tiny bow at the waist. "We should go check on her. If we need herbs, we will come back for some." She tightened her hold on me, and then we were out on the street, moving quickly out of Maison Magique.

"You found something?" Penny said under her breath.

Gran caught up to us and strode next to her. "Of course she did. Trouble finds her, doesn't it? And you can't get much more trouble than Fossette!" She swung a hand in the air to punctuate the name.

Penny let out a hiss. "There are people who can see you, Celia!"

"Bah, let them."

My eyebrows climbed. Gran was in a mood. "Yes, I found something."

Penny's hand tightened on my arm. "Not too fast then. We will draw attention."

Which is how we ended up stopping at two more stores, buying a bag of dried sage, two small notebooks, and a new pen. The pen had me excited, almost more than the information I'd scooped from the armorer.

"It's not really magical," Kinkly said.

I shrugged. I liked it, and Penny wanted us to look like we weren't in a hurry. "It's nice. It can be my souvenir from my trip to Paris." I smiled, twirled the pen, and tucked it into my bag.

We were almost at the doorway that led out of Maison Magique... almost.

The two guards who'd been chasing Remy stepped in front of us from the shadows near the door.

"Who are you, and what is your business here?" The guard on the left spoke English clearly, although with a good French accent.

Penny snorted. "My goddaughter and I have been doing some shopping. Is that an issue?"

"Perhaps." He pointed to our bags. "Empty them."

Penny tensed, her hand tightening on my arm. "Is this necessary?"

"Empty them or be thrown into the pit." He smirked, his stupid skinny mustache dancing over the top of his thin lip. "I only need a reason to make it happen, old one."

"Disrespectful!" Kinkly buzzed around our heads, flashing her colors. "Did Karissa put you up to this?"

The two guards shared a glance, and I knew, just like Kinkly did, that it was true.

"It's fine. Honest."

I shrugged, even though my heart was in my throat, and flipped the bag open. I reached in, feeling past the piece of leather, and started pulling things from the depths. If they wanted to know what was in my purse, I'd show them, and then some. "Here, put your hand out so I can make sure it doesn't get dirty."

Now, a smarter man might have refused my request, but the guard on the right stuck his hands out, cupped. I put my bottle of Advil into them first. Then the handful of loose tampons that always resided in the bottom of my bag, thin strings dangling. Next was a whiskey flask. I sloshed it, unscrewed it, and took a drag before I capped it and stuck it in his hands. Two more styles of feminine hygiene items later, one still wrapped, the other more of a light days product, and he was shoving the things back at me.

"Fine, that's fine. Go."

I took my stuff back and dumped it into my bag. The guard on the left wrinkled his nose.

Penny and I stepped past them, and then we were on the ramp going up and out of the Maison Magique.

"Clever girl," Penny whispered. "Men are so predictable."

"Just the idea of blood makes them uncomfortable unless it's on the edge of a sword," Gran said.

After that I focused on the ramp that I had, naïvely, thought would be easier than stairs.

Halfway up I leaned against the wall and struggled to breathe. "I have decided I hate ramps too."

Kinkly sighed. "I keep telling you, you need to get more fitness!"

"And I keep telling you, I like pastries!" I said. "They cancel each other out!"

We finally made it to the top and continued to Roderick's place. All the way back, I was fully expecting some sort of booby trap, or surprise pop-goes-the-fairy-queen, but it didn't happen. Neither Karissa nor Crash bothered to stop us.

We were the first ones back to the mansion, which meant we were the first ones to hear Feish's ranting.

"I am supposed to be here, you stuck-up glinking fish!"

I hurried my oh-so-tired legs up to the main dining hall, wondering just what the hell was a glinking fish, and then decided I was better off not knowing. Feish had squared off with the butler, Pierre. She was dripping wet and almost naked, fresh out of the Seine. The butler's face was splotchy red and . . . were those gills flapping off the side of his head? I hadn't pegged him as being one of Feish's kind.

"Get out," he snapped, and then burped up a bubble.

"*You* get out!" she threw back. I got myself between them and faced the butler.

"Feish is with us."

His eyes went wide, not with surprise, more like barely contained rage. A string of French flew from his mouth, and I was pretty sure there was some pointed cursing going on, but I ignored it and turned to Feish. "You made it!"

"How did you get here before me, and that one is a glinking fish, he should have his guts pulled out!"

I smiled up at her. "Tell me how you really feel."

"He should have his guts pulled out!" She stomped a foot and then shook her head, her side gills flexing and flapping with all the irritation.

I hugged her tight. "I'm glad you're here. What happened though? You look like you were in a fight."

"I need some clothes, I had to leave some behind when I got tangled in a net."

I ducked out of the room and saw one of the maids peering around a corner. "You got any dresses or something for my friend?"

The maid bobbed her head and took off.

A few minutes later, she brought a loose, colorful dress with a simple narrow belt to cinch it in. Feish discarded what remained of her tattered clothes, yanked the new dress on over her head and tied the sash. "I hate glinking fish," she muttered. "He was so rude!"

I smiled. "Yes, he is rather rude." He reminded me of Feish when I'd first met her, standoffish and pissed that I'd dared to step into Crash's domain.

"Where are the others?" she asked. "More came, yes?"

"They are out, looking for clues." I slid into a chair and pulled the leather piece out of my bag. One little piece of leather and two words. "Mortimer Abbey. That mean anything to either of you?" Kinkly and Feish shook their heads.

Penny got moving. "There is a library here. Let us look for information."

The library was lovely, stacked with books. Most of them were in French, but one of the maids helped us find some English books about Mortimer Abbey.

Flipping through the pages, I discovered it was the most haunted abbey in France (fantastic), with a history of deaths and legends connected to it. Other than that, nothing stood out. I mean, there are a hundred places in France that had death, ghosts and legends. There was nothing to suggest the first witch's first challenge would be there.

An hour and a half after our arrival, our friends started to filter back in.

We'd taken the books from the library to the dining hall, seeing as that was our makeshift war room.

Footsteps behind us turned all of us around. Sarge was the first one through the door. "Anything?"

"Yes, you know Mortimer Abbey?" I asked. Sarge paled, and I grimaced. Of course it was bad news.

"How did you get everyone here?" Feish muttered. "You shrink them down after all? And how so fast?"

Kinkly flew over to her shoulder. "We came through the demon fae pathway."

Clutching at her chest, Feish stumbled backward. "Ocean goddess, I am glad I swam! You are idiots! What did you let out by going through?"

"Nothing!" I shook my head. "We didn't let out anything at all."

But here's the thing, the second I said it, I could see the magic flowing off Remy, and I heard Crash saying something about Remy taking me down a dark path. "Maybe one person?"

Feish slapped her hands to her head. "One! You should have said none!"

"I didn't do it!" A gust of air slid out of me. "Crash is the one who opened the way!"

Feish's mouth hung open, giving credence to her name. "He did? What kind of a fool is he now?"

"Well, Karissa's with him," Kinkly said. "So, a pretty big stupid fool."

Feish let out a yell, and Kinkly started zipping around the room as our other friends showed up, and that is what the cranky butler, Pierre, came in on.

Complete and total pandemonium.

"ENOUGH!" He roared the word, but there was a definite 'wetness' to it. Feish glared at him, and he glared at her.

In other words, love was in the air.

He tugged his shirt and smoothed it at the front. "Dinner is served."

I held up a hand. "Not right now. Give us an hour."

His eyes swung to me. "I will not."

Feish stomped up to him, and he smartly backed away. "You will mind your manners, Glinker!"

Spluttering and cursing once more, he left, and I

held up both hands. "Mortimer Abbey. Sarge, you said you know about it. Why? How?"

Sarge settled into a chair across from me. "Because it's where the werewolf line began. Every werewolf knows Mortimer Abbey is the beginning. But it's also incredibly dangerous."

I took a breath. "Well, it's where the first witch is, or at least it's where we need to start our search for her. So, tell me about it."

Sarge nodded and spread his hands on the table. "There are over two hundred years of history, but I'll try to keep to the highlights."

Suzy slid into a seat, and Eric and the others did the same. "Two hundred years? I thought werewolves have been around longer than that?"

"They have been," Sarge said. "Just let me explain."

I nodded and he dove into the story. One that I had not seen coming. Not by a long shot.

CHAPTER
SEVENTEEN

"Mortimer Abbey is home to the mother wolf. *Garrache*," Sarge said softly. "She is both feared and revered. Kind of like your first witch." He nodded at Penny, who nodded back. "The grounds of the abbey are deeply haunted, bathed in blood and spells, and at the center of it is the *garrache*. She is the one who . . . if a secret about the first witch is hidden at the abbey, or the path leading to her runs through it, people probably have to go through our mother wolf first." He looked at his hands. "Just the idea of being in her presence makes my knees weak."

"Highlight reel only," Kinkly reminded him.

"Right, right. Basically, she was the last surviving wolf from the first pack of werewolves to ever be created. Depending on who you ask, she could be upward of two thousand years old. Some say she was around at the birth of Jesus." He shrugged. "She's not just any shifter. She can call other wolves to her, and even turn wolves against their friends. And she can call in bad weather. Some say she can even control the ghosts that reside there with her."

I frowned and tapped my fingers on the table. "Is she a ghost?"

"No, she is very real. But she can be there in front of you one moment and gone the next. I don't know if it's just speed or something else . . . like a spell." Sarge looked at Penny who shook her head. "But if that's where you need to go, I'm not sure I should go with you. She could turn me against you, make me hurt you. Werewolves have a strange sense of honor, and she would be the same. She will want to prove she is smart, and not just a thug."

"But you know the most about her," I pointed out. "And I trust you, Sarge. I know you are strong enough."

He closed his eyes. "I know you do. That's what scares me. What if she has Corb?"

If this was the first step toward finding the first witch, that seemed like a possibility. "Even more reason for you to be there. Penny, what should we expect? What kind of challenges could we face? Like a riddle or something?"

She shook her head slowly. "No, if she is still the Fossette that the stories speak of, she will make a game of it. The three challenges will be a range of things if I were to guess—"

A knock on the door of the dining room paused her. We all turned, the door was pushed slowly open, and...

My jaw dropped. "Remy? What in gawd's name are you doing here? How did you find us?"

He gave a slow smile, his cheeks dimpling. "You didn't exactly hide your steps."

Sarge cleared his throat, and then a low rumble slid from him. "Who the hell are you?"

Remy held his hands up, palms facing us. "I think you could use some help with what it is you wish to accomplish, yes?"

I didn't dare glance at Penny, but Gran ghosted up in front of me. "I have a strange feeling about this one, Bree. Be careful. I doubt it's a coincidence that he showed up now, right before you need to step into a deadly situation."

I winked at her, but she was between me and Remy, so he smiled back. As if I'd winked at him.

Poop. "We might need help, but we might not," I said. "You tell us what you know about the first witch, and then we'll decide whether you're useful to us . . . or if we should tie you up and hand you over to Karissa."

His smile slid a little. "You wound me, *ma cherie*."

It took effort not to roll my eyes. "Yeah, well you left me behind to face the guards without you, so you aren't exactly Prince Charming, now are you? Consider this tit for tat. Only if I leave you hanging, you'll face a werewolf, not a mustache-twirling joke of a guard." I smiled even though my words were hard.

Sarge laughed softly. "Oh, I do love it when you pull out the badass."

Remy's smile didn't slide. Nope, it widened. "Oh, I like this much better. I will tell you about the first witch." He drew a breath and tucked his hands behind his back as he slowly paced the room. "There is power in threes, you know this, yes?"

I vaguely recalled my gran saying something about threes, but I wasn't sure, so I just nodded like I knew what the heck he was talking about.

Gran sniffed. "Everyone knows about threes."

Sure. Sure.

Remy kept on going, not hearing Gran. "The first witch knows she is the key to more than one spell. Her blood. Her bones. Her soul. All of these things are valuable. She also has her own spells to fill, her own power to grow, and she knows that those who are brave enough to seek her out are powerful. So she sets traps. That way she gets what she needs and ensures any who reach her are actually worthy of a favor."

"Like a Venus flytrap," Eric said. "She offers something, then takes those that come to feed. As it were."

Remy pointed a finger at him. "Yes, my tall, sometimes hairy friend. That is exactly what she is. She might even present herself as weak at times, but that is not true." He made his way to sit beside me, and the rest of his speech was directed at me. "As you pass each challenge, you will gain a clue to take you to the next. Until you face Fossette herself. And that is when the trap will truly close. She is no easy-going *grandmère* who will bake you a batch of croissants and pat your cheeks. She tried to kill her own children, and only by a fluke did any escape." Remy's green eyes were serious as he regarded me. "Why do you seek out the first witch? What power are you wanting?"

"None," I said. "She has one of my friends who was dumb enough to come looking for her by himself." Not strictly true, but I didn't yet trust him enough to tell him the full story.

He leaned back. "Hmm. Well, there are a few other witch hunters in town. You should watch out for them."

"Like you?" Eammon had been quiet up until that moment. So much so that I'd almost forgotten he was there. "You have the smell of a hunter about you, Frenchie."

Remy turned to Eammon. "Everything in the shadow world is a hunter, leprechaun. Even you."

Eammon glared at Remy. "Cocky bugger. Just like Louis."

"He's nothing like Louis," I said. "I could snap Louis in half like a twig. And Louis would never have apologized."

Remy leaned back in his chair and spread his hands

to the sides. "I did not mean to start a disagreement. If you can pass each of the first witch's challenges, you might make it all the way to her. But I would not want to face her alone. She is . . . crazy. That is the only word you can say. She has lived alone, with no company other than her cats for hundreds of years."

Was it weird that it sounded to me like she had it right?

"Cats?" Feish burbled. "How can she have so many cats and no bitches to help her watch them?"

Everyone looked at Feish and she looked back. "What?"

I sighed. "Is that everything?"

He shrugged. "That is what I would say is the bare minimum. If you have specific questions, I will do my best to answer them. I am no hunter of the first witch, but her legend is very much alive in France."

That was more than I would have gotten from Crash. Or Robert, for that matter. Damn it, I did not need to be checking out another man, no matter how smoking hot he was. What was wrong with me? My hormones were out of control. I drew a breath and pushed all thoughts of hot Remy from my head—difficult with him sitting right beside me. "Thank you."

"*Mais oui.*" He smiled like he knew what I was thinking about him. Double damn it.

Penny began to pace the room, taking up the space that Remy had occupied, tapping her cane as she went.

"I believe you are right, Bree. I think you should take Sarge. And one other. Each challenge will present itself, and then we can draw from the team here for further missions. If Robert was with us, I'd say take him and Sarge."

"But he's not," I said. "So, who would be best to deal with a grumpy werewolf granny?"

Sarge all but choked where he stood against the wall. "Please don't call her that if you see her in person. Please. Promise me."

Suzy and Feish had their heads together, obviously discussing what they could bring to the table for this challenge, and Kinkly danced around the room, flitting from shoulder to shoulder. "I will come. You know that. I can help spot things you're too low to the ground to see."

"Thanks," I said. "We need another larger body too. In case I need someone to carry me and Sarge out."

Eammon smacked his hands on the table. "Tell me you aren't seriously discussing all this in front of . . . in front of *him*!"

I looked from Eammon to Remy, knowing exactly what to say to settle things. "He doesn't like Crash or Karissa, and he made it look like he was romancing me to piss him off."

Eammon did a double take. "Well . . . that's different then. Welcome to the crew, boy."

Remy threw his head back and laughed. "Gods. You

mean to tell me you immediately trust me just because I don't get on with Crash? Or Karissa?"

"Exactly. Good taste if you don't get along with that one." Eammon nodded.

I looked at Remy. "I do have one question."

His eyes swept to my face. "Of course."

Nothing like diving into the deep end. My suspicions had to be allayed if he was going to work with us. "Are you a demon fae?"

Remy's eyes widened. "No. Why would you ask that?"

I was not about to tell him that we'd come through the demon fae pathways. I stared hard at his face, seeing the bit of glamour there still, hiding the scars. I could call him out, but I wanted him to be honest. Okay, I wanted to know if he was lying. I looked at Sarge. "Can you smell a lie on him?" Was that a thing? No idea. But Sarge followed up and took a good long sniff around Remy.

"Seems okay."

Remy's eyebrows rose. "You . . . can smell a lie?"

"Only the best werewolves can," I said. Sarge faced me, his back to Remy as he mouthed one word.

"Liar."

Eammon huffed. "So, now that that is settled, why don't you go with Bree and Sarge to Mortimer Abbey?"

. . .

That was exactly what happened. Remy happily agreed to go to the abbey with Sarge and me, and Kinkly came along for scouting duty. The sun was just going down, and the pond we stood next to danced as the fish inside jumped for their evening supper. Ahead of us was the main house of the abbey. Not as large as the mansion we were staying in, but it was still an easy three stories. Behind it, I could see bits and pieces of rubble from another, no longer standing structure.

More than that, I could see a faint line of blue and white on the ground. Like shimmering paint. Who would paint the grass though?

"That's where the *garrache* will be." Sarge took a deep breath, and I realized he was scenting the air. "Near the ruins."

"Maybe we can just talk to her?" I offered. "Ask nicely?"

Both men looked at me like I'd lost my ducking mind. But I had to try for the simple route. I was tired, my body hurt all over, and I was struggling to focus on the task at hand with all the other big issues pushing in on me. Robert turning into a vampire. Corb missing and maybe dead. Crash's apparent reunion with Karissa. "I need to swear off men," I muttered.

Kinkly laughed. "You just figuring that out now?"

"Late bloomer." I started toward the main house.

"They won't let you in," Remy said. "This is a tourist destination."

I waved a hand at him. "So, I'll go around. The *garrache* is the one we want."

"No, no we don't want her." Sarge grabbed at my arm, but I stepped out of reach. "Bree. Trust me, we don't *want* to find her. We want to find the next clue and be gone as quickly as possible."

I kept on walking. "Quickest way to get this job done is to go straight through the mess. Not around, not over, not under. Straight through."

The smell of greenery and blooming flowers filled the air, and the weight of a late summer's evening pressed in around us. But that wasn't what I was paying attention to. Nope, I was headed straight for what I could see of the ruins of the old abbey. The gray stone was speckled with black in places, and as it came into view, I sucked in a breath.

There were ghosts everywhere, pressed up against the stone almost as if it were magnetic. It looked like a damn rave. I put my arm out, stopping Sarge. "Nope."

"See, I told you—"

I whacked him in the belly with my arm. "Just let me look."

I wasn't sure what I was looking for, actually, and there were so many ghosts blocking my view, I couldn't see anything beyond them. Remy stepped up beside me. "What is it?"

"Ghosts. Lots of ghosts. The space is thick like molasses with them." I stood on my tiptoes as if an extra inch was going to help me out. "Kinkly, can you head up there and see if you can see anything?"

"You got it." She shot off my shoulder in a burst of sparkles with only a mild hitch to her flight.

That blue on the ground? Flared the second Kinkly flew over it, then turned bright red and pulsing. I didn't need anyone to tell me we'd just tripped the alarm.

Next to me, Sarge was shaking. "Damn it. This is bad, Bree. She knows I'm here. I can feel her presence."

"What can we do to help?" I reached for him, and he took my hand, squeezing tightly.

"I don't know. I . . ." He pulled his hand free and took a step back, then another and another. "I can't stay here, Bree. I . . ."

He spun and took off, back the way we'd come.

I would never have called Sarge a coward, but this wasn't the first time he'd left me in a lurch. He was my friend, but there was no denying he was a bit more like the cowardly lion than a fearsome werewolf.

"Sarge!" I called after him, but he kept on jogging. And I didn't have the energy to go after him. This was what I'd been afraid of—being left to my own. Or going in with just Remy, who I still wasn't 100% sure of. I touched my head, wondering how I'd gotten into this mess. No, no I wasn't going to catastrophize. Maybe this would be okay. Maybe the *garrache* was a really lovely woman who would be happy to help us find the first witch.

Yes, yes, I was the queen of lying to myself.

"That is unnerving," Remy drawled and put his hands on his hips. "You sure you want to go in?"

I nodded. "I can't let Crash get to the first witch before I do."

"You assume she won't wrap up the blacksmith and eat him," Remy said.

"Can't have that either," I muttered.

"Why not?"

"Because." That was the only answer I was willing to give my new . . . friend? Was he a friend? I looked at him and squinted. "You got any amazing talents I should know about?"

Remy shrugged. "Good looks and charm."

"Neither of which are very effective in a fight."

Kinkly shot back to us. "There is nobody in the ruins. Just whatever ghosts you see."

"A trap then." I nodded. I mean, I'd figured it would be a trap. It would have been too easy to walk in and dig around for the next clue. "Is it common knowledge that the first witch has three challenges?" I made myself get moving.

"I don't know if it's common." Remy kept pace with me. "But I am sure that anyone who dug around could find it out. Especially seeing as she supposedly offers a favor or boon to the one who makes it all the way through."

Kinkly sat on my shoulder. "You said there were ghosts?"

I nodded. "I'm going to try to put them to rest."

We reached the outer edge of the ruins, but not one of the ghosts looked at me. That was weird. Ghosts were typically drawn to me, and they liked to get chatty when they realized I could see them.

"Hey, you all okay?" I asked.

Not one head turned my way. I reached into the milling crowd and grabbed the ghost closest to me. Dragged him out.

He stumbled and struggled to stand. "Where am I?"

I grimaced. "You don't know?"

He shook his head. "Last thing I remember, I was looking for the first witch. I came to Mortimer Abbey. My wife is sick, I need a spell to heal her. . ." His eyes widened. "The wolf woman! She bit my head off!"

He wobbled, and his head slid sideways, then bounced to the ground.

I swallowed hard and let him go. "Be at peace."

That connection I had to the dead flowed through me and he sighed, his ghost falling to pieces in front of me, spreading out and dispersing as the last of the sun's rays slid through him.

Remy put a gentle hand on my arm. "Bree? What did you learn?"

"Well, she likes to bite heads off. And the ghosts here are probably all the people who've come searching for the first witch." I stared at the numbers and suddenly wondered if Corb's ghost would be among them. My guts lurched. No, I would not think like that.

"So now what?" Kinkly said.

It was a valid question. One that I didn't really have an answer to.

Lucky—or unlucky—for me, we didn't have to go looking for the *garrache*.

Because she found us first.

CHAPTER
EIGHTEEN

The low grumble of a wolf was what reached me first. Only I didn't know it was a wolf rumble because it was so deep it vibrated through my bones, like the feeling of an oncoming train. Worse, I couldn't pinpoint it or where it was coming from.

The ghosts suddenly went still, frozen in their respective places, a low moan rolling through them, which added to the chorus of deep growls.

"Well, that can't be good," I whispered. I could have pulled out my knife, but I kept myself still. Maybe I could talk my way out of this?

"*Garrache*, we aren't here to hurt anyone. But others are coming for the first witch, and they *will* try to hurt her." I tried not to think about Corb, and how the *garrache* might have pulled his head off too.

The rumble began to huff, and it took me a moment to get that she was laughing at me.

"So much for that." I took a step toward the ruins, then another and another. "Kinkly, stay high and look for clues, okay?"

"Okay!" She was gone in a flash. The evening sky was dark blue, and while the sun had set, we weren't into the full night yet.

Remy hadn't moved. "Can I suggest something?"

"Sure." I kept scanning the area as the rumbling grew louder.

"The house might give us a chance," he said. "The *garrache* is rather... large in her wolf form."

I didn't have time to question how he knew that.

Because right then I saw her. She stepped out of the shadows on the far side of the ruins. The size of a damn horse, she had a pure silver coat that glimmered and caught the fading light. "Wow, she's beautiful," I whispered.

She bared her very silvery, rather sharp-looking teeth, and then I was running for my ducking life.

The sound of her big, padded feet behind us was all it took to drive me, and at some point I passed Remy, hit the front door of the main house, and slid through it. "Shut it, shut it, shut it!"

Remy didn't hesitate, and we got the door shut just as she slammed into it.

"Your friend, the fairy?" he breathed out.

"She'll stay out of range." I leaned on the door as

the *garrache* threw her body at it, the wooden door creaking under the strain. "So much for making nice."

Remy tugged on my arm. "Come, maybe we can find a way through the house and sneak out the back?"

It wasn't the worst plan.

Might have been better if I didn't feel something slide over my entire body. The bracelet on my wrist cooled, and then both it and my pendant warmed against my flesh.

"A spell!" I hopped and danced, smacking at my chest. Remy groaned and went to his knees.

"Damn." He shook his head and then went down on all fours, fell to his belly, and that was it. He was out cold.

"Seriously?" I shook off the spell—the bracelet and pendant had been enough to protect me, apparently—and took a breath. The banging on the door ceased.

My gut instinct was that the *garrache* being quiet wasn't necessarily a good thing. I grabbed Remy's hands and dragged him across the tile floor and into an alcove with a small fountain bubbling above us.

Ducking down, I slowed my breathing as the locking mechanism clicked and the door slowly swung inward.

The woman who walked in had to be seven feet tall if she was an inch. She was thick with muscle from head to foot, and her floor-length silvery hair left no question as to who I was dealing with. She wore a long white robe that was split up the sides to show off her legs. Actually, she'd probably selected it because it made walking easier. With high cheekbones and full lips, her face was intriguing.

Brilliant blue eyes swept the room, and I held perfectly still. Not like Remy was moving.

"Where are you, little pigs?" she whispered, and I frowned. Had she called us pigs?

Shit.

This wasn't going to be a challenge. If I didn't do something quick, it was going to be a damn slaughter that left us both floating around the ruins with our heads bitten off.

What had Sarge said? Werewolves have a weird sense of honor, and while it can come and go, they love to prove themselves smarter than someone else. Because they are always thought of as thugs.

An idea began to form, one that might give us a chance. It would probably just piss her right off, but it was worth a try. We were about to be eaten.

I stood with my hands up. "We can't outsmart you. I'm sorry we even tried."

She smiled, showing off what seemed like an excess of teeth. "English? Interesting."

I didn't move. "We were told there was a challenge. That we would have to outsmart you. But I can see that is not going to work."

Her eyebrows went up. "You think you can charm me?"

I took a guess. "The last one who got past you

worked his charm on you, didn't he? The ducker did the same to me. A siren, right?" Guessing, I was guessing here that Corb had gotten by her.

A narrowing of eyes and a flaring of her nostrils was the only indication that I'd hit the mark. I went on. "He charmed me, told me I was his mate, and then left me when I needed him the most. Rather cowardly if you ask me."

Remy's hand circled slowly around my ankle. Gently squeezing. He was awake at least. Maybe he could spring up and help.

Despite the discussion I was having, I had no false ideas about the danger we were in.

"The green-eyed one," the *garrache* said. "The siren."

Relief radiating through me, I nodded. "Yup, that's Corb."

She let out a growl.

"Not the first time he's broken the heart of a werewolf either." I frowned, thinking about Sarge.

She all but vibrated with anger. "He made a *fool* of me."

"No, he made a fool of himself." I pointed at her. "Do you really think he's going to flirt his way to Fossette?"

Her eyes narrowed, and she bared her teeth. "You are here for Fossette, but you have a friend who went ahead of you. The siren."

"Well, yes, it's complicated." I grimaced. "We aren't friends really, not like before."

Her head tipped to the side in a gesture I'd seen Sarge make a hundred times.

"With men, it mostly is complicated. What about that one at your feet? He is pretty." She waved a hand at Remy.

I put my hands on my hips and let out sigh. "I don't know about him yet. I think he is a trickster. He could help, he might hurt, but he'll smile the whole time, and that will make it difficult. Right now, I can use all the help I can get, so he's with me. Sort of."

The *garrache* gave a slow nod. "He does have some Loki energy about him. He will be fun, but he will be dangerous to you and your softness. Your heart could break against his energy if you are not wary. Assuming you had a chance to get out of here alive. Which you do not."

I barked a laugh. "I am not giving my heart out to anyone anymore, thank you very much."

Her lips twitched. "Why not?"

"Because it's a terrible ducking idea to give away your heart." Alan, Crash, and even Corb had hurt me in different ways. "When you don't know how to pick a good man."

"Tell me your story. I am bored here, often alone, and you are strangely entertaining." She paused. "And then I will make your death quick as a boon for your entertainment."

I pursed my lips as I pretended to mull this over. She was still going to try and kill me, which wasn't great, but I'd be buying myself time. "Do you mind if I walk while I tell you?"

She waved a big hand at me. "Go ahead. You cannot escape me."

I pulled my left ankle out of Remy's grip and strode across the small space. "Well, the truth is this. The council of Savannah sent me here to find the first witch before the members of the Dark Council can get to her. They, of course, want to steal her soul and create an army of vampires. Now... my kind of ex-boyfriend..." I wasn't even sure Crash fit that description, but it made for a better story.

"You mean the siren."

I shook my head and my hands at the same time. "No, he was... he just kissed me and told me he loved me. We were never really together," I said and noticed her eyes sweep over me. Judging me. "No, my ex is the blacksmith, you know of him?"

Her eyebrows went up higher and her mouth bobbled open. "Karissa's ex-husband?"

Jaysus. That's how he was known here too? Of course it was. "Yeah, so he turned out to be working for the Dark Council, and he's here looking—"

"Everyone knows he works for the Dark Council." She waved a hand, cutting me off. "I am more interested in what he saw in you. Because there has been no one for him since he and Karissa parted ways. No one.

And you, a little human in her middle age with a soft middle has caught his eye? How is that so?"

I glared at her. "Maybe it's because I don't give a duck what anyone else thinks anymore? Maybe because I'm tired of people thinking I'm less than because of my age, the size of my ass, or the simple fact that I'm a woman?"

I was in her face without realizing I'd moved, my finger jammed into her chest. I took a step back as her eyes glittered down at me. "Sorry, that's a sore point."

Her slow smile was oddly genuine. "I am only curious because he swore off all women. You have a pull on him. On men, it seems, as if you were siren. Only you do not smell like a siren."

I blew a raspberry, at myself more than her. "Anyway. He's here with Karissa, and there is another team coming through with No-face Bruce. If he hasn't shown up, then he will be here soon."

"So many." She shook her head. "And all so the army of darkness might rise again. Terrible."

I didn't disagree. "I am trying to protect Fossette. The council asked me to bring her back to Savannah."

"You believe them?" She laughed. "That *is* foolish of you."

"I don't believe them," I said, and realized that was true. They'd always kept things from me before. Why would this time be different? "But Fossette's soul is one of the ingredients to that damn spell. Teams upon teams are coming for her. Someone will take her. What happens if it's someone from the Dark Council who gets to her?"

The *garrache* sighed, and it sounded like a distant howl. "Then we are all doomed."

Indeed, we were doomed if that was the case.

"I want to help, but I can't help keep her safe if I can't find her."

She clasped her hands in front of her. "Did you ever consider that if you find her, then someone else might find *you*? Like your blacksmith. Or the siren. If they sent you, then they believe there is a chance you will find her. You yourself could lead danger to Fossette."

I hadn't considered that.

I grimaced and threw my hands in the air. "What then? What do I do? Just let her be taken by ducking No-face Bruce?"

Her eyes swept over me. "You are not lying? I find this strange."

"Why would I lie?"

"Because everyone lies," she said. "Everyone."

That was a rather bleak way of looking at the world, but I couldn't really refute the point. The people I loved had lied to me in an attempt to protect me. The men I'd loved had lied so they could use me. "I . . ." I didn't know what to say.

Her breath was warm against my cheek. "You are like me."

I blinked and found myself looking straight into her eyes. Her breath smelled like winter pines and the earth. Not bad, just . . . earthy. Woodsy. "I am no werewolf."

Her smile widened. "No, not like that, perhaps—"

There was a sound outside, so slight it was barely perceptible. The scratch of something on the building wall maybe? The pressure of a footstep on the gravel? I found myself crouching over Remy's body as I pulled my black blade.

The air changed, and the *garrache* swung away from me to face the main doors of the mansion. "I do believe I have more visitors."

CHAPTER
NINETEEN

More visitors to the *garrache* could only mean one thing to my mind. "It's either No-face Bruce or Crash," I said quietly.

Kinkly shot in through the window. "Look out, it's Bruce!"

Only it wasn't much of a warning, because no sooner had she finished than he busted in through the main door with a large shotgun in his hands. His face danced and fuzzed. He might have been smiling; he might have been frowning. "Silver shot, little bitch."

The *garrache* tipped her head to the side as he lifted the gun.

The moment slowed. I could see she had no idea what he had . . . or what he intended to do to her. Or maybe she just didn't think it was possible a gun could kill her? I didn't know. What I did know was that we needed her alive.

I leapt up and slammed my body into hers as the gun went off. The boom rattled the small space, and something sliced across my back, pulling a scream from me as we fell to the floor.

My back was on fire as I pushed up to face No-face Bruce. "You're quite the hunter, aren't you? With your great big shotgun to make up for your very tiny pistol. I guess that's the only way you're ever going to know what it feels like to hold a great . . . big . . ."

"Le zob!" The *garrache* rolled to her feet, snarling.

"Yeah, what she said!"

No-face Bruce chambered another round. "I'll kill you both."

"Run," I said to the *garrache*. "I'll deal with him."

"I will not run!" She snarled, and I didn't have to look to know she'd shifted back into her wolf form.

"If I can't kill him, you can!" I snapped. "But you are the guardian of Fossette. Which means you need to be alive!"

Bruce swung the gun toward me, and I slashed at it with my knife. Not really knowing what to expect.

The knife cut through the barrel like it was soft dough. Grabbing the tip, I yanked it downward (out of the gutter with you), bending it so it was a twisted-up pretzel somewhat pointed back at my friend Bruce.

"Shoot with that, le zob!" I stumbled backward, doing my best to ignore the still-raging fire along my back. I was going to have scars from his damn buckshot.

I glanced down, but Remy was not at my feet any longer. When I looked back up, he was behind Bruce. He gave me a slow smile and a wink.

"Not nice to pick on women," he said, and Bruce whipped around.

Remy slammed a fist into the side of his head, and then the two men started trading blows, throwing each other into tables, against the wall, and then out the side window as if we were in some sort of action movie.

I stayed put. Because I had no doubt that Bruce would not have come alone.

Unfortunately, I was right.

A flurry of wings filled the air, and I found myself staring at a dozen solid black beasties about the same size as a fairy, but from top to bottom none of them sported a single dot of color, not even in their eyes, their teeth, or the insides of their mouths. "Kinkly, what are they?"

Kinkly gasped. "Don't let them bite you, they are venomous!"

I dodged the first couple, slashed and cut one in half, then another. They were quick little duckers. "What are they?" I yelped as I back-handed one and sent it flying into the wall with a thump.

"Demon fae, they must have slid out of the pathway!" she cried and hid in my hair. "Bree, don't let them bite you!"

"Trying," I grunted as I took out three more,

slashing and stabbing. But they were fast, and despite my best efforts I knew that I was going to get bit at some point. Gritting my mouth shut, I stomped one that got close to my foot, grabbed another with my free hand and squeezed until I felt something pop.

"Listen here, little assholes!" I barked and the remaining demon fae lined up to look at me. There were six left out of the dozen I'd started with. "I suggest you take your wounded and get out of here before I finish you all off. Understood?" I felt my power with the dead slide into my words. I threw the body from my hands at the flying formation of solid black demon fae. They caught their partner, only to let the body fall to the ground.

"You have no say over us!" one of them cried out.

Anger and frustration rolled through me, exacerbated by all the irritation of the day and the fact that my back was literally on fire from the buckshot. A different power rumbled deep in my belly. "GO!" I roared the word, and they screamed and scattered. I made my way to the window. The two men were not there. I looked up as the door opened and Remy limped in. "He's gone for the moment."

"What is he? Why can't I see his face?"

"He's a skinwalker. The worst kind of shifter." He held his hand around his middle. "Did you get the next clue?" His eyes widened, and he took a half step back. I turned to see the *garrache* slink back into the room, circling around me in her wolf form.

"You tried to save me, why?" she growled.

"Because." I threw up my hands and instantly regretted it for the pull on my back.

"That is not an answer."

I sighed. "I'm tired, *Garrache*. Tired of people trying to kill each other. I'm tired of people thinking the worst of me. Of you. Of Fossette. For reasons they've been told, not because of anything they've learned first-hand." I tipped my head back and looked at the ceiling. "You are trying to protect Fossette. So am I. That is reason enough to keep you safe. Or try to. You didn't even know what that shotgun could have done to you. Why? Don't you know about guns?"

"Nothing," she said with a sniff. "Guns are nothing to me."

I shook my head. "It would have killed you. You have no idea what the world is like now. That gun would have *killed* you and left the first step to Fossette open wide."

She gave a low whine and licked her chops. "You cannot be correct."

I touched a hand to my face. "Kinkly. Go get Sarge. He needs to be here."

"The wolf you were with?" The *garrache* wrinkled her nose. "He ran when he felt my power."

"Smart man," Remy muttered.

Her eyes shot to him. "Says the trickster."

My muscles were shaking, and I let myself sit down. "Bruce will be back. With another gun. With more of those demon fairies. That's not good, *Garrache*. If we weren't here, they would have killed you. Not just taken the information and moved on."

She huffed and growled but didn't argue.

A few minutes later, Sarge stepped through the door, just after Kinkly swept in. He saw the *garrache* and went to his knees, bowing his head. "Goddess."

Kinkly flew to my shoulder and hunkered down.

The *garrache* strolled over to him, sniffing him all over, ruffling his hair with her snout. "Boy. Will silver shot kill me?"

He didn't lift his head. "The humans have discovered it is a way to disable us, long enough to remove our heads. About eighty years ago."

She stepped back and sat down, her body slowly morphing back into her Amazonian woman form. "Then I will have need of guidance. Very few have come this way for Fossette in the last few years. In a hundred years. But now they come nearly daily." Her sigh was fatigued. "With new weapons. New ways to hurt."

I looked at Sarge. "Maybe you could stay with her. Help her."

His eyes were wide. "You would leave me with the *garrache*?"

"Maybe it would be enough to show her that we are on her side. It wouldn't be forever, Sarge," I pointed out. The *garrache* looked at me.

"And you would have the next step given to you?"

It should have been an easy question, yet it wasn't. Because what if I led the people to Fossette? I rubbed a hand over my face. "Maybe. I don't know."

Both men choked as if I'd elbowed them in the guts. Kinkly came out from under my hair. "To find Corb, we have to keep going. That's also the only way we're going to find Robert or help keep Fossette safe. You know it, Bree."

I looked out the window. "No-face Bruce is going to keep trying too. The *garrache* is right. He won't just come back here. He'll follow me. I could lead him right to her."

"Not if you are clever," Sarge said. "And you, my friend, are clever. You are smarter than anyone has given you credit for." His big hand was warm on my shoulder, but I flinched. He glanced at my back and let out a low growl. "Bruce?"

"She saved me," the *garrache* said quietly. "She threw her body at mine and took the shot meant to steal my life."

Sarge nodded. "That is our Bree."

I closed my eyes, feeling strangely emotional. "Is she safer if we leave her alone, or is she safer if we try to find her? I don't know." Corb was an issue too, of course. Despite his stupidity, I didn't want him to die. Any more than I'd wanted Alan to die. No, check that, I'd wished for his death more than once.

Robert though . . . I had to go on for him.

"You must go on," the *garrache* said. "I will send

word to Fossette that you are . . . less dangerous than the others. And that you saved me. She will see it as a play for sympathy, but she was not here. She does not know you. Yet."

I turned to look at the *garrache*. "Take care of Sarge. He's my brother from another mother."

Sarge laughed, but the *garrache* dipped her head at me. "I will protect him as if he were my own pup."

That sobered him up. "Bree."

I threw my arms around him, and he carefully hugged me back. "Be safe. And help *her* be safe."

He kissed me on the forehead. "Bree, if anyone can do this impossible thing, it is you. Don't forget that. Don't doubt yourself."

I took a step back, and the *garrache* took her place in front of me. "I will give you the gift of the wolf, for while you seek Fossette you will need all the help you can get."

"Wait—" Sarge said.

But the *garrache* pushed him back and touched her fingernail to my chest, right at the hollow of my throat. And pressed. Hard and deep. My eyes watered, but I was proud of myself for not flinching. Okay, so I flinched a little. She released me, and I gave a slight shake of my head. Because, despite the sensation of pressure, there was no indication anything had happened to me. "I got nothing."

No, that wasn't quite true, I saw something in my mind: a cave of some sort. Deep underground, with lights flickering here and there. I could feel a pull in the direction of the cave, and instinctively I knew it was the next place we had to go. Small people were rushing about near the cave, and it took me the space of a second to realize they were leprechauns like Eammon. More helpful yet, there was an extremely handy sign sitting out front of the cave, telling me what I was seeing. Thank Jaysus for that. I blinked, and the vision was gone.

"The wolf will come to you as she sees fit. You are no werewolf, Bree, but this power is a boon from me to you. In your mind, I have also given you the location of the second trial. Fossette never gave any of us her actual location. We only know the next step to her."

Remy put his hand on my arm and tugged me backward. "If you know, then we should go. Because the skinwalker will be back. Sarge—" He looked at my friend. "I broke ribs on his left side. They won't have healed yet."

Sarge grinned. "I'll ducking re-break them if they are." The men shook hands quickly, firmly. Sarge held on a little tighter. "Take care of her."

Remy didn't even look at me. He gave a bow over their joined hands. "On my word, I will do all I can to protect her. As long as she lets me."

I grinned, and Sarge laughed. "Yeah, he's getting it faster than Crash ever did."

My grin slid. "Sarge, Crash will be coming here with Karissa. Be careful."

He looked at me. "The *garrache* is right... they will look for you now. They will follow Bruce, and Bruce will follow you. Knowing that you've got the next location. Go find Corb and save that witch, Bree. But, above all else, try to stay alive."

I managed to speak past the sudden rolling of my guts. "I can do two out of three, for sure." Then I really thought about what I'd said: only two out of three people were going to survive. What the hell had possessed me to say that?

Kinkly tapped on my ear. "We should go back to the house to start."

She was right.

Remy and I slipped out of the manor and across the open lawn. Ghosts flitted here and there, all around. "Here I'd thought they'd be the biggest problem we'd face," I said.

"What?" Kinkly asked.

"The ghosts. There are hundreds of them, and I thought..."

"It's probably your connection to the dead," Kinkly said. "Or something like that."

I felt Remy's eyes on me, but I didn't look at him as I spoke. "You're okay, Remy? You didn't get hurt?"

"Hard to hurt my kind," he said. "But thank you for asking."

So polite. So precise with his words. Different than before. I did glance at him then, and found him watching me warily. Like maybe I'd bite.

"What?"

"You are . . . not what I expected. Not at all. You saved the *garrache*. You kept me safe and left a friend to protect someone who tried to kill you. I am not sure what to make of you, *ma cherie*."

I kept my pace even though I could feel my back starting to spasm, the muscles right pissed off. I rubbed at my lower right hip. "Yeah, well, I'm just chock full of surprises."

He laughed. "I bet you are, Bree. I very much bet you are."

CHAPTER
TWENTY

Feish met me at the door to Roderick's place. "I knew you would figure it out, even if I was not with you. Probably faster if I'd been there."

I nodded, but I knew she wasn't going to like that the next location was an underground cave, which wouldn't be conducive to her talents. I was going to have to leave her behind. Again.

"I'm going to sleep for a few hours, then we'll talk." I put a hand on her shoulder. "Okay?"

"I'll get you tea." She patted my hand, her webbed fingers cool. "And Eric is making meaty pies. I'll get you one."

Yeah, she was going to be pissed as all get out. But what could I do? Suzy met me at the bottom of the stairs that led up to the bedrooms. "You know where you're going next?"

I nodded. "Yes."

She looked past me. "Feish isn't going with you."

I shook my head. "No. If I am to take only those who can help, this next challenge is not . . . she can't help there."

Suzy walked up the stairs with me and let herself into my bedroom. She shut the door behind us. "There is something else you need to know about."

I snorted as I stripped out of my leather armor, placing it across a chair. Down to my underwear and bra, I headed to the connected bathroom. "Let me shower first."

Hot water could do wonders for the aches in the body and the mind, and I let it pour over my face as if it could wash away the day I'd had. No-face Bruce. Leaving Sarge behind. Going face to face with the *garrache*.

I already had an idea of how I might slip away from the mansion undetected by No-face and Crash and whoever else might be interested in following me. But it would mean taking only one of my friends with me. I sighed and dipped my head under the water, sloshing away the suds. Reluctantly, I turned the water off and wrapped up in a big towel, then threw a fluffy white robe over that. I looked like I'd been eaten by a marshmallow, but it was warm and clean.

Suzy sat on the edge of the bed. "Come, I'll braid your hair for you."

I sat at Suzy's feet, and she started pulling the

strands away from my face. She was quiet for a moment, and I just closed my eyes and waited.

"We had word from Roderick."

"Good or bad?"

She tugged a little harder than necessary in my opinion. "Depends. He said someone else found the first witch and is bringing her back to Savannah. Another team they'd sent out."

I frowned. "There is no way the first witch was found. The *garrache* would have said something."

"He was lying," she confirmed softly. "I could hear it in his voice. So could Eric. Roderick wasn't trying to hide that he was lying. He told us to come back to Savannah immediately."

Her hands wove through my hair, tugging gently, pulling it into a semblance of order. If only it were that easy to put other things into place. Like what in the world was Roderick up to?

"Why is Roderick trying to pull you off this case?" she asked quietly. "That is the true question, I think. What is happening back in Savannah? Or maybe he realized something more dangerous is happening here, and he is trying to protect you?"

I tapped my fingers on my knees. "No, I don't think he's trying to protect me." I paused, thinking. "Who has sway over Roderick? Just the council? Or could he be tied to someone else?"

"He is a vampire." Feish's voice came from the door as she let herself in with a tray of food and drink. She sat next to me and handed me a pottery tea mug. I cupped it in my hands and breathed in the mix of sugar and spice. "It could mean that another stronger vampire is controlling him. That would be . . . terribly horrible."

I took a sip of the tea and let it slide down my throat, nodding to Feish. "Caramel something?"

"I know you like the sweet. It's hiding the herbs that will help you sleep," Feish said and then grinned.

I almost put the tea down . . . almost. "Good, I need to sleep." I took another gulp and then carefully worked on the meat pastry from Eric. Kinkly fluttered in next and took a position up on Feish's knee.

"So," I said around a mouthful of food, "what exactly did he say?"

Suzy finished off my braid—French, of course—and sat down on my other side. "Tell Bree that she must not look for the first witch any longer—another team has her already. You must all come back to Savannah immediately for her own safety."

I frowned and scraped the last of my food into my mouth, my arm feeling suspiciously heavy. "Well, that doesn't sound like Roderick at all. What was he really trying to tell us then? That the danger is here? That it's in Savannah? That would be weird . . ." I yawned and my eyelids fluttered. ". . . because the first witch is the dangerous one. Her and No-face Bruce. Unless there is a new player?"

"Yes, very weird. Not going anywhere until you

sleep." Feish grabbed me under one arm and just about dislocated my shoulder dragging me to my feet. "Into bed."

My body was limp, and I really was trying to help, but all I managed to do was flop my limbs about.

"Seriously?" Feish grumbled as I went face first into the bed, in a strange downward dog position. She slapped my ass. "That might work with the boys, but not me."

I mumbled a laugh into my pillow and slid flat onto the mattress. Sleep claimed me, and I went deep into it, without a single dream to bother me. Thank Gawd for small mercies.

That being said, my brain was not on Parisian time. I blinked awake in the middle of the night and found myself staring up at the ceiling with my heart pumping ridiculously fast and sweat beading up along my face and neck. I put a hand to my chest. Yup, heart was out of control.

"Hot flash?" I asked myself.

"Unlikely," a deep voice answered.

Now, I don't remember moving, but I was suddenly on my feet, crouched, my knife in my hand. Staring around the room because I still had no idea where the voice had come from.

What if it had come from under the bed? I stumbled away from the bed and put my back to the closest wall. "Who are you?"

"You are dabbling where you do not belong,

Guardian." My midnight visitor spoke again, and I narrowed my eyes at the long curtains near the window. "This is not your town."

"I'm not ducking dabbling," I grumped.

"You came for the first witch. Word is out that you made a pact with the *garrache*. I would say that is dabbling."

He moved from the shadows near the curtains, revealing himself: average height, average build, striking white-blond hair. Or maybe it was just white—either way it hung down past his shoulders and caught the light of the moon, making him glow.

"The halo trick doesn't fool me. Nobody shows up in someone's bedroom in the dead of night with good intentions. So, what's the deal?"

"Roderick is my friend," he said softly. "But in terms of our kind, he is young. And rash. And *foolish*. He is helping you to stop something he doesn't understand."

Although I didn't see him moving, the vampire—because damn it, that's what he was—was suddenly across the room, twenty feet from where he'd been just a moment before. "And you want an army of vampires?"

Under other circumstances I would have called his laugh gentle. "Yes. Simply put, yes. Roderick is one of the few of us who would stop this. Why, I don't know." His voice rippled, as if he truly struggled to understand why anyone would oppose the concept of a slathering, mindless army of blood suckers.

"And you're helping the Dark Council?"

"Helped. Not helping. We have the first witch. She is on her way to Savannah even now."

I didn't lower my blade, though I wondered if it would do anything to stop him if he came at me. "If you already have her, why should you care that I'm here?"

It lined up with Roderick's story, but it didn't make any more sense now than it had earlier. I'd have bet a solid hundred that this vampire had some control over Roderick.

"Because you are trouble, Guardian. There is a reason *we* killed you all off. I suppose one or two slipped through the cracks." He sighed. "You have until tomorrow at midnight to leave Paris. I will give you that since Roderick is fond of you."

I blinked, and the curtains were fluttering, the window open when it had been closed just a second before. "Well, fuck."

The shakes caught me, adrenaline unspent and wanting me to do something with it. I sunk to the floor and reached for the bedside clock. Two in the morning. Less than twenty-four hours to figure out what we were going to do.

He was lying, I was sure of it.

I fumbled around for the bedside phone—old school here—and dialed a number I'd been forced to memorize. The line on the other end didn't even ring. He just picked it up.

"Dr. Mori," I said.

"Breena O'Rylee. What, may I ask, are you up to now? Our lessons were to start this week."

"Dr Mori. I'm sorry, I got called away on a job." I grimaced. "But I need your help." Seeing as he'd all but forced me to accept him as a mentor, I was hoping to get an easy yes.

He let out a heavy sigh. "Tell me."

I told him about the race to find the first witch, ending with my visit from the strange vampire who'd insisted that the first witch had already been taken, but by the Dark Council, which didn't match with Roderick's story. "Oh, and then there is the *garrache*. She said something about calling the wolf to me?"

He made a choking sound. "You are not ready for that yet."

"Ready for what?"

"A remaking." He sighed. "But you are there, and I am here, so I cannot truly explain to you how it will be."

I held the phone from my face. "Am I going to go furry?"

"Unlikely. It is not like . . . never mind. You might be able to call a companion to you—an actual wolf to help protect you. Or you might indeed shift. The third possibility is that you might be able to call the ghost of an ancient wolf to you. Any of those things might happen, and you will not have a choice. But . . ." He paused, and I waited. "The larger problem is the first witch, as you said. Follow your instincts, Breena. That is most important."

I nodded to myself. "Any other advice?"

"The tables have turned," he said quietly. "You know of which table I speak?"

I did. The table that showed Savannah in its entirety, with one side in the light and the other firmly in the shadows. "You mean my friends?"

"I mean everyone. It is as if someone spun the table, and all who were on it were flung off and repositioned. Every single person now appears on both the light and shadow sides."

I sucked in a sharp breath that had me coughing and thumping at my chest. "How?"

"Some form of a spell, perhaps? I am not sure what this means other than there is great danger."

A heavy crash outside my door had me spinning around as Feish and Remy burst in, a body hanging between them.

"He's hurt!" Feish burbled out, and I struggled not to freak out. Because it was Crash.

Crash was hurt.

And duck me, I still cared enough to fear that if he died, my heart might break into pieces that could never be put back together.

CHAPTER
TWENTY-ONE

Crash wasn't just hurt—he was bleeding out. "Put him on the bed!" I shouted as we got the lights on. "Do we know any healers? Where the hell is Karissa?"

My heart was on fire with fear, and there was no way I would let myself sink into it. On his back, Crash looked like he was sleeping if you didn't take into account the smears of blood across his face and bare chest, the river of it running down his body. His skin was pale, leeched of blood.

And that's when I saw the bite mark in his neck. I put my hands over it and pressed hard against the wound, feeling the pulse of each beat of his heart. "Crash, damn you! Do not die on me!"

"Karissa is not here!" Feish cried. "She could heal him. A vampire bite could kill him, Bree."

"Get everyone!" I yelled as the heartbeat under my

hands faltered a little. This was not happening. I was not going to lose him. Bad enough that we could never be together. I wanted to at least know his heart still beat under the same sun and the same moon as mine.

Because when I let myself think about him, I knew he'd always be in my life in some capacity. We were tied together.

"He's lost a lot of blood," Remy said. "He needs some *très* big magic to save him."

"Do you have any of that?" I didn't even look at him. And he took what felt like a long time to answer.

"No. Not for this."

"Then go find someone who does," I said. He might have stepped back, I wasn't sure. I closed my eyes and pulled my own magic up from the depths of my being, like I was digging through my purse to find the keys at the bottom. Death magic. I didn't want to take him any closer to death, but perhaps I could use it to save him. I held on tightly and made myself really look at him.

Black lines spun out from the wound on his neck, shooting straight to his heart. I kept one hand on his neck and pulled at the thin lines. He gurgled, moaning under my touch.

"Hang on," I whispered as I kept working at the black lines. Like spiderwebs, they stretched across his upper body. I fumbled for my knife—the knife that Crash had made—and used the tip to pry at the black webbing only I could see.

Kinkly shot into the room, and she cried out, "Who did this to him?"

"Vampire," I whispered because I could feel Crash's heart slowing. It was irrational, but I was afraid to speak too loudly for fear it would break something more. I kept working at the lines, the only thing I could think to do. Even though . . . he was dying. I could feel him slipping away.

Kinkly landed beside Crash's face and pressed her fingers against his cheek. "I will give him my energy. That will buy him time."

She began to glow, autumn-colored sparkles shooting off her tiny body and sinking into his face. Wherever they touched his skin, it pinked up—not a lot, but a little.

It was something.

Eammon stumbled into the room next. "What in the . . . sweet pots of gold, is that Crash?"

Without even asking, he stumbled over to the bed and took Crash's hand. "Boy, don't make me regret this."

I gripped Crash tightly enough that I felt his heart pick up a bit. "It's working," I breathed out. "Suzy, Eric!"

"I've got them!" Feish stumbled into the room. "What do we do?"

Eammon slumped. "Take his hand. Give him energy."

Feish didn't hesitate. She took his hand. "Friend,

don't die." I blinked through watering eyes at her as a sparkling burst of pale blue shot out of her and into Crash. His body arched up as if he'd been shocked.

Another cluster of the black webbing pulled off when I yanked at it with the knife.

"Working, it's working," I whispered. "Where are Penny and Bridgette?"

Bridgette and Penny stumbled in as Eric and Suzy each took one of Crash's hands. "Sweet gods below, what happened?"

"Vampire," Eammon groaned. "He needs energy to keep him alive while Bree be taking off the bite wound."

I didn't fully understand what Eammon meant, other than that what I was doing was working. Maybe. Hopefully. "Crash, hang on."

Penny put her hand on Crash's leg. "Boy, how did this happen?"

Bridgette slipped up as Suzy slumped back. "My king. I know you are strong enough." She put her hand in his and her energy flowed out deep green, like moss and things that grew in the dark. It sunk into Crash, and his heart steadied. The wound under my hand felt ... smaller.

Bridgette let go. "Almost."

I plucked off another chunk of webbing. "Most of it is gone. I'll give him energy too."

"No!" Remy lunged for me, only it was too late. I'd watched what the others had done, could feel it against my skin, and I just . . . offered the same to Crash. Why would that be wrong?

I breathed out and pushed my energy into Crash.

My friends' energy had possessed a color unique to each of them—autumn colors for Kinkly, green for Bridgette, blue for Suzy and Feish, a soft brown for Eric, pale yellow for Penny, orange for Eammon.

So when mine glittered black and gold, I was a little bit concerned. Worse, it slid from me in lines not unlike those created by the vampire bite, webbing across his body.

My energy slid over Crash like vines, snaking up over his chest and to his wound.

Whoops. I could feel that too. I shuddered. "Oh shit."

Because I'd gone from fear that he'd die to *damn it, that feels really, really good.* Like . . . catch my breath and gasp feels good.

Crash's hands found my waist, his fingers digging into me as he pulled me down to him. But I didn't dare let go of his neck. The wound was smaller, but it hadn't closed. Which meant me and that gold and black energy just kind of sunk onto his chest.

His eyelids fluttered.

"I said no!" Remy growled, grabbed at me, and then he was tangled up with me and Crash, and the three of us kind of rolled around on the bed. I caught a glimpse of Remy's energy, a piece of it sinking into Crash too. Dark like mine, flecked with a deeper red.

A girl's dream, am I right? Only I got an elbow in the nose, a knee in the crotch, and the whole time all I could think was that I couldn't let go of Crash. I couldn't lose him. Not like this.

Maybe in the back of my head I'd always hoped we'd eventually find a path back to each other.

Which meant the idiot had to stay alive so we could have that opportunity. Whenever that time came.

"Ouch, damn it!" I yelped as someone's head smacked into mine. "Stop it, Remy!"

"You can't do this!" he bellowed. "His magic . . . goddamn it!"

"Just stop rolling around!" I think a knee got jammed into my lower back. "STOP IT!"

Both men held still, and I was sandwiched between them, Crash at my front and Remy at my back.

Crash slowly opened his eyes. Blue flecked with gold, just like always. "Bree?"

"Who else would try to save you other than me and everyone here? We're your friends, you idiot." I dared to peek under the hand I had pressed to his neck. Beneath the wash of blood, there were two tiny pinpricks where, before, the bite had been an absolute tear through his neck. Crash turned his head with a wince.

Kinkly, Feish, Eammon, Eric, Suzy, Penny and Bridgette stood quietly watching. Tears on their faces.

Exhaustion in their stances. All in their PJs. "You . . . saved me?"

The shock in his voice was sad. Remy had an arm wrapped around my upper chest and hips. He gently pulled me backward. I smacked his hands. "Stop. Seriously, just stop."

"I swore to Sarge that I would protect you as much as you would let me," Remy whispered. "He has been bitten by a vampire, and while he will not turn into a vampire, that does not mean he won't suffer some ill effects."

I stopped fighting and let him help me out of the other side of the bed. "Crash. What happened?"

He sat up slowly, then bent forward, elbows on his knees. I moved around the bed so I could crouch in front of him, ignoring Remy's low growl of warning.

"We were watching the house."

"Karissa is here?" Feish burbled. "She could have healed you!"

"She was taken by a second vampire," Crash said. "Robert caught me by surprise."

I swallowed hard and let myself touch the spot on his neck that was now not even a pinprick. "Robert did this?"

Crash gave a slow, careful nod. "I made the mistake of thinking he would still be capable of reason. He is not. Do not trust him, Bree. No matter what you do." He took my hands. "Promise me. Fossette has him working for her now."

I nodded. "I promise."

Crash stood, wobbled, and Feish went to him. "Boss, you cannot go, you must—"

I held up a hand. "She's right. You should stay, at least the night, and let yourself heal."

I couldn't meet his eyes. I couldn't even look at him. Because I had been so ducking scared I would lose him for real, forever. The way we'd lost Robert.

"What about you?" Suzy tipped her head, and I pointed to the stairs.

"I am going to get some tea. Eammon, will you have tea with me?" It was as good a time as any to tell him about the leprechauns I'd seen in the vision the *garrache* had given me. And we were suddenly on an even tighter time crunch.

Eammon startled a little. "Well, I wasn't planning on staying up, but I guess—"

"Everyone else go back to bed. Feish, make sure Crash finds somewhere to rest and watch his door," I said quietly.

Making my feet move was important, and I got them going so that no one in the room saw my tears. Kinkly was not having any of it.

She was on my shoulder in an instant. "Dry your eyes. We saved him together. And your black and gold magic sealed up the wound."

I kept on moving, knowing I was leaving the others behind. Knowing already that the sequence of events that had unfolded tonight were no coincidence.

The kitchen called to me.

The butler was in there, puttering. "*Mademoiselle*," he said.

"Hot water for tea, please, Pierre," I said.

His eyes swept over me. "*Mais oui.*"

He flicked on the tea kettle and left the room as Eammon joined me. I motioned for him to sit on the trestle bench that was pushed up to the large table that was also used as a prep table if the gouges in the wooden top were any indication. I poured hot water into two teacups, dug around in the cupboard and pulled out a bottle of whiskey. I added some whiskey and cream to the hot water before sitting down.

Eammon peered into the cup. "This any good?"

"Best ducking tea I've ever had." I took a sip of the not-any-actual-tea-in-it drink, and hot whiskey burned a path down my throat. Eammon doctored his 'tea' and then joined me, letting out a sigh.

"What's going on?" he asked.

"We have less than twenty-four hours to find the first witch and get out of Paris before a very nasty vampire comes back to evict us. Or, more specifically, me."

The swinging door to the kitchen opened, and Remy slipped in. He was pale as he sat down across from us.

"Where are you going?"

I arched a brow at him. I could leave him behind, but he had proven useful. And strong. "We leave in ten minutes. No more questions from you, Mr. Don't Help Crash Survive."

Kinkly squeaked. "What? Aren't you going to tell the others?" she asked me.

"You're going to fly upstairs to tell Suzy what's going on, then meet me in the backyard."

"How are we going to avoid being seen?" Eammon asked and then slugged back another gulp of his tea. "Aye, this is the best damn tea I ever did have."

"I've got us a way." I didn't have my bag with me. It was in my room, along with my leather armor. If I could've, I would've left it all behind. I wanted to get out of here without Crash knowing.

Because he was still fighting for the wrong side of the table. As it were.

And because I didn't want him to get hurt again.

But it would be pure lunacy to leave without my weapons and my armor.

"I'm going to get my bag."

Eammon laughed at me. "Into the lions' den you go then. That one is going to try and kiss you for sure. At the least."

I swallowed hard, tipped my cup back, and drank the rest of it down in three gulps. Liquid courage, right? "Feish will have moved him."

Eammon laughed harder. "He'll have found an excuse to stay, right as rain."

There was a way to make sure that Crash didn't try anything. "Remy, you come with me."

He shot a look at me. "Of course."

Together, we went back up the long stairs to my bedroom. Eammon was right, of course—Crash was waiting for me, with Feish pacing in front of him.

"You have to help us! Stop helping the Dark Council!" Feish clapped her webbed hands together as if that would help make her point. "Why are you such a stupid man?"

Crash sat on the edge of the bed. "Because I was a boy when I made the choices that brought me here. I would change it if I could, Feish. I would."

His eyes swept up to me as I stepped into the room. I held up a hand. "I just came to get my things. I won't stay in here tonight with all the blood." Which was true: even if I had been staying in the house, I wouldn't have stayed in the blood-soaked bed. I glanced at it and noted that the blood was gone. "Did they clean it up already?"

"No, it's a vampire's house. The blood is absorbed," Remy said quietly.

I didn't like the sound of that, but it wasn't my problem in that moment. I gathered up my clothing, armor, and bag to make it look like I was just moving all my stuff to another room.

"Bree." Crash said my name, and it twisted around my heart.

My feet moved of their own accord. "Nope." I fisted my hands at my sides and then relaxed and wiggled my fingers loose. "Nope."

"Please, Bree, you saved me."

I spun and stared at him, hating that my eyes prickled. "Nah, you don't get to do that. You don't get to sit there and be sad and act like this is so painful for *you*. Maybe they were choices you made a long time ago, but you're a damn grown-up now. Make better choices. Stop hurting me."

I stomped out of the room, because I wanted nothing more than to just fling myself at him and hold him tightly and lie with my head on his chest. To make sure that his heart was still beating, even if it wasn't beating for me.

Remy followed me to one of the other rooms, his arms full of my loose clothing. I dumped everything on the empty bed and pulled on all my leather gear with a bit more force than necessary. I grabbed the black leather pants, the ones that worked like camouflage. We needed all the help we could get.

"You aren't affected by him anymore. Not like before."

I looked at Remy and realized he was right. I hadn't fallen under Crash's spell like before. "He was probably blocking me from feeling it still."

"No, he wasn't." Remy handed me one of my arm bracers. "The energy you gave him. I think it reversed whatever was taken or blocked from you. Because you do have some Dark Fae in you, and no spell of Karissa's could be powerful enough to truly take it from you."

Remy tipped his head to the side. "That's why he likes you so, isn't it? You feel like home to him."

I shrugged. "Maybe it's because I don't grovel at his feet and kiss his ass just because he's gorgeous."

"That too." Remy handed me my bag, and I slid it over my shoulders, then pulled out my fancy new cloak and slipped it on. Good enough. I had what I needed, and we were rapidly running out of time. Footsteps outside the door had me pausing, though. I put a finger to my lips and closed my eyes.

For lack of a better word, it *felt* like Crash. I was sure of it.

I pointed to the window and Remy nodded. There was more than one way to get out of here.

We slipped out the window and I wobbled on the edge of the roof. Before I could stop him, Remy jumped out, grabbed me around the waist and pushed off the roof. I clung to him, squeaking, because I didn't dare scream and have Crash run in and try to rescue me from something I didn't need rescuing from.

Remy landed us on the soft grassy lawn, bending his knees to take the impact. I got my feet under me and shoved away from him. "Next time a little warning."

He grinned. "Glad to think you believe there'll be a next time we leap off a building together."

I sighed and turned toward the back of the house. Digging around in my bag, I pulled out the little boat-shaped bone and ran my thumb over it. "Skeletor, you ready to run?"

I flipped the bone into the air, and it landed about ten feet ahead of us.

"What is that?" Remy asked.

"Watch." Even as I spoke, my undead-but-still-actually-dead horse began to power up and out of the ground, the boat-shaped bone disappearing as he emerged.

"*Mon dieu*," Remy breathed out.

"No one can see him, or at least most people can't." It struck me that most of my friends *could* see the horse, but then again, my life was weird and the rules seemed to be constantly in flux. Go figure.

Skeletor shook his head and blew out a snort across my fingers that smelled rather like death warmed over. I wrinkled my nose and kept walking. "Come on, we need to get Eammon and Kinkly."

Eammon waited by a quietly splashing fountain, and Kinkly shot out of an open window as we drew close. "I told Suzy and Eric. They said they'd tell Feish once Crash is gone. Penny said she already knew you'd be going. You know Feish is going to have a fit."

I grimaced. She was right, but Feish just wasn't the best fit for this challenge. And I had to do what I thought was best at this point.

Eammon slid off the edge of the fountain. "There's a reason you be taking me?"

I nodded. "We're headed to the Fortress of the

Commarque. Skeletor, you got that?" I grabbed Eammon around the waist and lifted him up onto Skeletor's back. Okay, I tried to. I got him partway up and then stalled out. He started scrambling, and I started shoving him under his ass, the two of us sweating and cursing in order to get him onto Skeletor.

Kinkly laughed. "You know, this is why no one sees you as a threat."

I grimaced and then Skeletor bowed, dropping himself low so I could get on. Remy of course leapt right up onto his back to sit behind me. "You could have done this first," I murmured as I patted Skeletor's neck. Then I shot a look at Kinkly. "If no one sees me as a threat, then my ruse is working," I huffed out.

Eammon grunted. "The Fortress of the Commarque, I should not be surprised. It will be a game of wits then, not danger like the *garrache*. That's why you're bringing me. Because my cousins are there, and you know I be the smartest."

Huh. They were his cousins?

I bumped Skeletor with my heels, and he took off. "The *garrache*'s information . . . it came to me in a vision. I saw leprechauns at the fortress, and I figured you'd be our best bet if we had to go up against them."

Remy held onto my belt. "The Commarque is not just a fortress. It's a system of caves, Bree. And you know what creature lives in caves in France, don't you?"

I grimaced. I did not want to know what creature

lived in caves in France, yet it was most likely we'd be dealing with it. "Do I win something if I guess right?"

His hands tightened. "No, no you don't."

"Then tell me fast and get it over with." Like a Band-Aid being ripped off. Maybe the sting wouldn't last.

Remy leaned forward, his chin brushing against my cheek, in order to be heard over the thud of Skeletor's hooves.

"*Le lou carcolh.*"

CHAPTER
TWENTY-TWO

I looked back at Remy. I'd fully expected to be horrified to find out what was waiting for us in the Commarque caves. I'd expected at least a gasp to escape me. *Something*. But I had a big fat blank in my head, because I had no idea what it was that I was supposed to be so scared of. "What the hell is *le lou carcohl*?"

"A giant snail," Kinkly said from my other shoulder. "A giant, hairy snail with tentacles."

I wasn't sure if she was teasing me or not. Skeletor chose that moment to leap over something, and I had to grab at his mane around Eammon's round waist to keep from tumbling off.

Eammon grunted as I squeezed him. "My cousins will still be running the Commarque. The Lutins always were a snobby bunch. Always thinking they be better than the rest of us." Eammon sniffed. "But the monsters in the caves? We'll be thrown to them if we're found unworthy."

A giant snail? I mean, how fast could a giant snail move? And how big was it? Like the size of Skeletor? Bigger? Did it even matter if it was a slow-as-molasses-in-February snail?

"We are there." Remy pointed to a hill ahead of us, sparkling with a few lights. I narrowed my eyes to see the Commarque flow upward, looking like it was part of the hill.

"It hardly looks like a fortress."

"It's old," Eammon said. "And me cousins like to keep it looking that way. Keeps the tourists coming, you know?"

Skeletor slowed his stride and then came to a dead stop. I looked down to see a faint glowing line just in front of his hooves. Just like I'd noticed at Mortimer Abbey.

"Okay. We're at the edge of it," I said. I didn't question why I could see the line in the sand, so to speak—I just knew that the minute we crossed it we'd be in the game with the Lutins and whatever snail they had up their sleeves.

Remy jumped off first and I followed, my knees half buckling as the pins and needles hit me. I grimaced and put my hands on my thighs as I stomped my feet. "Getting old sucks."

"Better than the alternative," Kinkly said brightly. "You could be dead."

I laughed and forced myself to stand up straight. "Fair enough, Kinkly. I just wish being alive didn't make me wish for the quiet of death some days." I felt more than saw Remy look at me but chose to ignore him.

Kinkly swung around and hung from a strand of my hair so she could study my face. "How do you want to handle this? When I slipped over the line last time, I think it set off the alarm."

She was right about that. "So we go through together. Any idea where we should go first, Eammon?"

He had his hands on his hips and was staring in at the broken-down fortress. "The Lutins will be there." He pointed at the highest spire. "They can watch over everything and get the satisfaction of being above everyone. High-handed little shits."

I wasn't sure he should be making comments about others being little, but I kept the thought to myself. "Then we head that way. Eammon, you lead."

He bobbed his head and took a step over the line in the sand that only I could see. It flared from a soft bluish white to a bright flaring red, like a flame, before settling into a soft pale yellow.

I frowned. The colors had followed a different pattern with *garrache*. The bluish white had been the same, but it had burst into a brilliant red and stayed there, angry and pulsing. This was different. But why? Or did it mean anything at all?

Eammon snapped his fingers. "Don't dawdle. We're going to need every second with this bunch that we can get."

He headed up the short slope that took us to the base of the highest crumbling tower. I looked up to see the lights that had pinpricked the building were blinking out one by one. The previously empty window spaces seemed to fill with moving shadows.

I grimaced and shook my head. I would not make up monsters where there were none.

Remy was at my side, and he kept pace easily. "You truly wish to find the first witch and help keep her safe, don't you?"

I nodded. "I don't want an army of vampires flooding over the world, thank you very much. Especially when the flood would start with Savannah." Thoughts of my hometown made my heart pang.

Eammon pointed at a black opening. "There."

Before I could tell him to wait, he hopped through and disappeared into the darkness. Remy put a hand on my arm. "Wait."

Kinkly fluttered her wings against my cheek. "I think Remy is right. Something feels off."

I looked around us, turning slowly. "Eammon, you okay in there?" I fully expected him to shout for us to hurry our asses up.

Nothing.

I reached for my connection to the dead, and it slid over me like a second cloak.

A few souls blobbed into existence, but they weren't like the ghosts from the *garrache*'s hideout. No, these were pale imitations floating in and out of existence. Even with my connection to the dead (or undead if you prefer), I had a hard time keeping them in view. I finally let them go. "There are no ghosts here, just whispers of souls. Eammon, where the duck are you?" I shouted that last bit, and Remy flinched as my words bounced around the fortress before echoing back at me. Only they weren't my words. They were tittering laughter from many different throats.

I grimaced. "They've got Eammon now. Damn it."

Remy stepped just ahead of me and snapped his fingers, a bloom of light appearing above his palm that pushed the darkness back. "Perhaps this will help us not tumble into the same situation as your friend."

He took the lead then, and I followed. Kinkly clung tightly to my ear, her fingers digging into the edge. "I don't like this. It feels bad."

She wasn't wrong. The whole vibe was bad, like the smell of a tomb unopened for a long time, mixed with the cold damp of a dead forest. I wrinkled my nose and kept my eyes searching for a clue as to what the hell had happened to Eammon.

Remy led us to a narrow staircase. "Up?"

"I doubt Eammon made it this far."

"Agreed," Remy said with a sigh. "But we will not find him standing here waiting."

I motioned for him to keep going. Because he was

right—we had to keep moving. Despite the whispers that flowed around us, escalating in volume.

"Shut your pie holes!" I snapped. "You're irritating me."

Remarkably, the sounds faded. For about three seconds. Then they were back full force, screaming at us, the voices battering our ears as surely as if we'd stepped into a boxing ring. None of the words were recognizable to me; gibberish and laughter, that was it.

Remy reached for my hand and hauled me up the narrow stairway. As we moved upward, Kinkly dove for my bag, shoving her way past the flap to hide within the depths.

At the top of the stairs, the room burst into light—as in fireworks exploded all around us, blinding us. I threw my hands up and clamped my eyes shut, but I was too slow.

Remy's hold on me didn't lessen.

I sure as shit wasn't about to let him go either.

"You think to get past us, do you?" The voice was . . . petite was the only word I could come up with. It lent the impression of someone female, exceptionally high-pitched, and small. Eyes watering from the blast of light, I tried to see what the speaker looked like, but all I got was a blurry image of a small body dressed in red.

"Where is Eammon?" I blurted out.

"You don't want to find the first witch?" She seemed surprised.

"Friends first." I dashed tears from my cheeks, but my eyes continued to water.

"Something in the air," Remy whispered. "Can you see?"

"No." I tightened my grip on him. "I don't think I'll be able to talk my way past this one."

"No," he said, "I don't think so either, *ma chere*."

The little Lutin woman laughed, and the sound bounced around the room, other voices joining in. How many of them were there? I tried to see, but no matter how I squinted, my vision was shot to shit.

"You want your friends? Then you can win them out."

Win *them* out? "Yes, wait, did you say friends?"

Who else did they have?

In the blurred vision that I did have, I saw the Lutin woman lift her foot and stomp on something. "In no time you be flat on your back, like all the others." A grinding of stone, the tower around us shuddered, and then the floor disappeared.

I'll admit, I screamed as we fell, and I think I peed myself a little—damn bladder. The fall was long, and after a while it turned into a slide, curling around as we went. I tumbled across Remy, and my bag was yanked upward so the strap strangled me.

And then we were plopped out of the tunnel and into . . . mud. I hoped it was mud. The light was dimmer down here, but my eyes were not faring any better.

I struggled to get up, the thick mud pulling at my feet and hands. "Remy?"

"I'm here," he groaned.

I swiped at my face, forgetting my hands were covered in slimy muck. "Kinkly?"

"Ugh, that was not fun." She climbed out of my bag and then flew around my head. I could see her clearly. We were in a circular mud pit, about thirty feet across. Other than the mud and the huge stone slab walls, there wasn't much down here. I didn't see Eammon either.

Wait.

"The mud," I said. "It pulls the stuff from your eyes, whatever she flashed us with."

Remy sighed. "Good, that's good."

I did a slow turn. "Eammon?" Footsteps in the mud led away from our location. I looked up to see several tunnels that dropped down into the pit we were in. "He's down here. I'm sure of it."

And maybe Corb was here too? Could the two of them have been the 'them' that the Lutin woman spoke of?

Remy offered me a hand, and I took it. Helping each other, we managed to get out of the thickest part of the muck and make it to the edge closest to the wall.

"Why mud?" I muttered.

"Maybe the snail likes it," Kinkly said.

I grimaced. "I hope you aren't right about that."

Remy made another bloom of light over his palm.

"There is only one path by the look of it."

We stepped out of the deeper muck and onto a path that at least had some hard footing underneath it. Still slippery, but better than being knee deep. Kinkly landed on the top of my head.

"Only place there isn't mud?"

"Yup. And I can see farther ahead this way."

"Eammon?" I hollered his name.

My voice echoed, and I got a much better response this time.

"Lass? Ah, no, that harridan got you too!" Eammon wasn't too far ahead of us. With his short legs, I could only imagine how hard it had been for him to get out of the main pit under the building. He waited for us to catch up.

"She said we had other friends down here," I said softly. "You think Corb could have gotten snagged by them?"

Eammon gave a crisp nod. "Would make sense. She could have snagged him on the front step like she did me. There is no seeing it. There was no warning or spell that triggered it."

I wanted to ask why we didn't get dropped down through the same trap door.

"I bet it had to reload," Remy mused out loud. "That's why we made it to the top of the tower."

He held up his hand, and I dug through my bag to pull out my completely non-magical flashlight. I flicked it on and scanned the walls of the round room we were in. The ceiling was easily forty feet above us, which was . . . daunting. How far down were we? "How in the name of gawd are we going to get out?" I muttered aloud. There was an opening on the far side —a tunnel that was as tall as the room we were in— plus a few smaller openings that we'd have to crawl through on our hands and knees.

I dared to call another name.

"Corb?"

His name bounced around the space, but at least no weird laughter bounced back to us.

Disappointment and relief warred within me. At least he wasn't stuck down here too. "Let's try the big tunnel first." I pointed at it with my flashlight. "I don't want to crawl unless I have to."

We slipped and slid our way through the big tunnel, using each other and the walls for balance. I was hungry, my body hurt, and what I wouldn't have done for a hot bath and a hot toddy.

"What I wouldn't do for a Klondike bar," I whispered under my breath.

"A what?" Kinkly hung over my forehead. "You want to go to the Klondike?"

"Never mind." I swung my flashlight around the big space and realized we were coming to a dead end. Awesome.

The brick wall in front of us blended into the muck. I put my hand on it and gave an experimental push. Nope, nothing.

"Shouldn't there be like a hidden . . ." There was a grinding of gears and the bricks shivered, knocking off the muck on them.

They shifted and groaned as a portion of the brick wall peeled back to show something behind it.

A spinning lock four feet across, made of gears and cranks, with three number plates numbered from 0 through 9.

"A way through. But how do we figure out which numbers to use?" The wall kept shifting until the spinning lock was joined by a ticking clock above it that did not give us a lot of time.

"Oh, duck me." I pulled my hand back. Thirty minutes to figure out the three-number combination.

Eammon had his hands on his hips. "It's a riddle. The Lutins love riddles, which means there is a way out—difficult, maybe nearly impossible, but a way out. And the clues must be in here somewhere." He waved his hand around the open space. I looked back the way we'd come.

"The small tunnels. The ones you can crawl into." I made myself run. "Eammon, you stay here, Remy and I will get the numbers."

Remy didn't hesitate. "Kinkly can fly between us and Eammon with the numbers."

Kinkly shot into the air, obviously pleased to have a role. "Yes, I can do that."

We slid to a stop. There were three tunnels that were no more than a couple feet off the ground. "The first tunnel will be the first number," I said. "I'll take it. Remy, you take the second one."

He ran to his tunnel, and I ran to mine.

"Kinkly, if we don't get out of here, you find a way out and go tell the others," I said. "Get Sarge and the *garrache* too." I was hoping that the *garrache* would help us get out of here if we got stuck, but I really had no idea. Honestly, I just wanted Kinkly to get out if she could, and she'd only leave us if she thought she was doing something useful.

"Just get the numbers," she said as I got onto my belly and began to crawl through the thick mud. I kept my flashlight in my mouth so I could use both hands and legs to pull myself along.

I tried not to think about the mud, about where it had come from and why it was so thick and almost sweet smelling. Nope, nope, I did not want to think about snail poop.

Damn it.

I gagged when a bit of 'mud' flicked onto my lips. I could not lose the flashlight. I wiped the mud off my face with the back of my hand as best I could and kept going.

Minutes ticked by and the mud was cold, but I was still sweating by the time I reached the end of the narrow tunnel.

Etched into the bricks was a ducking riddle.

And here I'd just been hoping for a number.

CHAPTER
TWENTY-THREE

Lying on my belly in the mud, I had a little pity party in my head. Why was this so hard? I was trying to do the right thing, yet I kept finding myself in increasingly difficult situations. Mud, snails, ghosts, monsters. All for trying to save the world from an army of the undead.

Now we were down to thirty minutes and three riddles, and if we failed to guess correctly, we were well and completely screwed. Gawd damn. The muck around me squelched and squeaked as I tried to adjust myself.

The flashlight shook a little in my mouth as I grumbled around it, shook off the heavy emotions, and made myself read the damn riddle again. A tiny stream of water ran down the bricks, keeping the riddle clear from the muck.

If two's company, and three's a crowd, what are four and five?

Propping myself up on my elbows, I took the flashlight from my mouth so I could say the riddle over and over again. I pressed one hand against the etched bricks, feeling for an indentation. Something. I counted the bricks surrounding the riddle.

"What the hell are four and five?" I tapped the flashlight, causing the light to flicker, then backed out of the tunnel, thinking. There was nothing in here but the riddle. So presumably the riddle was the answer?

"Kinkly, can you hear me?"

"Yes, do you have a number?"

"No. I have a damn riddle that's supposed to give me the number!" I yelled back. Number. I needed a number.

I was halfway out of the tunnel when it hit me. "Nine! The first number is NINE!"

Jubilation set in. Four and five made nine, and the certainty I'd gotten it right gave me the energy to push backward faster. I didn't care that the muck was up to my ears or that I was slithering through a too-tight tunnel.

I plopped out into the main room. "Remy?"

Kinkly zipped back in. "That other one?" She pointed to the third tunnel, and I knew she was right. Might as well get going on that.

I slopped over to the third tunnel and got down on

my knees, groaning a little, my knees popping and crackling like cereal. "I'm going to pay for this later."

Kinkly buzzed around my head. "At least you fit in the tunnels. A few months ago, I'm not sure you'd have been able to slide through even with some oil."

I shot her a dirty look, although she might not be wrong. "See if you can help Remy." I bent at the waist, stuck the flashlight back in my mouth, gagged on the muck, and started my second army crawl.

"Hurry it up!" Eammon yelled.

Like I didn't know we were on a timeline.

This tunnel dead-ended in a grate instead of a brick wall. On the grate was a plaque made of steel etched with—you guessed it—another riddle.

I am an odd number. Take away a letter, and I become even.

"Seriously?"

I ran my fingers over the grate . . . and fingers reached back and wrapped around mine. I screamed and pulled backward, unintentionally dragging my new friend closer to the grate. Only . . . it wasn't a new friend.

Eyes I knew all too well stared back at me. "Corb!"

"Bree," he whispered my name. "I'm hallucinating, I know I am. Goddess knows I don't deserve to see you now. I am so sorry."

I tightened my hold on him. "How did you get stuck on the other side?"

"I don't deserve to—"

I yanked him so hard his head bonked onto the grate, sending a reverberation through the small space. "We don't have time for what you do or don't deserve. How did you get stuck on that side, Corb?"

He blinked several times. "Time ran out. I thought this was an escape, but I can't find a way out, Bree. I've looked. I've been here for days."

I fumbled through the muck to my hip bag, pulled out my knife, pressed it against the bars. As I'd hoped, the knife that Crash made me cut through the metal as if it were nothing.

I cut through the row, top and bottom, and Corb pulled the broken bars onto his side, silently giving me the plaque with the riddle. "Come on." I began to slowly back out of the narrow tunnel, Corb's face right in mine. But I didn't mind. We were both covered in mud, but he was alive. For now, at least. We needed to hurry the duck up.

"Yous got ten minutes left!" Eammon hollered.

I plopped out of the tunnel, and Kinkly spun around my head. "The number?" I pointed as Corb slid out of the narrow tunnel after me. She squealed and freaked out. "You found Corb!"

I had indeed.

I also had the plaque in my hand. "Take this to Eammon. It's the answer to the last number. See if he can make anything of it."

Kinkly took the small plaque and zipped away. Corb reached for me, but I was already up and moving to the middle tunnel. I leaned into the opening. "Remy?"

"I cannot see a number, *ma cherie!*" he called back, his voice echoing.

"Do you see a riddle or words somewhere? Some kind of clue?" Why would the setup in his tunnel be different than the two that I'd dealt with?

"I'm coming out."

A moment later he scrambled out and pushed to his feet. He looked past me, his eyes wide. "You found a new friend."

"An old friend. That's Corb," I answered, but I was already on my belly and pushing my way into the tunnel. "Keep an eye on them."

I didn't really know what Remy was supposed to do if we didn't figure this out. The muck was slicker in this tunnel, wetter and less sticky. I crawled all the way to the end, where the mud turned into nothing more than dirty water. There was no wall, no grate. Maybe the riddle was in the bottom of the tunnel? I swept the flashlight beam under the water but saw nothing.

What had the Lutin said? *Flat on your back, just like all the others.*

I rolled onto my back, and there was the riddle, etched into the ceiling.

What three numbers give the same result whether they are added or multiplied?

"Math. I hate math." I started back out the tunnel, because the answer would not be in there. As I moved,

I rolled the damn riddle over in my head, again and again. But math really was not my strong suit, and riddles weren't my jam either.

I plopped out of the tunnel and sat there. "What three numbers give the same result whether they are added or multiplied?"

Remy shook his head.

"Four minutes!" Eammon hollered.

Remy helped me up, and I looked over to where Corb sat in the mud. I held a hand to him, and he took it and let me pull him out of the mud.

"We have a riddle to solve."

We got to Eammon in no time, but I felt our time ticking away. Three and a half minutes. "Seven," Eammon said. "The answer to the second riddle is seven."

I gave him the last riddle.

He tapped his nose. "I got it. One, two, three. Third number, number three!" He lifted a hand, and I grabbed hold of him as he reached for the dial.

"Wait."

"Why in the world would we wait?"

"It's too easy. One two three? That can't be it. It has to be a single number!" I said. My gut told me as much.

Eammon didn't argue with me. "We have less than two minutes."

Three tunnels. Three numbers. It hit me like a plop of mud to the face. "What number do they add to? Six. That's the number."

I grabbed Eammon's arm in excitement. He grinned back at me. "Damn it, girl, you are smarter than you look covered in muck."

I grimaced as he put the last number in, speaking the three of them out loud. "Nine, seven, six."

That . . . was not right. I smacked his hand away from the spinning lock. "No, nine, six, seven!"

"I told you that was the last number!" Kinkly yelled as she pointed at the plaque she'd brought to him.

But it was too late. He'd put in the wrong numbers. "Can you do it again?" Kinkly fluttered between us. "Is there a way to start fresh?"

The walls around us shook and groaned, the muck under our feet heaving.

Corb took my hand. "Water, lots and lots of water is coming. That's how I ended up where I did. The grates in the small tunnels open, and water floods in."

And he'd swum through it, being a siren, and gotten trapped on the other side.

The wall in front of us cracked open, straight down the middle, and laughter flowed up from the bubbling mud.

"Lost, you lost, and now the *lou carcohl* will have you!"

I fully expected to fall again, this time into some lair that held a horse-sized snail.

That is not what happened.

The brick and stone wall in front of us opened wide, starting from that split in the middle, and as it opened, water shot out of the three narrow tunnels that contained the clues. They were pipes, not tunnels. The water softened the muck around us. Corb scooped up Eammon and put him on his back. "We have to go in."

"That's where the snail is!" I pointed out. "Will the water lift us up high enough?"

Corb stared at me. "High enough for what?"

I pointed at the ceiling. "We fell in through a chute, what if the water lifted us back up to it? Could we climb?"

Something moved in the looser muck around our feet. Remy grabbed my hand and yanked me to the side, away from it. "I think . . . perhaps that is the best idea. Back to the main room."

Scrambling and lurching, we flung ourselves back the way we'd come.

The funny thing about adrenaline is that it really does lift you up when you are down. We made it back to the main room in no time. Kinkly shot straight up the shaft we'd fallen down.

"Here!" she called, her voice echoing in the chute.

"Keep going, Kink!" I hollered. "Get out if you can, go to Penny!"

It was the best I could do. Because I wasn't sure that the rest of us would make it.

Of course, I hadn't counted on the fact that Corb was a siren.

He handed Eammon off to Remy. "I need her help to raise the water level quickly."

My help?

Corb grabbed me around the waist and hauled me to him. "Your magic sings to mine, Bree. It makes me stronger."

And then he kissed me. Covered in mud and about to face a monster, he kissed me.

The worst part? He wasn't wrong about that blood-singing business. The world dropped away around us as he took the kiss deep, his tongue tracing mine, our lips crushing together as if they wanted to become one. His hand was buried deep in the back of my hair, and the other was wrapped tightly around my waist so that I was held against every inch of him. Another time, I might not have complained. But as it was, I had no interest in kissing him.

Didn't matter that I felt sharp tingles and the flow of the ocean singing to me. I was not a siren, but there was undeniably a spark between us. That had never been the problem.

His lies though? And his manipulation? Yeah, that was the problem.

"Don't do that again," I snapped.

He pulled his head back, breathing hard. Without completely letting go of me, he raised his hand, and the water on top of the muck lifted.

"Boy, you never were that strong!" Eammon barked, startling me. I'd forgotten he and Remy were even there. I couldn't stop staring at Corb. I'd been afraid he was dead, and despite how things had ended between us, I'd never wanted him to get hurt.

He'd been my friend.

Maybe he could be my friend again.

"She brings out the best in me and makes me stronger," Corb said, his eyes never leaving mine. "And sometimes the worst."

Ouch. No, not ouch. I frowned. "That's not me bringing out the worst in you. That's you acting badly. Asshole."

Corb nodded. "Let's discuss it when we aren't fighting for our lives?"

"Agreed. But it's still not me." I would not let him, even for a moment, blame me for his own issues. Nope. Just one more reason why Corb would never be anything but a friend. At best.

He took one hand and made a fist, then spread his fingers wide. The water . . . well, for lack of a better word, it stiffened beneath us, giving us solid footing. Inch by inch, it lifted us toward the opening thirty feet over our heads. Slowly, but we were moving.

"*Mon dieu*," Remy said. "Hurry."

I looked over my shoulder to his face. Only he wasn't looking at me. He was staring at the space beneath us. I followed his gaze and wished I hadn't.

Tentacles flopped and danced in the muck. They were easily two feet thick around the middle, covered in what looked like hair, and there were a lot of them.

As in, I couldn't count them all. So much for the snail being horse-sized. I gripped Corb a little more tightly. "Quiet, everyone."

I mean, could tentacles hear? No idea. But I sure as shit on the bottom of my boot wasn't wanting to test that theory.

We were nearing the opening. Corb was sweating, the rivulets running through the mud on his face and dripping off his chin. I squeezed him as hard as I could, offering him whatever energy I could. We needed him strong to get us all out of here.

He didn't look at me, but his arm tightened around my waist.

Remy and Eammon reached the opening of the tunnel first. Remy had Eammon on his back as he reached the lip. He could put his feet on one side, and his hands on the other in a plank position, facing downward.

I was not tall enough to manage that. And there was no way Corb could carry me all the way up on his back. Remy gave a quiet grunt as he started up the wall.

Corb had not done the math on just how much shorter I was than him and Remy.

"I'm too short!" I yelped. But Corb had already let me go. I was standing on the water platform he'd created. Corb got himself into his plank position and sighed. I thought he was just waiting for me to grab a hold of him. I was wrong.

I gasped as he took away the footing of 'hard' water beneath my feet.

Because the second it was gone, I was falling.

Straight down into the waiting tentacles of the *lou carcohl*.

CHAPTER
TWENTY-FOUR

Laughter from that same damn Lutin woman boomed through the space as I fell. I stared up at Corb and Remy staring back down at me. Remy tossed Eammon to Corb and dove in after me.

Remy did.

Not Corb.

As he dove, the bottom of the shaft closed over with an iron sliding door that just missed cutting him off at the feet.

That was all I had time to see before I hit the murky water. It was thicker than regular water, though not as thick as the mud, and impossible to see through.

I sunk a bit, fought to get my feet under me, and then jerked and lurched my way to the surface. Something under my feet moved, rolling and twisting. A tentacle.

Remy surfaced a few feet from me. "*Ma cherie*, this is a terrible, terrible first date."

I stared at him. "You think this is a date?"

"Why not?" He carefully made his way across to me, dodging a tentacle. "It has adventure. Passion." He winked, and I rolled my eyes. "We don't even know if and when it will end."

I knew he was trying to distract me.

Because what normal girl wouldn't freak out in this situation?

Good thing I wasn't normal. "Let's find a way out of here. Then we can talk about a date, okay?"

His eyebrows shot up. "You think we'll survive? I rather doubt it at this point."

I shrugged as I grabbed hold of one of the tentacles. "My life isn't done yet. I'll survive. I'm not sure about you."

His laughter was . . . genuine. "Bree, what are you doing?"

"Going straight to the monster." The tentacle was hairy and slimy, but it didn't wrap itself around me the way I'd thought it would. It just kept flipping and flopping about. Shimmying along it, I found that it kept itself mostly out of the mud. The water that had swept in was already draining away rapidly, back out the pipes that had brought it in to us.

As I worked my way toward its origin, it continued to lift itself free, which allowed me to move more easily too.

Remy caught up to me. "This is a terrible idea."

"Most of mine usually are, yet I'm still alive, and those I've faced, not so much." I grinned across the tentacle at him, and he grinned back. For the first time, I could see that he was being open with me. Maybe it was the threat of death.

"Why did you dive in after me?" I asked.

He scooted along, keeping an eye on the tentacle. "It is complicated."

"Not really. It's a simple question," I said.

He sighed as if he held the weight of the world on his shoulders. "I . . . I gave Sarge my word that I would do all I could to protect you. I couldn't let you face this alone."

"You barely know me."

"Perhaps I know you better than you realize. You are here to save your friends. To stop an army of the undead. You've won over the *garrache*, and now you are scooting along to face a monster that has not been seen in a thousand years. You are not young; you do not fit most people's idea of the heroine of a story. You're clumsy, you make mistakes, and you aren't particularly fast or strong if I compare you to other supernaturals. You are just . . . you. And I'll admit that it is somewhat fascinating and . . . refreshing."

That was a lot of words.

I didn't know how to react to any of them. Strike that, I absolutely did. "And you're a trickster."

"I am. That does not mean I can't tell the truth. It

means you can't trust me to do what's expected." He paused. "So maybe that makes you a trickster too?"

We were approaching the big wall with the lock. Darkness lay beyond the seam that had been torn open.

The tentacles lifted us high and slid toward that darkness, picking up speed, as if we were on a slide at the park. A hairy, muddy slide. I held on tight with my legs and grabbed a handful of hair in front of me to stop the movement.

"Not so tight, *s'il vous plaît*."

I looked back at Remy.

That hadn't been him speaking.

He held a hand up, light blooming just in time to illuminate two large googly eyes staring back at us. Large, as in the size of garbage can lids. I tightened my hold on reflex, and the two eyes swung toward me, bobbing as if they were attached with strings.

"Not so tight, please. I'm sorry if you didn't understand the French."

So polite. I loosened my hold on the hair. "Lou?"

The eyes boggled back and forth. "Sure, you can call me that. I haven't talked to anyone in so long, I'm not even sure I know my own name anymore. But Lou sounds good to me."

The *lou carcohl* withdrew his tentacles and left Remy and me standing on somewhat steady ground. There was very little muck here. I inched closer to Remy. "Can you light up the whole room?"

Lou grunted. "Well, of course, I'm not a complete heathen."

The tentacles flipped around as if they were hitting light switches, and the space suddenly bloomed with bright light from sconces in the side walls.

My chest tightened at the sight of Lou in all his glory. He was the size of a house. A two-story house. His shell was covered in the same hair as his tentacles, his face was . . . well, his eyes were on stalks that bobbed around, and his mouth was shaped like a parrot beak, razor sharp. Across his shell was a series of scratches, like he'd been in a fight. But I didn't even want to think about the kind of predator that might've caused that damage to the giant snail.

"Excuse me," I said, and his eyes swung back to me. I opened my mouth to ask about a way out, but I realized we still needed the second clue that would lead us to the first witch. "Where do we go next?"

"Go?" Lou's eyes narrowed. He didn't have eyelids, mind you—it was more like the eyes themselves actually squeezed horizontally. "You can't go. You just got here! I haven't had company in so long!"

"Well, I understand that," I said. "But *when* we go . . ." Not like we knew the way out. "Where would we go next? This was our second stop in finding the first witch."

Lou's eyes dilated. "That's all you want?"

Remy slipped a hand in mine. "Caution, Bree."

He wasn't wrong. But there wasn't a lot of time to

be cautious. "Lou, do you understand that the first witch is key to the raising of a vampire army?"

"I do," he grumbled. "And I agreed to help protect her. I just didn't think it would be for this long! And with no visitors! You are the first in . . . many years."

I sighed. "Lou, I am trying to protect the first witch. The same way you are. But this might not be the best way for you to protect her."

Remy's hand tightened on mine. "My friend, don't you want to feel the sun on your face again?"

Lou sighed. "Oh, that sounds . . . marvelous. But I would be leaving my post here."

Remy's hand tightened gently on mine, pulsing a little. He was up to something. "What if we stayed in your stead? For a little while?" Remy offered. "You tell us what we need to say should anyone come through while you are gone, and then you can taste the sweet summer breezes once more, *mon ami*."

Lou sighed again and his tentacles flopped around, twisting together. "Yes, I want that. But I can't. The first witch would know! She would fry me up in butter and make me for her dinner, she said she would."

I stared up at him. "Lou, how big were you when you came in here?"

"I've grown a lot." There was pride in his voice, and while I couldn't see him smile, I could feel it. "Bigger than any of my siblings. We were all in here, but they are gone now."

Gone? "They left?"

"I ate them."

My guts clenched. So much for any softness I was feeling toward this particular monster. "Right, as one does."

Remy choked on what I assumed was a laugh. He covered his face and pulled himself together. "Lou, truly, if you wish to take a walk, we will watch your post for you."

His tentacles flicked around. "Maybe. But if someone should come through . . . and open the door properly, who will eat them?"

I was having a bit of a time following this. "Wait, so if we'd opened the lock properly, you'd have eaten us?"

"Yes, that's what the witch told me. But she never said anything about me eating anyone who didn't open the lock properly. She just said they'd die. But you didn't die, so that's wonderful." He reached out with a tentacle and tapped each of us on the head. "And now I have friends!"

Good gawd, this was bad. "Of course!" I chirped back merrily, feeling the proverbial noose tighten around my neck. "But like Remy said, you should go for a walk. Tell us what we need to do, and we can go from there."

"Oh, there is nothing to tell." Lou turned and began a climb up the side of the wall, his tentacles and the suction along the base of his body aiding him. "I don't know where the next place is. Like I said, the first witch gave me nothing to pass along."

Whatever hope I'd had in my chest was dashed. The first witch had to be found. She had to be protected even if she was as bad as Missy, even if she was worse. Remy pulled me into a side hug. "One step at a time, *ma cherie*."

Lou skidded to a stop upside down. "She's your cherry?"

Remy cleared his throat. "She is a beautiful woman. It is an affectionate term."

"You should kiss her then. Before . . ." Lou trailed off.

Did I want to ask? Yup. "Before what?"

Lou sighed and reached for us with his tentacles. "Before I get back." He picked us up and set us in the center of where he'd been sitting for hundreds of years, eating his siblings.

"Right, because you don't want to see him kissing me?" Like a kid watching his parents kiss.

Lou laughed. "No, no, because when I get back, I'm going to eat you both."

Well, *fuck*.

CHAPTER
TWENTY-FIVE

Lou, the cannibal snail, who'd seemed harmless for a few minutes, disappeared up into a hole to the left of us, his body inching along.

"He's going to eat us," I breathed out.

"Yes, I heard," Remy drawled. "So, what are we going to do about it?"

I made myself jog over to the side wall below the tunnel that Lou had just started through. If we followed him, closely, quietly, maybe we could make a run past him. Not exactly heroic, but I didn't think Remy or I stood much of a chance of killing the giant snail. I pulled Remy close and . . . well, he had different ideas than I did.

I wanted to whisper to him.

His lips landed on mine for that last kiss Lou had talked about.

Welp.

Whatever magic had sung between Corb and me was blasted away by the surge of heat that curled through me from Remy's mouth and hands. If I'd had a clearer mind, I probably would have realized it felt similar to kissing Crash. Only this heat had no smoke to it, no scent of coal fires. This heat was the crackling of magical fire, lighting up my blood and obliterating thoughts of anyone else.

I slid my hands up into his hair and held his face close as he groaned and grabbed at my ass, lifting me up so I was astride his waist, which only sent my hormones into overdrive. I was panting. So was he. This was insanity, but I struggled to remind myself this was not the place. Nor the time. As good as it felt, as much as my clothes suddenly wanted to fall off, I knew we had to stop. I forced my face away from him.

"Remy. We have to follow him. Stealthy. Then make a run for it."

He nodded. But in the bright lights I could see the bob in his throat. "Yes. You are right."

He let me go and pulled his shit together, only adjusting his pants once or twice. Working together, we managed to scale the wall to the base of the tunnel. The angle inside was steep but not vertical, which meant we managed to follow Lou up with only a little bit of slipping.

He was far enough ahead of us that I couldn't see him.

I kept searching the top of the tunnel to make sure Lou hadn't swung around for a return trip on the ceiling. But he was not. No tentacles.

A few branches and roots stuck out of the mud here and there. We used them to help our climb until one popped free, and I realized it was not a root or a branch but a large bone. I put it down and kept my gasp to myself.

The light around us began to change. We lost the lights from below, sure, but the light ahead was helping. Which meant we were on our way out.

Remy jerked me suddenly to his side, then pointed at our feet. A tentacle lay mostly buried. Waiting.

Now that I saw it, I couldn't unsee it. Tentacles lay all around us. Like a damn mine field.

We moved as quickly and carefully as we could.

There was shouting outside.

It sounded like Corb and Eammon having a screaming match. That would help cover any sound we might make, but it would not save us if we stepped on a 'mine.'

Lou's body was blocking the last bit of the tunnel. There was a small opening to either side of him. I pointed to make myself clear. We each needed to take a side. Remy nodded, pressed his lips quickly to mine, and then went to the right.

I refused to think about that kiss or the one that came before it. We had to survive a ducking snail before I could even consider . . . anything.

The thing was . . . I was considering. As I stepped over another tentacle, as I worked my way quietly toward the left side opening, I was very much considering.

Because Remy was this strange mix of all three men who'd captured my attention. A bit of the fire that I loved in Crash, solid like Robert, cheeky and charming like Corb. But he was also a self-confessed trickster. What if he was playing a part? I mean, let's be honest, that was quite possible. I lifted a foot and carefully set it on the other side of an extra thick tentacle.

"No such thing as a perfect man," I whispered. Damn it. I whispered it *out loud*.

That extra thick tentacle closest to me flipped up, and I bolted. Scrambling across all the tentacles, I set off every damn 'mine' in my way. I was already made, so might as well draw him to me.

"Who is that?" Lou yelped. "Who is stepping on my lovely arms?"

I fell, grabbed at a tentacle and, for good measure, yanked a handful of hair out. "Me!"

He screeched, high-pitched like a schoolgirl whose pigtail had been yanked. I kept on running. I wasn't fast, but I was moving. More than that, I was dodging the blows of the thick tentacles.

Kinkly saw me first if her screech was anything to go by. "She's here! Corb, help her!"

All I could do was keep moving, jumping and dodging those hairy tentacles. Until I wasn't. One grabbed me around the ankle and yanked me up so fast I lost my breath. Scrambling, I somehow got my knife in hand. Another tentacle wrapped around my wrist, squeezing down and pressing my bracelet into my flesh—and into the bottom of the tentacle.

I dug around in my bag and found one of the boxes I'd picked up from Death Row. With all I had in me, I threw it at Lou. It broke open and poofed over his body like smoke.

Lou screamed and let go of me, all but flinging me away from his body. I flipped over and over in the air and landed not on the ground but in someone's arms.

Remy had caught me. "*Ma cherie*, what did you do?"

"Nothing." I winced as I touched my wrist, then looked at the giant snail. His tentacles were turning to ash, disintegrating into nothing as he literally fell to pieces. "It looks like he's been salted."

Extremely salted.

In a matter of minutes, Lou was nothing more than a pile of ash under a large shell.

Remy put me down slowly, and I limped toward what was left of the great brute. A beak lay inside the shell, and inside it were eleven shells of various sizes. Lou's siblings. I grimaced but found myself staring at them.

Letters. Each shell had a letter etched into it. I flipped them around, one at a time, moving them until they made sense. Remy, Kinkly, and Eammon helped. We worked as a team until we had it spelled out with the exception of the giant 'S' that I'd thought was just a scratch in Lou's shell. No, it was a letter and as much a part of the riddle as everything else here.

"Mont St Michel." Remy breathed it out. That was our next stop.

I turned around in time to see Corb leaving. He'd heard the answer to the riddle and . . . "You're an ass, Corb! We saved you, and you're just going to leave?" I yelled after him. "You aren't a good friend! And you aren't a good man!"

I didn't like the tears on my face. I was exhausted, my body hurt, and it stung like hell for Corb to walk away from us . . . again . . . after everything. "Keep running," I hollered. "Just keep on running, you ass!"

Eammon sighed. "That boy, I thought he was better than this."

That was the problem. I'd thought the same.

Remy helped me stand, and I'll admit, I wobbled hard. "Skeletor?"

My undead horse manifested into being, and the three of us mounted up. "Take us back to the mansion, Skeletor."

He pawed at the ground once and then leapt forward, throwing me back into Remy's arms. I closed my eyes. Let the tears fall. Not because I'd thought that Corb was going to suddenly be the man in my life. But I had thought that finding him, saving him, would mean something. That he'd come back to our friendship, or at least our group of friends.

I didn't like being wrong about people.

I didn't like being used. Again.

The truth was, Corb was exactly that: a user. And I had to harden myself against anything to do with him ever again. He could not be trusted. I had to let him go.

BACK AT THE MANSION, there was a damn uproar. Feish was pissed that I'd left her behind again, and we were dragging mud through the entire place, which set off the butler and all the maids. Crash was gone. All things considered, that was good, but I couldn't deny it only deepened my sadness.

"You'll come with me this time," I said to Feish with a heavy sigh. "Just let me get cleaned up first, okay?"

Feish slapped her webbed hands together. "I'd better come with you!"

"It's a water trap," I said carefully. Remy had told me about Mont St Michel as we rode back to the mansion. It was an island cathedral with only a narrow bridge leading in and out. It had been shut down for repairs for weeks, leaving the only viable path through the water. Water that was infested with God only knew what.

I rinsed the worst of the mud off in a hot shower, but everything hurt. Everything from my ankles to my neck, shoulders, and . . . my heart. Damn it, that hurt as much as everything else combined.

"I drew a bath for you," Suzy called out. "We had a tub brought up."

I wrapped myself up in a towel and, still dripping, headed into the main bedroom. A massive copper tub had been brought up and was filled to the brim with steaming water and bubbles. "You are . . . an amazing friend."

I promptly burst into tears. Suzy wrapped me in a hug. "It was a hard one?"

"Corb was there. We saved him and then he left us . . . he would have let me die, Suzy. Remy came after me. Corb didn't even help after he saw the snail's tentacles." I sniffed against her shoulder. Sure, I knew I made no sense to her, but we could always talk later.

She shook her head. "He's not who we thought he was. But I'm coming with you to Mont St Michel. If there is water, you know I'll have your back. Feish too." She paused. "There is something that has been calling me in that direction since we arrived. So that has to be good, right?"

I nodded. "A girls trip then."

Suzy laughed. "You bet. A girls trip. Soak for a bit, rest, and then we have to go."

She left me there, and I dropped the towel. I moved to get in the tub and caught a glimpse of myself in the reflection on the window glass.

I was not the woman I'd been a few months before.

I didn't know who I was looking at anymore. And I didn't just mean the changes in my body. I could feel a new strength inside of me.

I was sad about Corb, but I also knew that I was right. He had chosen his path, and our friendship was beyond repair. That kiss . . . maybe that had been more about saying goodbye, saying he was sorry in the only way a siren knew how to apologize. I snorted. Or he'd just done it to soak up enough of my power to save his sorry ass.

Sighing, I stepped over the rim of the tub and slid down into the lavender and sage-scented water. The smell curled up my nose and pushed away the scent of centuries-old mud. Even though I was clean, I dunked under the water and let myself float for a moment before coming back to the surface.

A knock on the door twisted me around. "Yes?"

Remy stepped through, wrapped in a robe. "Mind if I join you?"

I probably should have said no, but I didn't feel like being alone. "I'm too tired for anything, Remy."

His smile was lopsided but tired. "I just want to be close to you, Bree. I will even keep my shorts on." He let his robe fall open. He was wearing snug-fitting boxer shorts. His scars were showing across his chest and collar bone, along with a set of tattoos that slid over his hips and dipped down into his shorts.

Honestly, I could use someone hugging me right about then.

I thought about telling him to duck off, but I didn't want him to go. I sighed and turned my back to him. "Don't push your luck. But you can join me."

He slid into the tub, and I pushed myself backward until I was leaning against his chest.

"If I weren't so tired, yes, I'd tell you to go. But . . . I'm sad."

His arms came around me, careful not to touch anything sensitive, like boobs or nipples. One went across my upper chest, the other around my waist to hold me to his very hard, mostly naked body. "Losing a friend usually is."

"I haven't lost a lot of friends. I just can't believe he'd turn on me, on us, like that." Keep talking, stop thinking about the body behind me.

Remy sighed and shifted so we slid deeper into the water. "I cannot speak for him, *ma cherie*. But I do believe he cares for you, perhaps as much as he is able."

His words softened the blow to my heart a little. "Maybe. Or maybe he was just using us all along, me included."

"He is a male siren. They are not meant for one person. Though I think . . . from what I overheard Suzy saying, he believed at one point that *you* could be the one person for him. I saw how your magic interacted with his, so it is plausible. Sometimes a magical connection makes us think that a person is right for us. That is how it was for Karissa and Crash by all accounts."

I snorted. "I have a lot of weird magic, Remy. I could interact with a lot of different people, I think." And from what I'd seen, that was exactly the case.

He sighed. "Guardians are like that. They must be able to connect with many. Which is why they are rare, why they get killed off, and why they are so very valuable. Look at what you've done here. You befriended the *garrache*, you kept the *lou carcohl* from eating us for long enough that we could escape, and then you killed him. If you had not taken care of him, something none of his siblings managed to do, we would never have found the last clue . . . While nothing may be going as you planned, you are making strides where no others have."

The hand closest to my face cupped my cheek and turned my head to him. "And you even have a trickster feeling strangely loyal to you."

His thumb ran across my cheekbone. "You might not see the light that shines from you, Bree. But others do. You are the light in the darkness. Do not be afraid of it."

His touch was so very gentle and not at all demanding. "That's why Crash wanted me?"

Remy shrugged. "Perhaps. Or perhaps, like me, he saw someone worthy of throwing caution to the wind for."

But he didn't lean into me. Didn't push. He was waiting for me to make the move. To initiate the kiss.

His eyes were dilated, and I knew that he would kiss me back if I leaned in.

I didn't.

"You're going to have to wait," I said. "I don't want . . . to believe you are one thing, only for you to show me something else and break my heart the way others have."

His smile was soft. "For you, I think I would wait a very long time, *ma chere*. A very long time indeed." He kissed me gently on the forehead. "We need to plan for the next step to get to Mont Saint Michel."

I turned and leaned my back against him again, letting him hold me. Letting his warmth and the warmth of the tub seep into me. "What are you, Remy?"

He startled. "You didn't guess?"

"Witch?" That guess was only based on the fire he could conjure in his hands.

"Half. My mother was a witch, my father is fae." He sighed. "A darker fae, like Crash. We grew up spending our summers together, he and I."

Well, that was interesting indeed. Like cousins? No, there was too much animosity for that. "And Karissa too?"

"Yes, she and I have always . . . disliked each other, to put it mildly. Crash and I were friends once, before he started with her." He sighed again. "But that does not help us decide on Mont St Michel."

No, it didn't. But I liked that he was being open

with me. "We leave in an hour. No point in hiding our tracks now. Corb knows and he probably is on his way."

Kinkly shot into the room. "You want food or . . . oh. Sorry."

"Just soaking," I said. "And yes, please on the food. We'll come down."

"Soaking, yeah sure." She laughed and zipped out of the room as fast as she'd come in. I was just glad my gran hadn't shown up. I frowned. Where was she?

"I have to go find my gran," I said, untangling from Remy. The heat from his body left, and I felt the cold immediately.

"I will meet you downstairs." Remy stood first which meant I got a very good look at his body. Yup, very nice in all the right places and covered here and there with bubbles that really added to the look. He turned his back, and I sighed. I really needed to get laid.

CHAPTER
TWENTY-SIX

Dressed in basic jeans and a T-shirt, I made my way downstairs. Apparently, all the muddy leather armor I'd come in with was being rapidly cleaned. I hoped it would be ready in time, but I'd wear it even if it was covered in muck. There was no way I was going out without my armor.

The threat of the vampire's late-night visit was heavy on my mind seeing as we were rapidly running up to his deadline. The kitchen smelled like Eric's cooking, and the bigfoot was working around all the tiny cooks, speaking French with them. They looked to be working together.

"I know I haven't been much help," he said over his shoulder, his big eyes wide. "But I've been learning so much!" His obvious distress moved me.

"You are making sure we are fed, Eric. That is worth everything. Honestly, when the going gets tough, I just think 'I want one more bite of Eric's pastries,' and it's usually enough to get my ass in gear." I sat down in one of the empty chairs, and Eric came over and put a plate of something in front of me.

"In that case, I better keep it up."

Penny, Suzy, and Feish had gathered there and, of course, Kinkly. "Where is my gran?"

"I'm here," Gran said as she stepped through the far wall. "I've been talking to the other resident ghosts. Trying to get information from them."

I nodded. "Any luck?"

"Only that the vampire who visited earlier has come before. He is friendly with Roderick, Bree. This could be a wild goose chase. If the vampire is being truthful, and the first witch has indeed been taken, then what?"

I rubbed my hands across the table, feeling every indentation from years of use. "There is still Robert. Even if the Dark Council has Fossette, we still have to find him. And there are more ingredients to the spell, but with each one we lose to them, the greater our chances of bleeding out."

Penny grimaced and tapped her cane against the stone floor. "Do you want to just give up then? Go back to Savannah?"

I shook my head. "She took Robert. I don't know how she drew him to her, but we can't just leave him like that. Even if it's just to send him back to the grave properly, we have to finish this." And lose another friend. My heart thumped painfully inside what felt like a too-tight chest. "We can't leave him like this. We can't."

Gran nodded. "Any more than you could leave any of your friends. I understand, my girl. I do."

Her soft words eased a little of the tightness.

"Then you aren't still mad at me?" Because even though we'd talked, I'd been worried.

"No!" She raised her hands in the air. "No, child, Karissa is a tricky bitch. No matter how you used that spell, she knew it would hurt you. And cut you off from your fae bloodline. From your grandfather. From Crash."

Her mention of my grandfather caught me off guard, but Remy stepped into the room before I could open my mouth again.

"I think I can get us a boat," he said. "Actually, I'm sure of it. Not pretty, but it will work."

Feish sniffed. "That boy is coming?"

I smiled at her. "Yes, Remy is coming along."

"Crash doesn't like him," she pointed out.

I shrugged. "Remy doesn't like Karissa."

Feish's eyes went wide. "No? That makes me like him better. He is acceptable then. Though he is not getting a bitches' ring."

She clapped her hands over her mouth, but I pretended not to have heard what she'd said. So Feish had gotten us best friend rings? That was my guess. A look at Suzy, who grinned and tapped one of her fingers and a thin gold band on her middle finger, confirmed it.

It was decided that Remy, Feish, Suzy, and Kinkly would come along for the last leg. Eric, Eammon, Penny, and Bridgette would leave the house and start back across France, heading for a safe house Penny knew of in England. Just in case things went sideways. Gran would lock onto Penny and go with them. We didn't know if Fossette would be able to sense Gran as a ghost.

Just in case we didn't get back in time to avoid the vampire's threat.

My leather armor was handed back to me, including the camouflage cloak.

I hugged Penny tightly. "Be careful. Look after them."

"I will be," she whispered into my ear. "And you be careful too. She will be angry when you find her, and I know you will. If she hasn't already been taken, I know you will find her, Bree, so be on your guard."

Bridgette squeezed my hand, drawing my attention to her. "I'm sorry that I haven't been more help."

"You got us here, Bridgette. And you helped save Crash. We could not have managed any of that without you." I gave her a quick hug. "Be careful, be safe."

I didn't like how we were all saying our goodbyes —like we weren't going to see one another again. Eric and Suzy hugged for a long time, clinging to each other. I hadn't been able to watch. I knew how they felt about each other. *That* was love, real love.

Finally, Suzy broke away from him and turned to me. "What about Sarge?" she asked quietly, wiping the last of her tears away.

"He's safe with the *garrache* for now." That was what I told myself. "We'll pick him up after."

After. After we were all safe.

Those who were leaving got their overnight bags, and ours, and then we watched as they got into the French equivalent of an Uber and drove away. I checked the clock. It was closing in on noon. We'd spent a long time dealing with Lou and the Lutin riddles.

Once they were gone, Remy led us toward the river's edge. "My friend said this boat is unsinkable," he said to me. "I figured with your luck that was important."

I snorted. "Don't tell me your friend named it the Titanic."

Remy swept his hand toward the river, and I followed the movement. A small boat, barely big enough for the four of us, waited. And etched into its side was the name *Titanic II*.

"Oh, I don't like this," Kinkly muttered. "Even I know that story, and we aren't all going to fit on a floating door."

"Well, one of us would fit," I laughed, then pursed my lips. "No motor. Which means we're rowing."

"No, I can propel us," Feish said, and before I could ask any follow-up questions, she dove into the river and came up behind the boat, her webbed hands settling on either side of its butt.

We got in, one at a time. "You sure?"

"I am sure," Feish answered, and then we lurched forward at a speed that I wasn't sure a motor could have matched. I fell onto my butt on the bottom of the boat and into a puddle of water.

"This was your friend's good boat?" I yelled over the rushing wind and splash of the water on the side of the boat.

Remy helped me sit up. "I never said it was a good boat. But it's hard to detect a boat like this. And we want to get as close to the island as possible before we are seen. In a manner of speaking, that makes it a very good, very dependable boat."

I frowned. "Seen by what? We never did figure out what we were up against."

"It's haunted," Suzy yelled. "We know that much. But other than that, could be anything."

I clung to the edge of the wooden boat as we zipped down the Seine and moved out into more open water. I'll admit, the speed and rocking of the boat, combined with my fatigue, had me nodding off. Remy slipped an arm around me, and I laid my head on his shoulder and closed my eyes.

I'd taken several Advil before leaving the house. Eaten the food Eric had made. Said my goodbyes. But none of that made up for missing a solid eight hours of sleep. Of which I had not had in how many days?

"Too old for this shit."

"Far from it," Remy murmured into my hair. "You are no more human than I am. Which means you have a longer life ahead of you than you realized. You just haven't tapped into all that you are yet."

I kept my eyes closed. I wished that I hadn't given up my connection to the fae. Not because I didn't want Robert back, but because all it had done was put him into the terrible position of having to relive his death. And it had put me into the position of possibly having to . . . put him back to being a skeleton.

My heart twisted up, and I didn't like it. Didn't like the feeling of having to say goodbye to another person that I cared for. Another friend, another family member.

We bumped along on the water, and I let the movement lull me. I dozed off and on. Dreamed of Corb. Dreamed of Crash. Dreamed of Robert.

But it was the dream of my grandfather that pulled me down deeper.

"Altin," I said his name as he sat across from me in the boat. "You're my grandfather."

"I am." He dipped his head toward me. "I loved Celia very, very much."

"Are you dead?"

"Mostly." He shrugged. "It is different with the fae when we die. We are never truly gone."

I reached for him, and he took my hand. "If I was cut off from my fae side..."

"No, never!" He laughed, but I didn't for a second feel like it was at me. "Karissa could no more cut you off from your fae side than she could change who you are as a person. She may have thought that's what it would do, but she didn't make the spell herself. The one who did has a different objective." He leaned forward. "What she gave you opened you up further. It pushed you closer to being a fully-fledged guardian."

I stared at him. "I don't feel any different."

"It will take some time, another few weeks. The potion is not meant to be fast-acting."

I looked past him to the approaching island. "Do we have a chance at making it to the first witch?"

His eyes were kindly. "There is always a chance. There is always a way to make things . . . right. Even if we don't see it at first. Look for the paths that no one else can see, Bree. Trust yourself, trust your friends." He looked past me. "That one, he . . . he could be good for you. Different than the blacksmith, less brooding. More open." He shrugged and grinned. "But you do not need advice about your love life from me. I certainly do not have a good track record. I . . . should have stayed with her. I know that now."

I clung to him. "I'll take whatever advice I can get. Have you been watching me?"

His smile was wide, so radiant it was obvious why my gran had fallen for him all those years ago. "Your life . . . is a beautiful tapestry of light and dark, granddaughter. Just like my Celia's. Follow the path you choose, don't worry about anything else."

His fingers slipped from mine, but before I let him go, I asked one more question.

"What monsters wait for us in there?"

"The worst kind . . ." he whispered. "But you will face them head on. You have it in you, Bree. Protect your friends. Don't let fear gather in your heart, only love."

His hand slipped fully from mine, and I jerked awake. The boat was slowing, and when I lifted my head, the sun was well past noon, dipping toward sundown. Mont St Michel sat maybe a mile away from us.

"What now?" Suzy asked quietly. Feish swam up to the side of the boat and burbled in the water.

"There is nothing down here. Not a single fish."

"Nothing?" Suzy put her hand into the water and closed her eyes. A shudder rippled through her from head to toe. She shook it off and opened her eyes. "Nothing," she confirmed. "There is no life down here. Something has hunted all the life away from this area."

"Hunted?"

She nodded.

"Get in the boat, Feish," I said, grabbing at her, lifting her into the small rickety wooden thing that was barely large enough to contain us. Remy helped steady Feish as she all but fell in.

"Why am I out of the water?"

"Because if something is eating all the life down there, I don't want it to get you too." I picked up one of the paddles and dipped it into the water. Remy took the other, and between the two of us we got the boat moving again.

"I would be faster," Feish grumbled.

"I don't want you to get eaten." I patted her knee. "I like you too much. Maybe I'd have left Corb down there to push us along, though."

Feish laughed, Kinkly snickered, and even Suzy gave a chuckle. They were the same species, and he'd been her mentor once upon a time, but she was nothing like Corb. "He'd deserve it," she said. "Seriously, what is his pea brain thinking?"

"Probably looking for a pussy cat," Feish said. "That's all the men want."

Remy choked on a laugh but wisely kept his mouth shut.

After that, the only sound was the paddles dipping in and out of the water. The drip of the water off them.

Or so I thought. I dipped my paddle in, and although the sound of splashing water followed, it didn't time quite right. I blinked and looked carefully over the edge in time to see a fin of some sort swish under the boat.

"Remy, your side," I whispered. We were maybe thirty feet from the rocks at the base of the island.

Close enough to swim if we had to, but I didn't want to have to.

Remy looked over his side and pulled back with a low hiss. "Melusine."

"Who?" I kept my voice low.

"What," he replied. "Melusine is a what."

Another splash, and the boat began to move backward. Suzy dipped her hand into the water and closed her eyes. "Her energy is strong, Bree. I can stop her. But you have to keep going."

I twisted around to fully face Suzy. "What are you saying?"

"She's . . . got some siren blood. Her magic is not the same as mine, but I can keep her busy." Suzy stood and shucked off her top and kicked off her boots.

"Wait," Feish said. "I'll come with you."

Suzy shook her head. "No, you need to go with Bree. Get her through the next obstacle. I'll be okay, honest." She smiled, but I could see the uncertainty behind it. And I thought about what she'd said earlier about feeling drawn here. I wanted to stop her, to ask her some hard questions, but she dove into the water before I could, barely a splash marking her entrance. She bobbed up a dozen feet away from the boat and began to swim away from us, making a bit of noise.

The bottom of the boat thunked as if something bumped it, and then I saw a flipping fin and a glitter of scales as it swam after Suzy.

What the hell was a melusine? Some sort of fish?

A body undulated up near the surface, feminine in form until you got past the waist. There were legs that were not legs, but fish tails. Two of them. I'd seen a variation of that before. "That's the damn Starbucks girl." I was standing up, as if I would dive in after her.

"Row," Remy said.

I dropped to my seat and grabbed a paddle, rowing while I watched Suzy draw the melusine away. "How dangerous is it?"

"Very," Remy grunted as he paddled hard.

Then I couldn't very well let Suzy be the only bait. "Feish, come on." I stood, and without dropping a single piece of clothing, I jumped into the water.

Remy yelled. Feish followed, and then I was underwater and fighting to get to the surface.

I really should have asked Remy a very important follow-up question.

Is there more than one melusine?

Because there were.

And I was staring one in the face.

CHAPTER
TWENTY-SEVEN

The melusine looked just like any other woman, if you discounted the deep green hair and massive predatory eyes that were black with rings of gold around them. And the double tail— that was a definite giveaway.

In the back of my mind, I could absolutely see why Starbucks used the melusine as an emblem. I couldn't look away from her, not because she was beautiful, but because I was terrified she'd eat me.

Her smile was slow, and she showed off the tiny, sharp teeth that I associated with piranhas.

A fool to come into our realm. Her voice kind of floated through the water, like an aquatic thought bubble.

I flipped her off with both hands, lifted a foot, and kicked her in the chest. I was propelled backward and felt Feish grab one of my hands. She dragged me to the surface, and then we swam for the shore. Fingers dragged along my legs, scoring the leather pants. I kicked harder, catching something hard this time—a head by the feel of it.

"Damn it, Bree!" Remy yelled from the boat, and then there was another splash. Had he dived in?

If not for Feish, I'd have sunk. Not because I couldn't swim. Because of all the leather armor. It was heavy, and now it was soaked through, along with the cloak and my hip bag.

"This was a terrible idea!" Feish burbled. "They are very fast!"

A moment later, I felt the rocks under my feet, and I stood up.

"We can't leave Suzy," I said. "Feish, go help her!"

Because clearly I was of no use in there.

Feish didn't hesitate, just turned and dove back into the water. Remy was getting to shore on my right as I stared into the water.

I was on a false shore, with at least another fifteen feet between me and the actual shoreline. The sea floor dipped down deep before the water grew shallow once more. Damn it all!

The water was clear, and I could easily see a pair of melusine circling around me. Waiting for me to step off my outcropping. The water was just above my knees, so they could have easily grabbed me. But they were waiting. I looked out into the deeper water.

Thrashing, a spray of water shooting into the air.

My friends were in trouble. "Remy, what will call the melusine?"

"Blood is the best... wait, no!"

I had my knife out in a flash and ran its edge across the crook of my arm, in one of the few places that the armor didn't cover. Right where Robert had bitten me. I hissed at the sharp pain.

The blood hit the surface of the water, just a drop, and the two melusine went wild below me, spinning around my outcropping so fast the water actually pulled away from my feet. They were creating a whirlpool.

I looked out into the deeper water.

The thrashing had stopped.

That was good.

"Oh shit." It was less good that several leaping melusine were darting straight toward me. I'd gotten their attention all right.

I had no idea whether Suzy and Feish were okay.

A hand reached up and grabbed at my foot, now clear of the water. The outcropping sat in the center of a whirlpool.

"You shall not enter the cathedral, you little fool."

One of the melusine pulled herself up onto the edge of the rock so her upper body was doing the little mermaid trick as she braced herself on her hands and the water spilled out around her.

"Listen, I just need to find the first witch so I can save her scrawny ass from a bunch of assholes who want to put her in a boiling pot to make vampires!" I snapped. "That's it. Why is it so damn hard to believe one woman might want to help another? Why does it always have to be about hurting each other to get to the top?"

Yelling, I was yelling again.

Her googly eyes didn't so much as blink. "Because the world is all about which fish is bigger, and the big fish—" she clicked her teeth together, "—eat the little fish."

I took a half step back, loading my weight on my left leg, preparing for her charge. When it happened, I kicked out with my right foot and caught her in the jaw. I *felt* the bone break. She screeched and flipped herself back into the spinning whirlpool.

"Try to eat little fish with a broken face," I yelled. The whirlpool slowed, the melusine circling around the one I'd booted in the face. She writhed and clutched at her mouth, blood blooming out around her.

And then they attacked her.

I didn't think about whether it was a good idea or not, I just knew with every fiber in my being that this was the distraction I needed. I dove for shore, kicking and swimming for all I was worth as the melusine turned on their wounded comrade.

These were not the kind of women I wanted to be friends with. Unlike the *garrache*, they were ruled by no honor system. I floundered hard as I swam, got my feet on real rocks, and fell forward as hands pulled at me from the shoreline.

Remy yanked me up and into his arms, hugged me tight, and then started dragging me along. "Your friends are hurt."

I ran with him, cursing my lack of stamina, cursing the rub marks I could feel developing where my armpits rubbed against my sides, cursing myself for not moving quicker. I could see Feish and Suzy clearly now. Feish was sitting up with Suzy in her arms, holding a hand to Suzy's middle.

"No," I breathed out, as if I could keep her from dying through sheer defiance. The amount of blood, though... it was too much. Even I could see that.

We reached them, and I fell to my knees. "Suzy."

"You drew them off just in time," Feish burbled. "I got her to shore, but we were too slow."

Suzy reached for my hand. "Tell Eric I love him. That he was the best thing that ever happened to me."

I clutched her hand tightly. "This is not your time, Suzy. It can't be, so don't be saying goodbyes. You need to..."

"A melusine's bite isn't fatal," she whispered and twitched, her eyes darkening. "Not to someone like me."

I watched as her body writhed and danced as if on the end of a fishing line. "But it *will* make me one of them." She closed her eyes, and when she opened them again, they were bigger and darker, with just a hint of the blue.

"What can we do?" I tightened my hold, feeling the loss already. "Suzy, we can't just leave you here. They kill their own!"

Her smile should have terrified me. Her teeth were falling out, leaving little tiny piranha teeth behind. She spat the bigger teeth out and shook her head. "Then I will show them a new way, Bree. The way you showed me. I . . ." Her body convulsed and she shook it off. "I knew that I would not be with Eric forever. But he loved me like no one else ever has. Pure. And you were my friend, both of you." She looked to Feish. "That's something sirens are not supposed to have. This is the next step in my journey, and it isn't with you. It's my time to go."

I pulled her into my arms and hugged her again, not caring that I was dripping snot and tears. "Did you know? When we left for France?"

She shuddered. "I felt the pull of this water, Bree. I felt it and knew it was my time to make a change, though I didn't know it would be like this." She pushed away from me. Her eyes were not quite as big as those of the other melusine, but her legs had morphed into two long tails, each with fluttering fins at the end.

She cupped my face with her hands. "Be safe, Bree." She kissed me on the lips, and her siren magic coursed through my veins, pushing away the fatigue, the fear, and leaving only love—the love of a friend who would be my friend no matter what. Even so, the sadness was heavy.

Another friend, I was losing another friend. She turned to Feish and embraced her. "It's up to you to keep her safe now, Feish."

With a flip of her new fins, she slid away from us into the water.

Gone without so much as a splash.

"We can't stay here," Remy said after a few minutes. "I know you want to watch for her, but if she is smart, she will hide from the others for a while."

"She is the smartest!" Feish yelled at him. A burbling sob fell out of her, and I caught her in my arms and held her for a moment.

"She is the smartest siren we know, Feish, and she will show the melusine a different way. We'll come back and see her again. I promise you that." I stared out into the water. "I promise you, Suzy, we'll come back."

Maybe we'd be able to bring her back from this. It was a slender hope, thin as a fishing line, but it gave me something to hang onto. I forced myself to my feet, helping Feish up, and Remy helped me.

"We need to go," I said softly.

And just like that, we had to leave Suzy behind. My throat was tight, and the tears flowed freely down my face as we made our way up the rocks, to the base of the cathedral.

I pressed a hand to the stone. "How do we get in? And is this where the first witch is hiding?"

Or was it just another test? The thought of fighting off another monster was enough to make my legs shake.

"I don't know," Remy said. "But we have to keep going. We're almost there."

He was right. We were closer than ever, and despite the losses we'd suffered, I knew we had to keep going. I slid my hand over the stone wall.

"Could it be like Death Row, Feish? Is there a simple stone we need to push in so we can step through?"

Feish stood next to me and put her webbed hands on the wall. "Could be we just use the front door." She grabbed my chin gently and turned my head toward the bridge and the main entrance to the cathedral.

"I don't think that's a good idea," Remy said, "as much as it's the obvious entrance."

I turned to the water's edge and watched where it lapped against the island. And the small depression it slid into. No, sucked into.

"What about an underwater front door?"

"With the melusine?" Remy shook his head. "They'd be guarding it . . ." He trailed off and all three of us peered into the water. Suzy was out there, dragging the melusine around, drawing them to her. She was the new girl. They were distracted.

Not a word was said between us. The three of us

just turned and ran toward that depression under the island. Feish got there first and dunked her head underwater.

"Not too deep, we can walk in, good amount of air pockets. When the water goes in, air pockets gone, but then the water dips back out, air pockets back," she burbled. "I go first. You got a light, guy who hates Karissa?"

That was an improvement. At least she was talking to Remy.

He slid into the water right behind her and lifted one hand as a light bloomed in it. "Yes, but that leaves Bree in the back."

I hopped down into the water and hooked a hand through his belt. "If I get dragged away, I'll drag you with me." My head and shoulders were above the water, but each wave that came in drew the line a little higher. "We need to hurry. Go, Feish." Go fish. Another day I would have cracked a joke about losing at a child's card game. As it was, I felt like I was losing a real game, a gamble that was taking my friends from me. Robert. Crash had almost died. Suzy was gone.

The watery tunnel was just wide enough for us, just tall enough that no one would have to duck. It had been made for sneaking in and out of the cathedral, no doubt.

Remy shook a little. "I don't like tight spaces. I thought I was over it, but this is a bit much."

I smirked. "Odd thing for a man to say."

He barked a laugh. "*Excusez-moi*? Did you just make a sex joke?"

"Perhaps you aren't the man I thought," I said. "Feish, I don't think Remy likes small cats. Only very large cats."

"Like a tiger?" she burbled.

Remy started laughing. "*La tige*? Goddess, this conversation is—"

"About to get weirder," I muttered. "Probably likes them large and maybe those wrinkled up cats, the ones with no hair?"

Feish made a heaving sound. "Terrible. What is it with men and cats? All the books, I just don't understand! What does a cat have to do with love?"

Remy's laughter was good, and he was totally distracted from the fact that the space was getting tighter. "*Mon dieu*, this is a joke."

"No joke," I said. "Too bad for you that you don't like cats the way other men do."

"At least you don't have a cat for him to chase," Feish said. "I am happy about that."

Now I was laughing. "You aren't wrong. I do not have a pussy cat at home."

"No pussies for us," Feish burbled. "So none for Remy."

Honestly, I wasn't 100% sure that she wasn't playing along for fun, but I chose to believe she was innocent of what she was saying. It was funnier that way.

"Here, tunnel is tighter," she said, and that about did us in. Remy turned and faced me, his eyes wide.

"Bree, I cannot."

"You can." I put my hand on his chest, and it slid down to rest just above his belt buckle. "Look. Just face me and keep walking backward." The water swooshed in right then, covering our heads. I held my breath, Remy pushed hard against me, his body tight with nerves. I pushed back, went on my tiptoes and pressed my mouth against his, giving him a breath.

That slowed him down, the water receded, and I blinked up at him. "You got this, Remy. Keep going."

His eyes were locked on mine. "Talk to me."

"About what? My asshole ex who died and then haunted me, and whom I regularly stuffed into my hip bag, just for shits and giggles?"

His eyes widened. "No."

"Yes, so remember that is what happens to men who cross me."

Feish laughed. "I like that story."

His lips twitched. "That isn't true."

"It is. I was framed for his murder, too, but you'll be disappointed to hear I didn't do it. Anyway, he got caught up with a voodoo priestess and works for her now, and my name was cleared. He seems . . . well, I'd say happy, but I'm honestly not sure what he's up to." I shrugged.

"You sound sad," Remy said.

"Only that I don't get to grab him by the ear and

shove him in my bag." I grinned up at him. "It was a small price to pay for the life that I was forced to live with him."

The space around us tightened again and Remy's jaw ticked.

"I had a skeleton for a sidekick," I said. "That *does* make me sad because we thought we'd brought him back to life, but then he was snatched away by Karissa. It's . . . complicated. He was a guardian like me . . . I mean, when he was alive."

Remy's voice softened. "And you cared for him."

"I love and cherish all my friends," I said. "I don't take any of them for granted. Even the ones who only come to me when they need me. The ones who use me . . . I know how broken they are. Maybe because I'm broken too?" I shrugged and kept walking, pushing him along, the light in his hand flickering here and there. "The thing is, we don't all have to be hard. We don't all have to draw lines in the sand so deep they go to the core of us. We can love our friends, even when they are broken. Even my ex. I want him to be happy." I paused. "You know what? That's not honest. I'd be just fine with him being miserable for twenty years or so. To make up for our life together."

Feish burbled up ahead. "Hurt people hurt people. I read that. I think it's true. That's why you try so hard, Bree. Because you been hurt, and you can see it. So, you try to be the fixer."

I sighed. "Yeah, that gets me into a whole different kind of trouble."

Remy's hand drifted to my face. "But it's also what draws so many to you. Even me. I don't do other people's quests, *ma chere*. I've been alone a long time. You make me wonder what it would be to have others around whom I trust. Whom I love." He shook his head. "It's beyond weird."

I laughed, and the sound reverberated far louder. I blinked and looked up.

"We're out of the tunnels."

But we sure as shit stinks weren't out of trouble.

CHAPTER
TWENTY-EIGHT

The tunnel under Mont St Michel opened into a cavern with stalactites (or maybe stalagmites, I'm no geologist) and little lights buzzing around.

Because they were moving, I figured they were creatures that could possibly swoop down and try to peck or pull our eyes out. That was the way things were going, anyway. After all, we'd almost gotten eaten by a giant snail, faced a snicken, a wendigo, and a pack of ravenous mermaids. Pardon me, melusine.

Remy drew a deep breath. "Doors. But which one?" I followed where he pointed, and sure enough there were three doors arrayed in front of us. Of course there were.

"Let's go check them out."

As we drew closer to the doors, my grandfather's

words came back to me. Look for the path that only I could see.

The water was shallow now, sloshing around our ankles as the waves came in and out from the tunnel. The three doors were identical. There were no defining characteristics that would sway you to pick one over the other.

"Bree?" Feish said.

"Just give me a minute." I closed my eyes and pulled up the witchy part of me I'd inherited from my grandmother. I blinked my eyes and saw a sparkling path leading to the door on the left.

I shook my head to dispel the connection to my gran. Not because I didn't want it, but because I was going to face a witch who was known to steal the souls of other witches.

And almost vampires.

Was that why she'd taken him? To steal his soul? Or just to hurt us?

I made my way to the left door, thinking about Robert.

I touched the knob, and the door swung open, an intake of wind like a giant breath sucking me in.

Alone.

The door slammed behind me, cutting me off from Feish and Remy.

I tumbled across the floor and found myself at the bottom of a set of stairs. I grimaced. "Ducking stairs."

The space was dimly lit by a single torch in a

sconce on the wall. I lifted it free and started up the stairs. I wasn't worried about Remy and Feish. They would either be able to get through the door or they wouldn't. Either way, I had to keep moving forward.

"Is this an analogy for life? Keep moving forward, don't look back?" In a very short time, the stairs were making themselves known to my quads and my ass. You'd think by now my nemesis would not have such a hold on me.

You'd be wrong.

I counted the stairs. Ended up being just over fifty, so about five flights. High enough to take me up into the cathedral. "Should have taken the front door," I muttered.

"Then you would have died."

I looked up to see a ghost floating my way. Long robes, hair bound up in a tight bun, sharp eyes and a sharper nose. There was a glow about her that reminded me of Gran. "You're a witch?"

"I was. And you can see me, which means you're a necromancer."

I grimaced. "No, I'm . . . a guardian."

Her sharp eyes widened some. "A guardian? Perhaps the prophecy is at hand then. Two guardians are needed. Is there another?"

I could feel the blood run from my face. "She has Robert."

"The vampire pup? He was a guardian? *Mon dieu!*"

She put a hand to her face. "Come, I will lead you the rest of the way."

I had no reason to trust her, no reason not to. "Why are you helping me?"

"Because I was the first witch before her. I was killed to create the spell that brought about the first wave of vampires. When the spell was broken, my soul was freed, in a manner of speaking, and I was sent to watch over the next first witch."

I stumbled over a bump in the footing. "That still doesn't explain why you would help me."

"It will take two guardians to keep her safe from what is coming. Even now, I can see what will come if you do not both stand in front of her. The skinwalker is almost here. You must stop him." She twisted around to look at me.

"No-face Bruce." I growled and shook a fist. "Damn it!"

"Yes, indeed. Skinwalkers are immune from a witch's magic. They are our nemesis." She tipped her head. "It will take two guardians to stop him. Once he is stopped, there will be no others who wish to take her soul. Or at least none for many years. Many wish to kill her. I've warned her of the beautiful woman, but beyond that, I cannot see more."

Time, we were just buying ourselves some time. But I'd take it. "If we stop him now, then we should be good, no vampire army?"

"Until another chooses to chase down her soul." She bowed her head to me and kept on moving.

"You don't sound French," I blurted out.

"Because I am not. I came here with Fossette to try and protect her, but the fool ignores me." She shot me a look. "You must be Celia's granddaughter. You have a bit of her look."

"I am," I answered but then did the math. "My grandmother was around when you were alive?" In the 1800s?

"Yes, of course she was! Tell me, is she well? Did she end up marrying Altin?"

"She is like you. A ghost." My brain was on fire. I'd had no idea Gran was that old! But my shock would have to wait. I held up the light as we came to another set of doors. My ghostly friend slid through the one on the left, and I followed. I mean, I didn't slide through it, I opened it and stepped through.

"Pity, she would have been the next first witch after Fossette dies. I am Belinda." She waved a hand at the room around us. "And you stand now in front of the first witch."

I had no eyes for the room in front of me, only the people that stood within it.

Maybe standing was an exaggeration.

Crash was on his knees, Karissa beside him. Robert was crouched at the feet of a slender, sharp-angled woman with pure white hair and eyes as dark as any cave. She slowly turned her face toward me.

"Who is this now?" Her English was heavily accented. Her lips parted, and she drew a breath. "You smell like a witch."

"Nope." I spat the word out. "Not a witch. I mean, my grandmother was, but not me." As I spoke, Robert's head swivelled my way, and he bared his teeth at me.

The first witch snapped her fingers, and both Crash and Karissa were flattened to the floor by a spell that I could just see the edges of. It sprung from her fingers like vines, wrapping around them both and holding them tight.

"There is a skinwalker coming," I said. "And while you might not like it, you do need protection. Seeing as he is immune to your magic."

She laughed, the sound echoing around the room. "Do I now? I have my new pet here." She patted Robert on the head, and he cringed. "And now I have two fae at my feet whom I shall also make my pets."

How the hell did I play this? She was no kindly old woman, hoping someone would happen along to save her. I looked at Karissa. "You are the queen of the fae. Ain't you got any juice in you?"

Karissa glared at me.

Crash answered. "She bound up our magic."

I had no idea how that worked, but I gathered neither of them could access their power. Awesome.

Fossette's power all but vibrated around her, and I wondered at the fact that we'd been sent to 'save' her at all. A witch this powerful didn't need my help. Horror slid through me.

"The *garrache* was right," I said. "Someone on the council . . ." Most likely a traitor on the council was using every resource they could plunder to find Fossette. Including me. I shook my head because I didn't know what to do.

"You spoke with Winifred?" She seemed genuinely surprised by that. "How is it that your throat was not torn out? Do not tell me that the bitch has gone soft."

I shrugged. "First. She could tell I wasn't lying about why I wanted to get to you. I'd prefer to keep your soul intact so we don't have to deal with a vampire army. Second. The three of us—" I circled my fingers to include Karissa and Crash, "—found you so do you not owe each of us a boon? A favor?"

I didn't actually want anything from her other than to keep her safe . . . and non-violent toward my friends, of course.

Her eyes narrowed. "Is that why the Dark Council wants me this time?" She snorted. "I will make you all my pets, as I did the others, and I will have all the protection I need."

She snapped her fingers, and Corb stepped out of the shadows, head bowed, a thick collar on his neck. "This one is lovely, so sweet in his words." She stroked a hand down his face and then slapped him. "But quite the liar."

I threw my hands in the air. "He's a siren, what do

you want? Of course he lied to you. He lied to me. He lies to everyone!" I pointed at Crash. "That one's a liar too." And then I pointed at Robert. "And so is that one. You know what they have in common?"

The white slashes of her eyebrows were high. "What is that?"

"Testicles." I flipped my hand out in front of me, miming a flopping fish. "They are always going to lie to get what they want, and they'll tell you they were trying to do right by you. You know who else they lie to? Themselves!"

Everyone was looking at me now, but I didn't care. We'd come all this way, to what? Watch No-face Bruce steal her soul? I think not. My rant would buy us a bit of time. "I don't trust any of them. I know why I am here. I don't want a vampire army, so even though you seem like a miserable old witch, I will do all I can to protect you!"

The sound of footsteps turned me around as the man of the hour arrived.

No-face Bruce stepped out of the darkness. "Then you'll die first, Guardian."

I drew a breath and pulled my own knife free. "Meh, I've heard that before. But I'm still here, Brucey Baby. And everyone else who said I'd die . . . well, they aren't."

He grimaced, which made his face dance and do weird things.

And then his body shifted until he was no longer Bruce.

He was Crash. "You sure about that?" His voice was just like Crash's.

My eyes narrowed. "You think showing me the face of a man who treated me like a cast-off is going to save you?"

I lunged at him, faster than I think either of us had thought I could move. One slash of the knife, and he had a slice across his chest, peeling back his shirt and the first few layers of skin.

Hissing, he slid back and shook his face so it danced and jigged once more. He tried Robert. He tried Corb. But with each man he showed me, I drew more blood.

He even tried Sarge.

That got him a kick to the knee.

The whole time, I kept myself between him and Fossette. "You can't have her, Bruce."

His face shifted until it was Roderick in front of me. "Thank you for showing me how slow you really are."

I didn't see him move. I just hit the ground, flat on my back with my forearms up as he snaked his face down to try and bite me. He wasn't a vampire, but he had a vampire's teeth. As I fought to keep him off me, all I could think about was Joseph, the vampire who'd very nearly killed me.

Crash had saved me then.

He wouldn't be saving me now.

Which meant I had to find the strength to do it myself.

An image of a wolf slid across the front of my eyes, superimposing itself on Bruce.

"Let the wolf come," I whispered.

CHAPTER
TWENTY-NINE

"There is no wolf to save you," Bruce snarled.

The image of the wolf turned toward me, opened her mouth, and howled. My ears registered no sound, but my body still shook with the vibrations. Then the wolf dove into me.

With a heave, I flung the skinwalker straight up into the air. His legs flailed, and I slammed my knife up and into his belly as he fell back down toward me.

Howling, he ripped himself off the blade. "You need more than that to kill me."

I didn't think, I just moved. The wolf was in me, feeding me strength, giving me the speed I needed. I slashed my knife through the air, my feet moving in the intricate dance that was a fight to the death. I knew in my gut that I had him on the ropes.

He grabbed my left arm and yanked it to the side.

Bones broke. I didn't feel pain, just the distant knowledge that they'd been broken. I'd heard them give way.

But as he jerked my arm, it drew me close enough that I was able to slam my knife into his neck, all the way to the hilt.

He stiffened and looked at me. His mouth drooped, and he slumped to the floor and fell to his side.

I took a step back, then another. "Duck me."

I turned and faced Fossette, still not feeling the break in my arm. "You good then? Can you let these losers go?"

Yup, I'd just called the three men I had a variety of feelings for losers. Because maybe they'd always been Mr. Right Now, not Mr. Right.

Or maybe, they'd never been meant for me at all. Ouch. I frowned.

Something struck me from behind and drove me to the floor, face first. My head hit the ground hard, and I couldn't shake it off. "You need to learn to finish off your mark," Bruce growled in my ear.

Well shit, maybe this was the day I'd join Gran.

I tried to lift him off me, but with only one good arm, I couldn't do it. I wasn't strong enough.

"No!" Robert bellowed, and then Bruce was off me.

I spun in time to see Robert and Bruce tangled up like a pair of hissing cats. Their blows were fast, brutal, and . . . I saw the flash of silver as it drove into Robert's heart.

"Robert!" I lurched forward.

He pulled the blade out, spun it around and stabbed it into Bruce's neck, right beside the wound I'd given him.

Bruce fell backward for a second time, only now I could see far more of his insides than I'd ever wanted to, his guts spilling out of a wound I hadn't noticed until now. I stumbled over to Robert, doing all I could with one arm to cradle him as he slid to the floor.

"You aren't a loser, Robert," I whispered. "You aren't. You're my friend, and I just wanted . . ." I just wanted him to have a chance at a life. To be able to talk to him for real.

"I am a fool," he whispered, and gave me a careful smile. "I will be your friend, always, Breena. Don't try and bring me back again. I can protect you better dead than alive." His body slumped and crumpled, flesh disappearing until he was the Robert I'd first met.

I couldn't help the tears that filled my eyes as he stood up and swayed, his clothing hanging off him. "Friend."

Sniffing back my tears, I made myself stand up, my broken arm dangling. I gasped and tried not to move it as the nausea of the break finally hit me.

"Bravo." Fossette clapped slowly. "It seems that my predecessor was right, it took two guardians to save my soul." She tipped her head to the side. "But there was another vision she had, of a beautiful woman killing me." Her eyes bored into me. "A beautiful woman who had immense power."

Oh. Duck. "Not it," I whispered. "I don't want to kill you. I . . ." How did I convince her? I could see in her face that she didn't trust anyone. That's why she'd hidden away. And yet if she'd surrounded herself with her friends, maybe she would have been okay?

From behind her there was some movement. A flash of webbed hands. I held my breath as a net dropped over the first witch. She screeched and flailed, which only tightened the net around her body. Her magic flared out all around us, bouncing off the walls, slamming into everyone.

Corb was flung to one side and slid down the wall. Karissa and Crash were thrown to the other side, and I just bowed my head as the magic washed over me. It was Feish and Remy, I was sure of it.

"We gots you now!" Feish yelled as she tightened the net. "We made a catch for you!"

Remy stepped out, holding the end of the line. "Good job, Feish."

She beamed up at him. "I hate Karissa too. We make a good team. And you made a good magical net!"

He'd won her over. I wanted to get up, but my legs were like damn rubber, and now that the adrenaline was gone, I could feel every bump and bruise, and that break . . . damn that was going to hurt me later.

Feish rushed to my side. "You hurt?"

"Yup." I pointed to my rapidly swelling arm. "Broken."

She clucked and burbled as she made a sling for me out of a strip of her shirt. "Here. That be better now."

And then she patted my arm. I about passed out. "No touching it."

"Right, right." She helped me stand. Crash stood to one side of the first witch, Remy to the other.

Fossette turned her head to Remy. "You . . . how *dare* you!"

"I warned you once that I wouldn't let you hurt anyone again," he said softly. "I meant every word of it." He tugged her to her feet.

Karissa, who stood just in front of Fossette, shook her head. "I cannot believe you thought she"—she looked over her shoulder at me—"was the beautiful woman with immense power."

We all kind of stood there, frozen for a split second too long as her words sunk in. It meant we were too long to stop her.

With a quick lunge, she leapt at the bound-up first witch and tackled her to the floor. Crash and Remy yanked her off Fossette, but again, not fast enough.

Foam bubbled from the first witch's mouth.

"You want her soul?" The question flew from me.

"No," Karissa snarled. "I want her dead."

Confused? Yup, me too.

"Jaysus," I breathed out as Fossette lurched and danced inside the net, her eyes rolled back in her head. "Why?"

Karissa was backing away from the first witch's

flailing body, from all of us. I had no way to stop her, but I knew we had to try. Whoever she was working for, she couldn't be allowed to leave. She smiled at me. "Just you wait for what comes next."

What the hell did that mean? "Yeah, well . . . you too."

Pithy, I know.

She snapped her fingers, and a tiny piece of paper floated to her. "*So* nice of you, Crash, to give me the list of all the Dark Council members."

"You're not on it," Crash said.

"Oh, I'm on it." She laughed and blew the paper toward him. "You think Scarlett, a mere pixy, was a Dark Council member? You hadn't even seen the list. I . . . adjusted it to show her name instead of mine."

While I didn't quite know exactly what was happening, I got the gist of it. "You weren't after Fossette," I breathed out.

"I was," he growled but never took his eyes off Karissa. "She was on the Dark Council. Apparently, so was my *ex-wife*."

Karissa laughed. "Oh, please, I begged them to recruit you all those years ago. I couldn't be married to a goody-two shoes. And then this one comes along and ruins all my plans to win you back." She flipped a hand toward me.

Her magic swept around my body and tried to drive its way into my mouth. It was thick, like plastic molding itself to my face.

Robert was not having any of that shit. "Not friend!" He shambled over to Karissa, and she flicked a hand at him, sending his bones flying.

Feish tried to help me peel the magic off, just enough so I could breathe.

Remy stepped up beside Crash. "Together." I took note that Corb had already slipped away, like the snake in the grass that he was.

The two men bumped fists and circled around Karissa. Her eyes widened. "You . . . no, you would never hurt me! You hate each other!"

I truly hadn't expected Crash to come after Karissa, let alone with a sword. Remy blocked the fairy queen from escaping, but he left the fight to Crash.

Apparently, Karissa didn't fully believe that Crash would hurt her either. She screamed as she stumbled backward, throwing her hands up, a spray of magic slamming into Crash. But that magic was sliced clean through by his sword.

Along with her neck.

Her body slumped to its knees, and her head slowly slid off her neck as she fell to the side.

The magic blocking my airway dissipated in a poof, and I drew in a deep breath.

Feish held me in a tight embrace. "I got you, Bree. I got you."

I hugged her back with my good arm. "I got you too."

The two men stood there, breathing hard, staring at each other. Sizing each other up.

"No pissing contests," I said. "No more fighting."

Crash slowly turned to look at me. The sadness there was . . . overwhelming. "I am sorry, Bree. For everything."

I saw so many possibilities in him. The potential of a man who not only loved me but made me laugh and kept me safe. A man who would walk with me through every fire I faced. Only . . . it was just potential. "You have work to do." I said softly. "A lot."

He blinked, and I knew he didn't fully understand that I meant he needed to work on himself.

I drew a careful breath. "You should go, Crash. I will never regret . . . any of it."

Okay, maybe I'd regret never actually having sex with him. I'd have to put that on my bucket list. Like climbing Everest. It's on the list, but is it ever going to happen? Probably not, but damn does it look aspirational.

His chest lifted slowly with a long breath. "This is a different goodbye then."

I smiled and chose to ignore the tear that slid down one of my cheeks. "It may have taken a while, but I know who I am . . . and what I'm worth. You fight your demons, and I'll fight mine. Maybe one day . . . when all the broken pieces are fixed, put back together . . . maybe then. But I won't live for potential. I won't live for maybes."

His smile was soft, and he bowed at the waist. "I'll be there, Bree, in the shadows. Watching over you. Always."

"No." I held a hand to Robert, and the skeleton shuffled to my side. "I've got my friends. You do you, Crash. Find yourself."

The confusion on his face said it all. He didn't understand. Maybe he never would.

Using Feish as a crutch, I limped away from the three bodies. Remy stepped up beside me. "You did good in there, young guardian." His wink seemed to convey a multitude of emotions. He was sad about something.

"You okay?" We wove our way out of the cathedral and out of the front gates before he answered.

"I . . . did not think Fossette would die," he said. "I thought perhaps she would see the light."

I looked at him, really looked at him. "You knew her, didn't you?"

He gave a slow nod. "She was my mother."

CHAPTER
THIRTY

Fossette was Remy's mother.

Well, that little bombshell rocked me back on my proverbial heels. As it was, rocking on anything was a terrible idea with a broken arm.

"I'm assuming there is a story there?" I offered.

"Yes, but now is not the time for it." He carefully put his arm around my waist, so that I was held on either side. "I will tell you later. I know what she was, I have no illusions. I have done my work." He smiled down at me, dimples showing.

"Cheeky French man," I said.

"I like him," Feish said. "If not the boss, this one is acceptable."

Her words had me looking over my shoulder. Robert shuffled along ten feet behind us. My chest tightened. When I looked at him now, I saw the man he'd been. Not just the skeleton he was.

Superimposed over himself, he lifted a hand and waved. "I am your friend, Bree."

"And you are trapped," I whispered.

One day I'd find a way to set him free. Either to a new life or . . . to a life beyond this one.

The day had faded while we were inside the cathedral. "How close do you think we are to midnight? That vampire . . ."

Remy answered me, "We need to get Sarge. We can hurry."

He half picked me up and we made it off the island using the bridge, snagged an Uber on the far side, and headed to Mortimer Abbey.

I could feel the weight of eyes on us again as we stepped onto the familiar ground.

Sarge met us first.

"Did you find her? Jesus, what happened to you, Bree?"

I shrugged. "The usual. We found her, and Karissa killed her."

A gasp from behind him, and the *garrache* stepped out. "Fossette is dead?"

I nodded. "We stopped the skinwalker. But . . . Karissa was working for the Dark Council. Actually, it turns out they both were."

Sarge frowned. "But why would she do that? Why not just take her soul?"

"That," the *garrache* said, "is a spell that takes time

and energy. To take her soul, they would need a powerful necromancer. Why did I not think of this before? Of course, of course!" She paced around the grass in the moonlight.

"Think of what?" I asked. "I don't understand why Karissa killed her."

The *garrache* turned to me. "Who is the first witch now? What if, all along, the ones who sought the spell already had the next oldest witch in hand? Killing a witch, that is far easier than trapping her soul. Unless she is already subdued."

The breath whooshed out of me, along with a single name. "Penny."

THERE WAS no time for anything else but to chase after our friends. "They were headed for a safe house in England," I yelled over the rushing of Skeletor's hooves on the French countryside. Feish rode with me, and Remy rode on the back of the *garrache*. She'd insisted on coming along.

I still had to talk to her about that whole *call the wolf to you* business. Because distantly, I could feel a connection to that same she-wolf who'd saved my butt.

Sarge raced alongside his great-great-grandmother (or however many greats were involved), and we were making good time. But we were still in France. And midnight was only minutes away.

"You don't think they'd actually come after us?" I asked. They being the not-so-friendly vampire who'd paid me a visit.

Feish thumped me with a webbed hand. "Of course they will! If they did not, then what? They will be seen as weak."

"We're trying to leave!" I didn't have a watch or phone to check the time, but my gut told me we were closing in on the deadline. Or maybe it was the sensation of being hunted.

I didn't like it.

"I can smell the ocean," Sarge yelled. "We're close!"

Maybe we should have taken another Uber. Or a train. But the roads were clogged, and Skeletor and the wolves were fast. Faster than any man-made machine that had to stop at a red light every five seconds.

Feish burbled, "This is going to be close."

I didn't doubt it. I could just hear the waves hitting the shoreline when an inhuman screech lit up the night behind us. Skeletor redoubled his speed.

"There, we need to get on the barge!" Remy yelled, and he and the *garrache* turned slightly to the left. We followed, the pack of vampires behind us.

I dared a glance back.

They were riding beasts that looked a little like the *garrache*, only their eyes burned red and they had more legs than she did. Bigger mouths.

"Don't look back," I yelped and dug my heels into Skeletor's sides. He pounded down the dock. The few people still working looked around at the sound of hooves, but they couldn't see us.

Well, except for the one old man who pulled off his cap and crossed himself as we galloped past. At the end of the dock, the barge was pulling away.

The *garrache* and Sarge made the leap look effortless. And I could only hope Skeletor could do the same.

I leaned into his neck and hung on tightly, or as tightly as I could with one arm, and Feish leaned over me and clung to my waist.

"Please make it, please make it," I whispered.

Skeletor didn't slow. He just pushed off the very edge of the dock and covered the distance between us and the barge, landing far beyond the wolves.

He slid to a stop, and we turned to see the vampires gather on the dock, watching us go.

Did they know that the first witch was dead? Were they working with the Dark Council too? I lifted my good hand and waved at them. With one finger.

The vampire who'd threatened me in my room lifted a hand back and then gave a very quick bow from where he sat on the back of his monstrous ride. "Guardian, your luck will run out one day. On that day, I will be there."

"Sounds like a promise," I shouted over the water between us. "I hope you're not a liar like the rest of them."

Even at that distance I could see the anger flash

across his face. Or maybe it was the open mouth hissing business he had going on.

After that last burst of energy, the barge ride was quiet. Both Skeletor and Robert were back in my hip bag, safe and sound. Feish had somehow found a tiny kettle and set to making me a pot of tea. Wincing, I pulled out my flask and chugged back a few gulps, then handed it off to Remy. He took two pulls and handed it to Sarge, who then handed it to the *garrache*. No, not the *garrache*. Winnifred.

With a warming belly, I carefully lowered myself down so I could lean against one of the shipping containers.

"Your arm needs to be set properly," Sarge said. "I can see from here that the bone is not sitting right."

"It will have to wait," I said. "We don't have a doctor here." I looked at him, and he and Remy were having a silent exchange of eyebrows lifting.

"I'll hold her," Remy said, "you set it, and then I can alleviate some of the pain."

I sighed. "Really? I'm not going to fight you if you're trying to help me." I moved so that I was closer to Sarge and just closed my eyes. "Make it quick, please."

I'd barely let the words out of my mouth before he gripped my hand and gave a quick twist.

I screamed, letting the whole world know we were there. Which worked weirdly in our favor.

Remy put a hand on my shoulder, and a whoosh of

his magic slid through me, numbing the pain. He wasn't healing me, but it helped. Boy did it ever help.

"I feel drunk," I whispered.

"Essentially, yes." He pulled me against his side. "I enhanced the effect of the whiskey in your blood."

"Ah-mazing," I sighed and closed my eyes as he got my still-broken but now-set arm back in the sling.

Feish pushed a cup to my mouth. "This helps heal too."

The smell was, as always, questionable. I slurped it down with a grimace and then forced my eyes open. "I see Eric."

The bigfoot was peeking around one of the containers. I had to be seeing things. He stepped out. "It is her! I knew that scream!"

My brain was fuzzy, so there was a lot of confusion as to what had happened, but I eventually worked through it. Penny, Eammon, Bridgette, Kinkly and Eric had been waiting on the barge, knowing it was their best bet for getting away quickly, without ending up on anyone's records.

I stared at Penny. "Fossette is dead. Who is the next oldest witch?"

She put a hand to her chest, and I closed my eyes. It was Penny, which meant we could keep her safe. But when I opened my eyes, she was shaking her head.

"She is older than me, but only by a few days."

"Who?"

She swallowed hard. "Missy."

The silence was heavy. Eammon cursed, breaking it. "That's why she was helping the council find the first witch! Because she knew she'd be next."

"And that's why Karissa killed Fossette," I said. "Just like the *garrache* said, it is easier to kill the first witch if you already have a hold of the next in line."

I looked at Penny. "Is there any way we could make it back to Savannah in time?"

Gawd in heaven. I sucked in a breath and blurted out my next thought before she could answer. "That's why Roderick wanted us to come back! Because he'd caught on to the Dark Council's plan. He'd found out Fossette would be killed, not captured!"

And he'd wanted me to come back to protect Missy. Why hadn't he just said that?

I pushed to my feet and a stream of curses that rhymed heavily with duck, punt, and blocksucker really fell from my mouth. Breathing heavily, I leaned against one of the containers. "Why couldn't he have just told us?"

"Maybe he couldn't," Remy offered. "Maybe he is bound to that vampire we left behind?"

Eric cleared his throat. "I know that the world is at stake... but where is Suzy?"

My heart ached all over just at the mention of her name, and he must have seen it because he lost color. "Did she..."

"No, no, she is alive." I held out a hand to him. "But she's not coming home, Eric."

We were surrounded by the water against the barge and the steady thrum of the motor, but my attention was focused on Eric as he stared at me with tears in his eyes. "Tell me."

He took my good hand and I sat down next to him. "She loved you, and she knows that you love her."

"Past tense," he whispered around the tears that fell from his big eyes. "Loved me."

I squeezed his hand. "She's not lost, Eric, just gone for a little while. She was attacked by the melusine, and that turned her into one of them. She's still alive, Eric. That's good."

"You can't save everyone, Bree." He let my hand go and turned away as his shoulders shook, and I sat there and stared at his back as he spoke. "That's not how the fairy tales work. There isn't always a happy ending. In fact, traditionally there is not."

He wasn't wrong. And he wasn't right. "But that doesn't mean you just give up," I said. "I am not giving up on her. None of us are."

The rest of the barge ride was very quiet. Everyone kind of sunk into themselves. Replaying one of the hardest jobs we'd ever had. A job that we hadn't completed.

The safe house in England was tall and narrow and had enough rooms for everyone. There were no witches around.

Which concerned Penny. "There should be at least a few signs of witches here. Where are they all?"

Me, I just wanted to go home.

Gran found me in my bedroom the next morning.

"You've been quiet." She sat on the bed next to me.

"I feel like I can't . . . like we aren't making a difference. We've lost friends, Gran. Suzy. Corb. Robert. Crash. Even though they aren't dead . . . with the obvious exception of Robert . . . they're still gone. And we haven't made so much as a dent in the Dark Council!" I let the pity tears fall. Exhaustion will do that to you.

"Honey girl, you have made a difference. Consider what you told me about that scene between Crash and Karissa." She leaned in close. "He's hunting the Dark Council members, I'm sure of it. If he kills them all, then he'll be free. Free to be whoever he wants to be for the first time in his adult life."

A knock on the door interrupted us.

"Come in," I said.

Remy poked his head in the door. "I have a place for us to eat. Something very French."

I looked at my gran, and she shooed me away. "Go. Your arm needs time to heal. We cannot move through the fae realm until it is more stable. You've talked to Roderick. You've talked to your new demon friends. They all know to watch for Missy."

She wasn't wrong.

Which is how I ended up on my first real date since my divorce from Alan—a date that had me laughing and smiling and seemed to lighten the very air around me. I noted that Remy was letting me see the scars I'd glimpsed beneath his glamour the first time we met. I'd seen them in the tub a bit too. I wondered what they were from but figured that was more like a second or third date question.

We avoided the heavy stuff like his mother being a powerful—and now dead—witch, stuff like Crash saying he wasn't giving up on me, like all the shit we'd been through in such a short time.

Funny how hardships could bond people so quickly.

Of course, the bathtub moment hadn't hurt.

Sitting at a French café in London was a bit surreal, but I was enjoying it. The sun on my face was warm. I was safe. I was wearing a dress size I hadn't worn in . . . well, I had no idea how long.

A hand curled around mine, and I tightened my fingers through Remy's. I was finally out with a man who seemed to have done some of his own damn work.

What could possibly go wrong?

"Bree!"

A voice I did not want to hear, a voice I'd really hoped was firmly in my past, jerked me out of my moment of peace. "Alan?" I spun to see him running toward me.

"Who?" Remy asked. "Wait, that's your ex-husband, is it not?"

But my gaze was fixed on Alan, who had a look of horror on his face and a note in his hand. He flopped it onto the table. "She sent this for you. You have to see she's trying to help. Bree, I know, I know what you think of me, but . . ." He leaned forward. "I am trying to change too. I want to help."

Did I trust him? Not one bit.

Did I think he was lying? Absolutely. I should have just pushed him away or, better yet, shoved him into my hip bag. But I found myself reaching for the note that his new boss had sent me. A voodoo priestess from New Orleans was reaching out to me, and it seemed like a good idea not to ignore her.

The note was messy, as if it had been hastily scrawled.

The siren is next.

UP NEXT!

Bree's story isn't done yet...

About the Author

Well, it's been a trip so far, hasn't it? Let me tell you, I am hopeful that 2022 brings a bit more light, a little more laughter, and a helluva a lot more great books (or at least better than mediocre).

There will be at least one more Forty Proof this year (with 9-12 total), two new first in series, and then of course, the wrap up of the Desert Cursed Series, Realm of Demons this spring.

I hope you continue to hang out, interact, review and in general stick with me. If not, well, all the best to you in future endeavours.

Click on Facebook or Amazon for the easiest ways to follow . . .

Check out my swag store for goodies Mayers Merch

Website for updates and books Shannon-Mayer.Com

And if you're brave, find me on TikTok, apparently I'm doing a dance off with KF Breene. 0_0 #KillMeNow

Printed in Great Britain
by Amazon